D0457515

# THE
# SWALLOWTAIL
# LEGACY

## Wreck at Ada's Reef

# THE
# SWALLOWTAIL
# LEGACY

## Wreck at
## Ada's Reef

MICHAEL D. BEIL

PIXEL+INK

**PIXEL✚INK**

Text copyright © 2022 by Michael D. Beil
Illustrations copyright © 2022 by TGM Development Corp.
All rights reserved
Pixel+Ink is a division of TGM Development Corp.
Printed and bound in November 2021 at Maple Press, York, PA, U.S.A.
Book design by Torborg Davern
Interior illustrations by Torborg Davern
Cover art by Becca Stadtlander
www.pixelandinkbooks.com
Library of Congress Control Number: 2020940461
Hardcover ISBN 978-1-64595-048-6
eBook ISBN 978-1-64595-102-5

First Edition

1 3 5 7 9 10 8 6 4 2

To my brother Bill, for being there

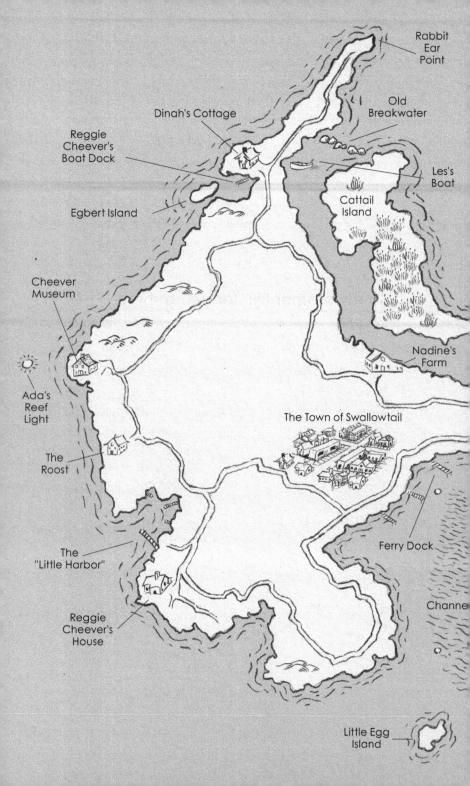

Rabbit Ear Point

Old Breakwater

Dinah's Cottage

Reggie Cheever's Boat Dock

Les's Boat

Cattail Island

Egbert Island

Cheever Museum

Nadine's Farm

Ada's Reef Light

The Town of Swallowtail

The Roost

The "Little Harbor"

Ferry Dock

Reggie Cheever's House

Channe

Little Egg Island

# SWALLOWTAIL ISLAND

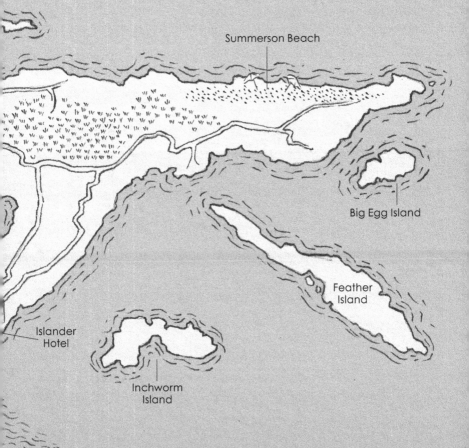

Summerson Beach

Big Egg Island

Feather Island

Islander Hotel

Inchworm Island

SWALLOWTAIL ISLAND

# CHAPTER
# 1

IT'S A DRIZZLY SUNDAY MORNING, the day after my twelfth birthday, and my family—such as it is—has arrived at Swallowtail Island in the western end of Lake Erie. All six of us stand on the foredeck of the ferry *Niagara* as it makes the turn at the buoy marked R3 at the entrance to the harbor. My ten-year-old sister Pip and I shiver in our thin cotton dresses, our arms pocked with goose bumps, as the town comes into view before us. Its two piers are like long arms reaching out into the harbor to greet us (Pip's interpretation), or to push us away (mine). As the *Niagara* bullies its way down the narrow channel, its bow pushing a wall of water, the previously unruffled surface is pulled and stretched like gray taffy. Moored boats dance in our wake as we pass, bows and sterns rising and dipping with each wave. Near the east shore a fleet of mallards steams south toward a dilapidated wooden dock, and above me, a single gull cries, then swoops down to see if I have anything to offer it. Pogo, our English setter, "sets" beside me, body quivering and tail high in the air. I reach down and stroke the top of her head, but she doesn't take her eyes off the gull for a second.

My heart leaps when we bump against the pilings at the ferry dock and lines are made fast: we have arrived. Without a word, Pip slips her tiny hand into mine; together our hearts pound out a rhythm that I am sure can be heard over the whining engine and shouts of dockhands.

Our stepfather, Thomas, gathers Pip and me along with his own three boys—Blake, Nate, and Jack—with his long arms. "Everybody ready? We should get a family picture. This is a big—"

"Let's not," I say. When I was five, and Pip three, our dad died when the small plane piloted by his best friend crashed into the Connecticut River a few hundred yards short of the runway at Goodspeed Airport. That same summer, Thomas's wife was killed by a falling tree branch while she was jogging in Central Park. Four and half years later, Mom married Thomas. They had been friends (nothing more, they both insisted) in college and reconnected at a class reunion. So we had kind of a *Brady Bunch* thing going for a couple of years but then, three months ago, Mom died, and what was left? Thomas and his kids, and then Pip and me. I don't know what we are, exactly, but it doesn't feel quite like a family.

"C'mon, Lark," Pip says, squeezing my hand. "We should."

I am saved from the indignity of a family selfie there on the foredeck by one of the ferry's crew: "Okay, folks. Need to ask you to move along."

We wind our way down the steep metal staircase and onto the gangplank. When I reach the end, I hesitate before taking the final step onto the worn wood planks of the pier but there is, I know, no turning back. For the next seventy-two days (yes, I'm counting) this is home.

I'm not off the hook for that family portrait yet, though. Thomas has already recruited a woman in a yellow slicker to take our picture in front of a sign that announces "Welcome to Swallowtail Island" and is busy composing the shot. "Lark, since you're the tallest, in the back with me and Blake."

I grunt and move into my assigned place. Sometimes it is easier just to do what Thomas wants and get it over with.

The woman in yellow says, "Smile!" and I do my best to provide something that at least *resembles* one. My teeth are clearly visible, so that counts, right?

With that little bit of torture out of the way, the other five of us leave Blake, not quite fourteen, in charge of our bags and the cage holding my budgie, Bedlam, and trudge toward town to get our bearings and to find a ride to the house that has been in our family since the 1920s, and where Mom spent her summers as a kid. The last time I was here was the summer I turned ten, the same summer that Mom first got sick. After that, it was like someone hit PAUSE on our lives. For the next two years, the only traveling we did was on I-95 between Connecticut and Lenox Hill Hospital in New York.

It was a lawyer who pressed PLAY, calling us into his office the week after Mom died to tell Pip and me that the house on Swallowtail Island now belonged to the two of us.

As we amble along Main Street, strangers in a strange (and strangely *quiet*) land, a light, ground-hugging fog filters out the town's imperfections—the peeling paint, the cracked and frost-heaved sidewalks, the shuttered storefronts—making it appear more charming than I remembered it to be. Slowly, though, the fog lifts higher and higher, until it hovers just above the tree-tops, and the sun begins to peek between the maple branches, highlighting Swallowtail's blemishes in a golden glow.

But who am I to call out its flaws? I mean, it's not like I'm perfect—ask anyone. When Thomas first told us that we were going to spend the summer on Swallowtail Island, it was his idea that I start keeping a journal, to help me deal with "my issues." He first brought it up when Mom got sick but I wanted nothing to do with it. "Trust me," I said. "You *really* don't want to know what I'm thinking most of the time."

"It's not for me," he said. "It's for you. *I'm* not going to read it. You're right—I don't want to know what you're thinking. But it's good for *you* to know, and sometimes the only way to do that is to write it down."

"What's supposed to go in it?" I asked.

"Whatever you want. What you'd like to say out loud but don't—that is, if there *is* anything that fits in that category. You're a very observant person. Unusually so, I'd say. But you're so much *more* than a mere observer. You're constantly gathering and analyzing data, plugging it into your own formula of how the world works. You're a born scientist. On top of that, you have a baloney detector that would make Holden Caulfield proud. So, observe. Gather. Rant. Draw pictures if you want. There's no rules unless you make them. Marcus Aurelius wrote in the morning. Seneca did it at night."

Thus began the unvarnished journal of Meadowlark Elizabeth Heron-Finch. I know, right? Twenty-nine letters, not counting that hyphen. ("A perch for the two birds," Mom explained.) My sister's is almost as bad: Sandpiper Alanna Heron-Finch. When my mom, Kate *Heron*, met my dad, Marc *Finch*, they decided that the bird thing was fate, so when we came along, they "had no choice" but to keep the ball rolling. By the way, no one calls us by our real names, *ever*. I'm Lark and she's Piper or, most of the time, just Pip.

For the moment, there's only one rule when it comes to my story: I promise to be honest. Otherwise, what's the point? But I should probably clarify: Just because I promise not to lie doesn't mean that I'm going to tell the *entire* truth. I'm not one of those people who is determined to share every unspoken thought with the world and I don't want to be. Here's the

God's Honest Truth about me: There are places in my own brain that, when I make a wrong turn and accidentally end up there, I turn around and get out as fast as I can. No need to go poking around places like that—who knows *what* I'll find.

Further west on Main Street, the town starts to perk up. No cars or motorcycles are allowed on the island, so it's not unusual to see horses and buggies sharing the road with electric golf carts and bicycles. To Pip, who has taken riding lessons at a stable in Chester for the past two years, horses are the best thing about the island. She loves them beyond all reason, and once prepared a PowerPoint presentation to convince Thomas to buy her one. I think they're very pretty, but the GHT (God's Honest Truth) is that I can do without them. A twenty-year-old palomino tossed me out of the saddle at summer camp a few years ago, and I swear he looked back and laughed at me when I hit the ground. And seriously, have you seen those teeth? I'll take a bicycle, thank you very much.

We stop in front of the old-fashioned drugstore where we arrange for a wagon to take all of us and our stuff to the house. The boys go inside with their dad while Pip and I stay out on the sidewalk. She wanders a few doors down to pet a horse that is harnessed to a small, Amish-style buggy while I peek through the front window at a stack of the local weekly newspaper, the *Swallowtail Citizen*. The headline reads "Tragedy Strikes Swallowtail 75 Years Ago," and next to it is a grainy black-and-white photo that takes up the top right quarter of the page. It shows the wrecked hull of an old-school wooden speedboat—like something from an old movie. There are several ragged holes across the bottom of the boat, the largest a good three feet long. Not all of the article is visible through the glass, but I'm able to read enough to learn that the writer is convinced that the speedboat crash that killed Albert Pritchard was no accident *and* that it was probably also connected to the death of the town's most important citizen, Captain Edward Cheever. Pritchard was Cheever's lawyer, and was returning from visiting friends in Leamington, Ontario, when he plowed into the rocks known as Ada's Reef just west of Swallowtail Island. When I've read as far as I can through the drugstore window, I go back to the top where I see that the article was written by Nadine Pritchard—Mom's oldest friend and the main character in just about every story from her childhood.

"Pip, you have any money on you?" I ask. "I need fifty cents for a paper."

"What? No. It's back in my bag. Come and look at this horse. Isn't he beautiful?"

"Yeah, he's great," I say, handing her Pogo's leash. "Hold Pogo for a sec. I'm going inside. Don't go anywhere."

Thomas is on his way out the door as I open it. "We're all set," he says. "The wagon'll be here in a few minutes. Supposedly.

Where's Pip?"

I nod in her direction.

"Oh, right. Horses."

"Can I borrow fifty cents?"

"Sure." As he digs two quarters out of his pocket and holds them out, I realize he already has a copy of the newspaper in his other hand.

"Oh. You already . . . that's what I was gonna buy."

He hands me the paper, along with a five-dollar bill. "Get some drinks for you and Pip. This may take a while. Remember the last time? The guy showed up an hour late and then he blamed us. Said *we* were in the wrong place."

Thomas is right. *Everything* on Swallowtail Island takes a while. Our house is only a couple of miles from the drugstore,

9

but by the time we pick up Blake and the bags and *clippity-clop* our way there, winding through the streets of downtown and then north on the unpaved Captain's Road, a good hour has passed. I don't mind; the sky has cleared up and I'm lying back with my head on my duffel, reading the rest of Nadine's story about the speedboat crash and ignoring the locals who stop to watch us go by, some of them shaking their heads and muttering about "summer people."

Shortly after we pass the protected cove known to the locals as "the little harbor," we come to a fork in the road.

"That's *our* house!" Pip cries, pulling me up by the arm to make me look at the carved wooden sign pointing to "The Roost."

The driver makes the turn and we wind down a long, dusty drive bordered by cornflowers and Queen Anne's lace with Pip still gripping my arm and vibrating with excitement. As for me, I'm *acting* nonchalant, but inside I have to admit that I'm incredibly curious if nothing else. I can't deny that I still haven't wrapped my head around the idea that the Roost actually belongs to Pip and me, and no one else. It sounds like something from an old novel.

Around one final bend, and the house and barn come into view.

"Here we are," the driver says, making a wide turn in the yard.

We're still moving, but Pip stands, so now it's my turn to

hold *her* arm so she doesn't do a face-plant into the dirt. Her mouth falls open, and she shakes her head in disbelief. "It's so beautiful! It seems like forever since we were here."

Sometimes two years *is* forever.

The house has definitely suffered a bit from neglect in the two years since our last visit, not that it was in perfect condition then. It's kind of New England-y looking, like our house in Connecticut, except that the Roost's siding and trim are badly in need of a paint job, and quite a few shingles are either missing or crooked. But the yard is neat and freshly mowed, and somebody has trimmed the shrubs around the house. With the exception of a couple of broken windowpanes, the barn—classic red with a gambrel roof, and surrounded by a good-sized fenced pasture—is in excellent condition.

The wagon shudders to a stop and all five of us kids (and Pogo) hop off, ready to explore, when Thomas predictably holds up a hand. "Wait. Everybody stop right where you are. Let's get the bags off the wagon and then . . . we need a picture."

Five groans. Maybe six—I swear Pogo joined in. She is ready to chase something—anything.

"Man," I say, hanging my head. "You're killing me."

He grins and lines us up with the house in the background. The wagon driver takes the picture, then climbs back aboard and waves goodbye. "Give me a call if you need a ride anywhere," he says. "Number's on the card."

Thomas thanks him, then says, "Now, maybe one of just Lark and Pip. It is their house, after all. The rest of us are their guests."

"Can I be opening the door?" Pip asks. "Where's the key?"

"Here you go," says Thomas, tossing her a red rabbit's foot with one brass key dangling from the chain.

She opens the door and then assumes a car show–model pose, pointing to the opening as a small bird flies out, missing her head by inches. Pip holds a hand to her heart. "Omigosh. That *scared* me!"

"Are you done?" I ask Thomas, so flustered by the bird that he drops his phone.

"He probably came down the chimney," he says. "Your mom mentioned something about that. Anyway, I got the picture, so we can go inside."

"Probably a swallow," Pip suggests as we crowd through the narrow door. "The island's named after them, there's so many here. I think it's a sign that we're going to have a *great* summer."

"'One swallow does not make a summer, neither does one fine day,'" says Thomas, mysteriously. We all ignore him as we do whenever he says something strange, so he adds, "Aristotle said that."

*Goody for him*, I think.

"It's a good thing we got here when we did," says Jack, eight, the youngest. "That poor bird would have starved to death." Jack worries about things like that. He's the kind of kid who shoos ants out of the house instead of killing them.

"Are you sure it wasn't a bat?" asks Nate, who is two days older than Pip, a difference that he never lets her forget. "I hate bats."

I set the newspaper and my backpack on the kitchen table. "It wasn't a bat. They only come out at night . . . when they turn into vampires." I whisper into his ear: "And go searching for the blood of little boys. Especially little boys with brown eyes and curly hair."

Pip stands in the middle of the kitchen, hugging herself as she takes in the whole scene. "It's *exactly* the way I remember it." She runs to the hallway closet, opens the door, and then points at pencil marks on the wood trim inside with a squeal. "They're still here!"

"Why *wouldn't* they be?" I ask. "You think someone's going to break in here and erase them?"

"I know, but it's Mommy! Katie, age five! She was so little! Here she is at ten, the same as me." She backs up against the wall and looks at me. "Who's taller?"

I lean in for a closer look. "Looks like a tie."

"No, it's not," says Blake. "Pip's—"

"Exactly the same height," Thomas cuts him off with a wink.

Blake takes the hint. "Oh . . . yeah. You're right."

Pip's face lights up even brighter. "And then she grew all the way to . . . here! Do you think I will, too?"

"Definitely," I say as I wander through the kitchen door into the wallpapered dining room and through that into the living room—*my* living room, I think to myself. A wide staircase divides the rest of the downstairs into two large rooms, the "official" living room with its stiff, rather dated furniture, and the room that Mom called the bird room, with walls of bookshelves and a small loft (reached by a ladder) in the bay that juts out toward the lake. (This might be the place to say that Mom, no doubt inspired by the family name, became a professor of ornithology at a university that everyone has heard of.) Anyway, the reason it's called the bird room is obvious: Resting on tables and shelves, hanging from wires, perched on curtain rods, sitting on the molding above doors and windows, and everywhere else you look are birds of every shape and size. A life-sized great blue heron in bronze anchors one end of the fireplace mantel, at the other is a mounted tree branch with a variety of carved and brightly painted finches (a gift from Dad to Mom on their wedding day).

Something about not seeing the house and especially this room full of memories for a couple of years gets to me. I feel my legs getting a little wobbly, so I settle into a chair before I do a face-plant onto the hardwood. Pip and the boys are running around—why are they *screaming*, anyway?—but I stay in the chair for a long time, composing myself.

Eventually, Thomas finds his way to the bird room. "There you are. I wondered . . . are you okay? You look a little peaked."

"What? I'm fine," I say, almost believing it myself.

"Oh. Geez. This room . . . I'd forgotten . . ." He looks a little weak in the knees, too, and he steadies himself with one hand on the mantel. He reaches up with his other hand and runs it down the neck of the bronze heron, turning his face away from me. When his shoulders start to tremble, I feel like I'm intruding on a private moment and decide to busy myself by airing out the room. I head to the far end of the room, where I push aside the curtains and turn the cranks to open the windows wide. As a faint breeze begins to replace the stuffy, stale air, Thomas wipes his eyes and forces a smile.

"Good idea," he says. "Let's open all of them. Then everybody out to the front yard."

I grab Bedlam's cage from the kitchen and race up the stairs, taking a sharp left into the room that Pip and I share. Both upstairs bedrooms have views of the lake, but the one on the left is smaller and has a pair of matching twin beds, while the one on the right has two sets of bunk beds for the three boys. Pip, a step behind me, runs straight to the French doors that take up much of the front wall and throws them open. Her hands cup her face as she steps out onto the narrow balcony that runs the width of the room and looks out at the western end of Lake Erie, letting the wind tousle her hair. "I feel like I'm dreaming. It's *too* perfect. I'm afraid I'm going to wake up and it'll all be gone."

I set Bedlam on an end table and pinch Pip gently on the

arm. "There. See? It's real. It is weird. . . . I mean, it feels like—"

"—like home? For me, too!"

"I was *going* to say that it feels like, I don't know, when I walked in here I almost expected to see Mom there on the bed, sitting up with a book on her lap. It's stupid."

Pip launches herself at me, throwing her arms around my neck. "It's not stupid. Don't say that. She *is* here . . . kind of. This was her room when she was a little girl. And remember, she used to say she thought it was haunted. Maybe—"

"OUT-RAAA-GEOUS!" Bedlam cries. It's his favorite word.

"I agree with Beddie," I say. "Mom was teasing us. There's no such thing as ghosts. So, which bed do you want this year?" The two beds are identical, with white-painted headboards and footboards, but every summer we came to the island, I gave Pip first choice. Most kids would probably pick one side and stick with it, but not Pip. And she always had a very specific reason for her choice. Two years ago, she picked the one on the right because she insisted that it was better for viewing the moon.

She spins, twisting her lips as she considers this Very Important Decision. She raises an index finger slowly, moving back and forth between the two before stopping at the bed on the left. "That one."

"You're sure." I look up to admire the mobile that the wind from the open doors has set in motion. Not surprisingly, it's made up of eight different species of birds, all with wings extended as if they're flying.

"Ummm . . . yes. Positively. My *Misty* poster is going right *here* next to me. And I can keep my books on the table." Pip has all of Marguerite Henry's *Misty of Chincoteague* books, and has read each one at least a hundred times. When I suggested that perhaps she didn't need to bring them all with her—after all, we're just staying for the summer, I said—she looked at me as if I'd grown a second head.

"Girls!" shouts Thomas from the front yard. "Come on down!"

Pip waves at him from the balcony. "Can we stay here forever?"

"How about we have some lunch and talk about that later," answers Thomas. When we come out the sliding glass door at the front of the house, he is sitting on a plaid blanket in the front yard, unpacking a cooler packed with sandwiches and cans of soda. "Turkey on the left, ham on the right. Everyone grab and go. Lark, will you open that bag of chips, please?"

"What kind of soda is there?" asks Jack, excited because he usually isn't allowed to drink it.

"Any flavor you like . . . as long as it's orange," says Thomas. "If you don't like it, blame Nate—he picked it out yesterday. By the way, people out here don't call it soda. It's pop." The way he says it sounds like *paaap*.

Jack looks at him as if he thinks his leg is being pulled. "You're teasing."

Thomas holds up a hand. "Ask Lark."

When Jack looks to me for confirmation, I nod. "He's right, Jack. You don't remember, 'cause you were so little the last time you were here. Wait till you meet some of the local kids. They all have a funny accent." I choose a turkey sandwich and sit on the low brick wall at the front edge of the property. The Roost sits high up on a rocky point of land above the lake, and directly below me, small waves break on a narrow beach that is strewn with driftwood and seaweed.

Jack joins me on the wall and holds out his hands. "Kate used to hold on to me so I could look out over the edge."

I set my sandwich down and grip his wrists tightly. "You okay? I can't believe Mom let you do this when you were six years old."

"It's not *that* scary," said Jack. "Dad! Can I go down to the beach?"

"Not now," says Thomas. "You'll have plenty of time for that later. We have lots to do today. We need to unpack, and make beds, and figure out what we're going to eat. I'll ride into town for a little shopping, assuming that the bikes are still in the barn. And the tire pump. Volunteers to join me?"

"I'll go!" Jack says.

"I appreciate the offer, Jack, but it's a long ride," Thomas says. "Why don't you stick around and explore the house? Blake, how about it?"

Blake mumbles, "All right, I'll go," through a mouthful of sandwich.

"Great. Thank you," says Thomas. "You can pick what you want for dinner."

"Gee, I wonder what that will be," I say, knowing full well that it's going to be chicken of some kind. Blake would eat chicken every meal of every day if he could. I swear the kid's growing feathers.

"Whose house is *that*?" Jack asks, pointing to the beautiful— and *enormous*—Victorian cottage half a mile north, perched on a rocky cliff much higher than the one we're standing on. "It's like a *mansion*."

"Some sea captain," I say. "It's a museum now."

"Not just any sea captain," says an unfamiliar voice. "Captain Edward Cheever."

We all spin around to find a man in starched khaki pants and a matching safari shirt with its short sleeves rolled right to his shoulders, the better to show off his impressive biceps and tattoos on both forearms. His steel-gray hair is cropped short and perfectly flat on top, as if it were done with a lawn mower—and he looks hard-boiled enough that it just might have been. I have a vague memory of seeing him before. It must have been three or four summers back, before Mom and Thomas got married, when he stopped by the house after a bad storm to see if we were okay. Just like that time, he seems to have just appeared out of thin air—none of us saw him coming and then there he is, standing three feet away. The only thing missing is the puff of smoke.

"Sorry, didn't mean to scare you," he says in response to our blank stares and open mouths. He approaches Thomas and as they shake hands, Thomas winces a little. "Don't know if you remember me. Les Findlay. Live down the road a bit. Saw you pass by and thought I'd stop and say hi."

"Right. Les. I'm Thomas. Emmery. Sure, I remember you. Good to see you again. Been a couple of years."

"Miss Pritchard told me you were coming. Told me about Kate. A real shame. My condolences. Always liked her. Anyway, Miss Pritchard asked me to get everything ready for you. Said you were planning to spend the summer."

"She was Mommy's best friend when they were kids," Pip says. "She's at a horse show—that's why she didn't meet us at the ferry."

"Coming back on the last boat tonight, I believe," says Les. With a nod at the folded copy of the *Citizen* on the blanket, he adds, "I see you're catching up on all the local news. That's quite a story Miss Pritchard spins."

I lift the paper and point to the picture of the destroyed boat. "The man who got killed—was he related to Nadine? She doesn't say, but he has the same last name."

"Sure is—was. Albert Pritchard was her grandfather."

Thomas looks over my shoulder at the front page of the

paper. "Wow. That must have been some crash."

Findlay points to the house we'd been looking at when he mysteriously appeared. "Look to the left of the museum, couple of hundred yards. See that buoy? That's where the wreck happened. Ada's Reef, it's called. Named after Captain Cheever's daughter. Or maybe his daughter was named after it—I forget. Nasty rocks a few inches below the surface. Pritchard's boat was fast, a double-cockpit Hacker, nineteen forty. He was probably going fifty when he hit 'em."

Sunlight is sparkling on the water, and I squint for a better look at the buoy. "The buoy has a light on it, right?" I say. "A red one."

"That's right. Flashes every second."

I let that sink in. "Was it—the light—there when the crash happened?"

Findlay nods, and the corners of his mouth turn up ever so slightly. "I see where you're going. Folks've been asking that question since the night of the crash: What was he doing on the wrong side of that buoy on a calm night? He knew the waters around the island like the back of his hand. Don't make sense."

"I guess that's why it's still selling newspapers," says Thomas. "People love a good mystery. Lark here is really good at solving them."

As Les Findlay talks, Jack zeroes in on his tattoos and follows every movement of those muscular forearms. Eventually, he works up the courage to ask, "Were you in the navy or something? Is that why you have a tattoo of a ship?"

Findlay holds out his right arm for all of us to see. "It's not a ship. It's a PBR—a kind of patrol boat. I took one up the Mekong River in Vietnam back in sixty-seven, sixty-eight. Funny thing is, when I left there, I swore I'd never set foot on another boat. Said I was gonna move to Montana, as far from the water as I could find. But here I am living on an island and runnin' a work boat—even kinda looks like the PBR. Only difference, most days nobody's shooting at me. I work down the marina, sorta semi-retired now. Life's funny, I guess." He pauses, looking as if he has something to add, but gives up with a shake of his head. "I'll leave you folks to your lunch now. You need anything, you know where to find me."

Actually, I'm thinking, *We* don't—"*down the road a bit" isn't exactly precise now, is it?*

Findlay tips an imaginary cap and disappears into the brush as quickly and as silently as he'd appeared.

"*Most* days?" I say when he's out of sight.

"What do you mean?" Thomas asks.

"What he said. *Most* days nobody's shooting at him. So, like, *some* days they are?" Maybe Swallowtail Island isn't as peaceful as it seems.

# CHAPTER
# 2

THE SLOW PARADE TO BED after our first day on the island starts with Jack, carried upstairs by Thomas a little after eight thirty. Pip, whose eyelids grew heavier and heavier as she read *Stormy, Misty's Foal* for the umpteenth time, is next, followed by Blake, who falls asleep with both thumbs on a video game. Nate, the middle brother who's afraid of missing something important every time Thomas sends him to bed, hangs in there for another half hour before he finally drops off. Thomas and I sit wordlessly in folding aluminum chairs on the front porch for a long time, listening to the waves lap up against the shore, and watching the flashing of the red light of the buoy off the captain's house. Occasionally, a boat rounds the buoy heading south to Port Clinton or Put-in-Bay, the most popular of the Lake Erie Islands. A few minutes past ten, Thomas stands and lifts Nate into his arms. "Well, that's it for me. And Nate. Don't stay up too late, okay?"

"Mmm."

"Lark?"

"Mm?" I pull my heels up onto the chair and wrap my arms around my legs.

He hesitates. Thomas has always had a hard time talking to me, even before Mom died, and now it's just plain awkward. And yeah, I know: My one-syllable responses don't exactly make it easy. The thing is, I know Mom's death has been hard on people besides me, but that doesn't mean I have to be sympathetic or something. It's only been three months, and the way I see it, I'm entitled to be unreasonable.

"Listen," he starts. "I want you to know how much I appreciate all your help . . . with Pip and all. And the boys, especially Jack. He really listens to you. I think he likes having a big sister. He never knew his mom, and then losing Kate . . ."

That part makes me feel like a schmuck. I forget sometimes that the boys have lost two parents, too—their mom and their stepmom.

"I know this isn't the summer you had planned, but let's try to make the best of it, what do you say?"

Without looking up at him, I say, "Mmm. Yeah. I will."

That's *four* syllables, if you're counting.

When I switch on the light on the bedside table, Pip stirs once but doesn't wake. Pogo, stretched across the width of my bed, lifts her head, looks around the room with her usual befuddled expression, and drops back to sleep. Bedlam calls out, "Hello!" from his cage.

"Shhhh!"

"Shhh!" he repeats.

"Stupid bird."

"Stupid bird," he says.

"Good night, Beddie," I say, draping his cage with a pillowcase.

"Sweet dreams," he says in Mom's voice, and I shiver.

The leaves of the poplar tree to the left of the balcony rustle in the breeze, and out on the lake a sailboat motors past the buoy. Standing at the screen door of Mom's old room, and sitting on the edge of the bed that was once hers while running my fingers across the spines of the books of her childhood, I find myself missing her more than ever.

"Coming back here may have been a mistake," I say aloud, though I'm the only one listening.

A sudden gust of wind lifts the curtain, and above me, something clatters against the wood of the exposed beams. All eight birds that make up the mobile are swaying in the breeze, and from time to time a tail or wingtip collides with a beam, sending that bird off into a spinning frenzy. Something about the way the light from my table lamp is shining on them makes me

notice the colors and
how perfectly each one
is painted. If I had to
guess, I'd say the
mobile came from
a museum shop or
maybe a zoo. It's
not junk, but it's not
exactly fine art, if you
know what I mean.

Growing up with
an ornithologist for
a mom, I would die
of shame if I couldn't
identify them: cardinal, eastern bluebird, goldfinch, Baltimore
oriole, house finch, scarlet tanager, and—yay!—the lovely eastern meadowlark. The eighth bird doesn't fit in with the others,
though. The other seven are considered "perching birds," but
based on the shape of his wings, number eight is definitely a
species of swallow. It also doesn't seem to be painted at all. Its
body looks to be made of metal of some kind, but the color is
a dull brownish-gray, not at all like the brightly painted bodies
of the others.

I stand on the bed for a closer look, hoping that the slats
holding up the mattress don't give out. Except for the strange
coloring, it looks alive, its pointed wings like those of a

fighter jet. I reach up and stop the mobile's movement with one hand, undo the brass S-hook at the end of the wire the swallow hangs from, and cradle its tiny body in my hands as I drop to my knees on the bed.

Holding it close to the light, the first thing that jumps out at me is all the color that wasn't visible while he was hanging from the mobile. Unlike his underbody and wings, which are, I realize, badly tarnished silver, the top of his head and much of his back is iridescent blue enamel that glows in the moonlight peeking through the windows—and I am *mesmerized* by how beautiful it is. I mean, I literally can't take my eyes off it. This is no toy or cheap souvenir from a day at the zoo; it *is* a work of art. Round and round I spin it in my hands, and with every turn I see something more. It feels fragile, hollow—yet it is oddly heavy for its size.

I'm pretty sure it's a tree swallow, but I can't be positive until I consult the well-used, much-loved Audubon guide that Mom carried everywhere she went, and is now in the side pocket of my duffel. It is a book filled with memories of Mom, and opening it takes me back in time to our long walks on the shore or in the woods near our house in Connecticut. Her notes, in the elegant, flowing cursive that I attempt to imitate when I write in my journal, fill the margins of nearly every page with the details of each bird sighting. I leaf through the color plates until I get to the "swallow-like birds," and there he is in all his glory: the tree swallow, *Iridoprocne bicolor.*

"Sparrow-sized. The only swallow in the East with metallic blue or blue-green upperparts and white underparts."

My question is: Why is a beautiful (and expensive-looking) swallow hanging from a mobile with a bunch of fairly ordinary carved perching birds?

Apparently, the question I should have been asking is: What happened to the *real* eighth bird when this high-class impostor took its place? *That* one, I'm happy to say, I can definitely answer. I wish I could tell you that I found it as a result of my superior sleuthing skills, but it literally dropped out of the sky. I stand up on the bed again to rehook the swallow to the mobile (it seems like the safest place for it), and when I grab hold of a beam to steady myself, I send something tumbling from the top of the beam onto the bed—a rose-breasted grosbeak.

"Well, well," I say. "Hello there, Mr. Grosbeak. I think it's time you joined your friends." I hook him onto the wire and send him on his way with a little push. "Happy flying."

I look around the room in search of a place to keep the mysterious little swallow safe and settle on the bottom drawer of my dresser, empty except for a stack of old soccer shirts I'd tossed in earlier.

"Don't go anywhere," I say, pushing the drawer closed.

Pip's bed is already made and she is long gone by the time I open my eyes. The smell of breakfast gets me moving, and the first thing I do is open the dresser drawer to stare at and hold the swallow in my hands for a few seconds. When I hear footsteps outside the room, I quickly set it back in place, cover it with a T-shirt, and close the drawer.

"You comin' down?" Pip asks from the doorway.

"On my way." I'm not sure why, but I decide to keep the silver swallow to myself—at least for now. Something about him makes me think that he has a story worth looking into.

Before I go down, I peek under the cover of Bedlam's cage.

"What are you doing?" he whispers, which makes me laugh—as it does every morning. He started saying it about a year ago, when his cage was hanging in the living room at our house in Connecticut. Every morning, Jack, the first one awake, lifted a corner of the sheet and whispered those words. After a couple of months of that, Bedlam surprised him one morning by saying it before Jack had a chance to.

After a breakfast of his "famous" waffles with blueberries

and maple syrup that we brought from home, Thomas points to an item in the "Island Activities for Kids" column in the *Swallowtail Citizen*.

I read it silently and set the paper on the table.

"Starts a week from today," he says.

"What is it?" Pip asks.

"Soccer camp," Thomas says.

When he says the word "soccer," everyone stops chewing and looks straight at me, mouths wide open. Blake is first to regain the gift of speech: "Soccer camp? I thought she wasn't allowed to . . . after . . ."

"After what, Blake?" I say. "The . . . *Incident*?" That's how it's known in the family: The Incident on the Soccer Field. I've started calling it the ISF just to save time. For now, here's all you need to know:

1. I was involved in an incident during soccer practice after school.

2. I got kicked off the team for the rest of the season. If I follow all the rules laid down by the principal and athletic director, they *might* let me back on next year. Then again, they might not.

3. The school agreed not to put it on my permanent record as long as I promised to get counseling. Since

adults freak out whenever the words "permanent record" are mentioned, Thomas immediately accepted the deal. So now I have to go have these deep, meaningful chats with a therapist every couple of weeks. Ugh.

One more thing: I am—well, *was*—the best player on the team. Not bragging, just being honest. A couple of boarding schools in Connecticut have asked me to visit their campuses, and the word "scholarship" has been mentioned. Which is another reason that Thomas was so worried about the ISF showing up on my permanent record.

"No one here knows about that . . . or needs to," says Thomas. "What's past is past. It's like Marcus Aurelius said, 'Our lives lie within the *present*. The past is done and the future is uncertain.' Anyway, Lark is moving on, and so am I. I think the camp would be good for all of you. Make some friends, get some exercise. The coaches are all college players, including one girl—sorry, young woman—from UNC. You could talk to her about what it's like playing there, Lark. It's mornings, eight to noon. You'll have the rest of the day to do whatever you want."

Thomas is pushing all the right buttons. It's my dream to play soccer at the University of North Carolina—home to players like Mia Hamm and Meghan Klingenberg and Tobin Heath—and I'm having a hard time coming up with a reason to say thanks but no thanks to this opportunity.

"I think we should," Pip says.

Jack and Nate agree, leaving only Blake and me.

"I'm kinda done with soccer," Blake says, glancing at the other options on the list.

"I think soccer's kinda done with *you*," I say.

He ignores my dig. "Can I do this theater thing instead?"

"Fine with me," says Thomas. "That leaves Lark—what do you think?"

"Sure. What the heck," I say.

"Excellent!" Thomas says, pleased and maybe a little surprised at how easy it was to talk me into it. Then his phone rings, and he takes it outside to talk, returning a few seconds later. "That was Nadine—she's on her way over. Let's get this mess cleaned up, whadayasay?"

"Eh, I say, let's leave it alone," says Nate, grinning.

Thomas throws him a sponge. "For that, smarty-pants, you get to wash."

Nadine arrives on horseback, much to Pip's delight. And not just any horse—it's a gray Arabian, the most beautiful horse I've ever seen. When she takes off her riding helmet, her long chestnut hair tumbles down around her shoulders and she looks remarkably like the girl in the pictures in Mom's scrapbooks from when they were in high school.

"Nadine!" Pip cries, running to hug her as she drops from the saddle. "It's so good to see you. Your horse is . . . the . . ." She shakes her head, unable to find the words she needs.

"This is a first," Thomas says. "Pip, speechless. How are you, Nadine?"

"So much better now," she says. She stops to admire the house for a second before hugging the boys and petting Pogo. Her eyes finally land on me. "Oh, my. Look at you." She pulls me in close, squeezing tight. "Seeing you standing outside this house, in that T-shirt, those shorts . . . good golly, you look so much like your mom it's scary. And seriously, have you grown since the—since the last time I saw you? It was only a couple months ago! How tall *are* you, anyway?"

"Five-eight. And a half."

"I'm so jealous. What I wouldn't give to be five-eight."

"And a half," Pip adds, stroking the mane of Nadine's horse. "What's her name?"

"That's Lulu. She's been with me for a year now. She's a beauty, isn't she? Can I park her in your barn for a while, out of the sun?"

I open the barn door and Pip leads Lulu inside and into a box stall.

"Now maybe a bucket of water," says Nadine, looking around. "Ah, here we go." She picks up an overturned metal bucket and fills it with water from a spigot on the wall.

Pip can't take her eyes off Lulu, so she stays in the barn when Nadine and I join Thomas and the boys in the kitchen.

"What can I get you to drink?" Thomas asks Nadine.

"We have orange . . . *paaap*," Jack says, collapsing into laughter as he says it.

Nadine looks at me, her left eyebrow raised. "Water would be great."

"Jack thinks it's very funny that you call soda *pop*," I explain.

Thomas yells out the screen door, "Pip! You'll have plenty of time to talk to the horse later. Come in and talk to Nadine."

"She really does have a bad case of horse fever, doesn't she?" Nadine says. "She's still taking riding lessons, right?"

"Oh, yes," Thomas answers. "Twice a week. And still trying to convince me to buy her a horse. I'd do it in a second if we had a barn. Boarding in Connecticut is not a realistic option. It's outrageously expensive."

"You know, I have a . . . no, I'd better not," Nadine says.

Thomas fills a Flintstones glass tumbler with ice and water and hands it to her. "What is it?" He looks out the screen door and shakes his head at Pip's stubbornness.

Nadine takes a long drink and sets the glass on the table. "I remember these glasses. Katie loved the Flintstones. And the Jetsons."

"We've got that one, too," I say. "And my personal favorites, Heckle and Jeckle."

"What I was going to say," starts Nadine, "is that I have the perfect horse for Pip. She's a rescue from south of Sandusky, but in good shape. Very sweet filly named Tinker. Her dam was a Chincoteague pony."

At the word "Chincoteague," I slap my palm to my forehead. "No. Way. If Pip were here, her *head* would have just exploded. *Misty* is her favorite book."

"Totally up to you, Thomas," Nadine says. "I could bring Tinker by and she could spend the summer here . . . if you want. No commitment. A little exercise would be good for her. And when I say she's sweet, I'm serious. She's the gentlest pony I've ever seen. I can help you get settled with hay—looks like there's already plenty of straw in the barn, and the pasture's in good shape. I even have a nice little saddle that'll be a perfect fit for both of them."

At that exact moment, Pip reaches the screen door and pulls it open. We all go silent and she stops in her tracks. "What?" she says when she sees the silly grins we're all sporting.

When we finally manage to pry Pip from the ceiling, Thomas, Nadine, and I take our drinks out on the front porch to enjoy the breeze and the view of the lake. Nadine tells us about how little Swallowtail has changed in the two years since our last visit—a new coffee shop on Main Street is the highlight. Thomas admits that the summer isn't going to be a vacation for him; before we left Connecticut, he contracted to do some work for the museum on Swallowtail as well as a couple of other museums on the mainland. Although he is a very talented painter himself, he supports the six of us by restoring valuable (and some not-so-valuable) paintings for museums and private owners. If you've ever seen an old oil painting, you know what I'm talking about. When they're new, the colors are crisp and bright, but over time, the varnish that's put on to protect the paint gradually gets darker and darker, until the painting looks basically like a muddy pond. He spends hours and hours (using his own secret techniques and formulas) removing those layers of varnish and grime until the painting looks like new again. He always says that cleaning a painting is a lot like painting one: You have to know when to stop.

"But enough about me," Thomas announces. "Tell us about yourself. What are you working on? Book number . . . What are you up to now? Seven? Eight?" After a very successful career as a journalist with a British TV network, Nadine returned to Swallowtail Island and wrote a bestselling memoir about her time in Africa. That was followed by several more books, most of them about not-quite-famous people who, in her eyes, deserve to be better known.

"Working on number eight. And lucky for me, I found the perfect subject right here on Swallowtail. For once I don't have to travel all over God's green earth interviewing people."

"That speedboat crash?" I say.

Nadine holds up a hand for me to high-five. "Yay! *Somebody* read my story!"

"I picked up a paper when we were waiting in town for our ride."

"The crash is interesting, to be sure, and it will sell some papers—which will make the editor happy—but it's really just one little piece in a thousand-piece puzzle. There's a woman on the island—Dinah Purdy, she's ninety-three. The book's really about her. She's absolutely *amazing*, and hardly anybody knows what she's accomplished in her life—which, believe me, is a *lot*."

"And if I know you, that's going to change very soon," Thomas says.

Nadine points north along the shore. "Dinah lives alone in a little cottage out on Rabbit Ear Point, couple of miles past the museum. Her father was Captain Cheever's first mate, and he built the place back in the twenties. Dinah left the island for college and law school in the forties—this is an African American woman we're talking about, the first member of her family to go to college. She came back every summer and spent two or three weeks on the island, and when she finally retired seven or eight years ago, she was determined to stay in the cottage even though it's pretty isolated, especially in the winter. I wrote a little story about it at the time. She said she wanted to spend the rest of her days reading good books, watching the

MICHAEL D. BEIL

birds, and listening to the waves."

"Doesn't sound half bad," says Thomas. "'In all things of
nature there is something of the marvelous.'"

"Marcus Aurelius?" Nadine asks.

"Aristotle," says Thomas.

"So . . . how is she connected to the speedboat?" I ask, but
before Nadine can answer, I add another question: "And the
man who was killed, he was your . . . grandfather?"

"That's right," says Nadine. "I'm still trying to figure out
all the connections. Like I said, this puzzle is complicated. I'm
spending my days—and nights—reading old legal documents
and talking to everyone who was alive back then. The list of
people who remember those days is getting shorter and shorter."

"Would you like some help? An assistant, maybe?" Thomas
asks, looking right at me. "Sorry, I don't mean to put you on
the spot, but this sounds like it's right up Lark's alley. I think
she'd be perfect. She's incredibly observant, and has a mind
like a bear trap—once it gets in there, she never lets it go.
*Way* smarter than me. Kate and I used to read mysteries aloud
to her, and she always figured them out before we got to the
end. And she was the only one—we would guess, but we were
wrong every time."

Nadine puts her hand on my arm. "I would love it. And I do
need the help. But I insist on paying you. How about a hundred
and fifty a week, and I promise, no more than fifteen hours.
You can come over in the afternoons."

"A hundred and fifty dollars a week!" I say. "You're serious?"

"Cross my heart," Nadine says.

On Tuesday morning, the boys head out to explore the shoreline while Thomas, Pip, and I take bikes across the island to look at Tinker, the piebald half-Chincoteague pony that Nadine is "loaning" to Pip for the summer. Although Nadine won't be home—she's teaching at a writers' conference until Friday—she has welcomed us to come over to check out Tinker for ourselves and to walk around the farm. Her house is modern with lots of glass across the front, and sits across a narrow channel from the southern end of Cattail Island, a low, marshy home to tens of thousands of birds. The horse barn is enormous, with a dozen stalls on each side of an indoor riding arena, but it takes Pip no time to find who she is looking for. And any chance that Thomas had of swaying her toward a new pink bicycle instead disappears the moment she lays eyes on Tinker. Six years old and standing a shade over thirteen hands, she is, Pip declares, "*perfection*."

For the next three days (Nadine promised to deliver Tinker Friday afternoon), from breakfast to bedtime, Pip talks of nothing else. One thing's for sure: Nadine doesn't have to worry about Pip being a responsible caretaker. No amount of ignoring, eye-rolling, or threatening can dissuade her from her mission to learn (and share!) the sum total of all human knowledge of horses before Tinker comes to live with us. She drags the rest of us to the library to get library cards so she can take out *every* book about caring for horses in the collection. For such a small library, it has a surprising number, providing her with enough ammunition to bombard us with nonstop equine trivia:

"Did you know that horses have sixteen muscles in each ear?"

"A horse's heart weighs about *ten* pounds!"

"Can you believe that a horse produces ten gallons of saliva a day?"

"One horse lived to be sixty-two years old!"

And on. And on.

The movies: *Black Beauty. National Velvet. The Black Stallion. Misty. Flicka.* (All, believe it or not, on VHS tapes from the library—and yes, the Roost still has a working VHS player!) Binge-watching *The Saddle Club* on her tablet. Fresh discoveries, like *Free Rein* and *Heartland*, and her new all-time favorite, *Ride.* That show inspires her to add a painted-on crest and red trim to a navy blazer she salvaged from the local thrift store and now wears everywhere. She scrubs every square inch of the stall she has chosen and paints Tinker's name on the door. After some hard bargaining with the manager of the grocery store, she uses her allowance to buy a twenty-five-pound bag of carrots, which she carries home on the back of my bicycle.

By the time we sit down for dinner on Thursday night, the rest of us are exhausted and cranky. After hearing the story (for the third time in as many days) of the Ash Wednesday Storm of 1962 in which the owners of Misty kept her safe in their kitchen, Blake announces, "I swear, if I have to hear one more story about how smart, or how strong, or how . . . *anything* horses are, I'm gonna jump off the cliff into the lake."

"Did you know that in nineteen forty-nine, a horse in Chile jumped over a fence that was *eight* feet high?"

Blake leaps to his feet. "Dad! Make her stop! She's driving us crazy."

Thomas motions for Blake to sit. "All right, all right. Calm down. Pip, honey . . . I think maybe it's time to give the horses a rest—and yes, I *know* they can sleep standing up. Let's talk about something else for a while, what do you say?"

"I can't help myself," she says. "I just love them *so* much."

"I know you do, and that's great, but you gotta give the rest of us a break," I say. "You're going to see Tinker in . . . nineteen hours. So from now until one o'clock tomorrow, you can't say the word 'horse.' Or 'pony.' Or anything to do with them. Deal?"

"Deal," she says, as if she has just bargained away her very soul.

I put my arm around her. "You know, if you stick that bottom lip out any further, a chickadee's gonna land on it."

# CHAPTER
# 3

WHEN THE FIRST DAY OF soccer camp ends, I wave goodbye to Nate, Jack, and Pip as they head for the Roost and I pedal off to Nadine's for my first day as her assistant. She has lunch ready and we have quiche and salad at a table next to her swimming pool.

"We'll get down to some work in a little bit, but first I want to hear about your day. Oh! And Pip! How are she and Tinker getting along?"

"We practically had to drag her away from the barn for soccer this morning," I say. "She would totally sleep in there if we let her. She's ridden every day, just around the pasture. Thomas doesn't want her to go off on her own yet, but she's wearing him down."

"She's such a good rider—she's going to be fine. So, how

about you? I can find a nice horse for you if you want."

"I'm more of a bike person," I say. "Nothing *against* horses, but—"

Nadine holds up a hand. "No need to explain. I get it. They're not for everybody. You remember Kira? She didn't like horses, either." Kira Langley had been Nadine's producer during the Africa years. She was killed by a stray bullet in Somalia, the event that led to Nadine's return to America. "So, first day of soccer. All good?"

"It was all right," I say. "I'm sure it'll be better once we . . . actually start learning stuff. Today was just kind of figuring who has some skills and who doesn't."

"You're in the former group, obviously."

"Yeah, I'm okay," I say. "There's one boy, Owen somebody, he's pretty good, I guess. He's kind of a ball hog, though."

"Owen *Cheever*?" Nadine asks, her eyes narrowing.

"I . . . *think* so. He has long hair . . . and all the best equipment. His cleats cost more than—"

"Oh, yeah. That's Owen Cheever. As in *Captain* Cheever. And the Cheever Museum. Owen's family are direct descendants. *And* they're right smack in the middle of this story I'm working on. Right about now, I think they'd like nothing better than for me to disappear—until July twenty-eighth, that is."

"What happens on July twenty-eighth?"

"If they have their way, this tranquil little island is going to be transformed into something very, very different. Come on inside. It's easier to show you on a map."

We gather the dishes and leftover quiche and carry them inside. The first thing I notice inside is a framed photo of Nadine and Kira on a console table in the foyer. They're in hiking gear, carrying packs and standing in front of a sign at the base of Kilimanjaro.

"We didn't look so great a few days later," Nadine says when she sees that I have slowed for a better look. "Eight days without a shower can do that to you. We *were* still smiling, though. Amazing trip."

"You guys look so . . ."

"Young?"

"I was going to say *happy*," I say. "And beautiful. I didn't know you climbed Kilimanjaro. I just read a story about this girl who did it for her sixteenth birthday instead of a sweet sixteen. *So* much cooler. I told Thomas I want to do it before all the glaciers melt, but he's like, 'We'll see.'"

"Something tells me you'll find a way," Nadine says. Then she touches the frame gently. "Hard to believe this was taken ten years ago. I still remember what we had for lunch that day, before we started up the mountain."

She then leads me into a room with an enormous table surrounded by ten chairs. But it's obvious that there's been no actual dining in this room for quite a while. Stacks of file folders and old newspapers, photographs, boxes of photographic slides, books about the history of the island and property law, and dozens of photocopies of handwritten legal documents cover every horizontal surface in the room including much of the floor, and the walls are covered in tacked-up maps, nautical charts, survey plans of the island, and more pictures.

"This is my war room," Nadine says. "It's more organized than it looks, honest. Take a look at this map of Swallowtail. Here's the ferry dock, and your house is about *here*, and the Cheever Museum is out on this point. Now, let's go back to eighteen eighty-nine. That's when Captain Edward Cheever is born—right here on the island. His only sibling, Gilbert, doesn't come along until nineteen oh-two, so they're, what, thirteen years apart, and are never close—which is going to matter later. Eventually, Edward gets married and has a daughter, Ada, who's born the same year as Dinah Purdy. He's happy for a few years, and then it all starts to fall apart. A flu epidemic hits the island the winter Ada turns twelve, and both she *and* her mother die, leaving the captain all alone. He lives a few more years, and then drops dead of a . . . well, they say it was a broken heart, but more likely, it was a heart attack, maybe a stroke. With me so far?"

"Got it," I say. In my brain, I've already started constructing a timeline.

Turning her attention back to the map, she points at the northwest corner of the island, tracing a dotted line across a big chunk of it. "Okay. So, when Captain Cheever dies, he owns all this land—everything north of *this* line. Something in the neighborhood of five hundred acres, or almost twenty percent of the island. A *lot* of land. Unfortunately, the only will that the captain leaves behind is one written in the thirties that, naturally, leaves everything to his wife and daughter. One little problem: they're already dead. So who gets it all? His only living heir, the brother he hates. Gilbert."

"Oh, man. That's terrible," I say.

"Yeah. It is. And the captain's relatives still own most of it. They gave, or sold, a few acres to the town, but all the rest is still in their grubby little hands. But hold on, we're not done yet. There's one not-so-little surprise in the will. This part is a little complicated. The captain had made a provision for his old friend and first mate, Elias Purdy—Dinah's father. He wanted to take care of Elias, who had lost his wife right after Dinah was born, so he did what a lot of people did back then. He left Elias a life estate in all the land north of this line and east of this one—including all of Rabbit Ear Point, where the Purdys lived in a small cottage. A life estate is a legal thing— it means that as long as Elias was alive, he could stay on the land. Technically, he didn't *own* it, but he had the right to live on it rent-free and couldn't be kicked off it. At the time of the captain's death, Elias was in his fifties, and Dinah was about seventeen and ready to leave for college. And the fact is, land on the island wasn't worth very much back then.

"But there's one more wrinkle, and it's a doozy: The life estate didn't end when Elias died. The will was written in such a way that the life estate passed on to Dinah and continued until *her* death . . . *or* when seventy-five years had passed. When the captain died, it probably never crossed anyone's mind that Dinah would still be alive, but . . . here we all are. And on July twenty-eighth, the seventy-fifth anniversary of the captain's death and the execution of the will, full ownership of the land—land that is now worth *millions*, by the way—will go back to the Cheevers."

"Are you serious? They're going to kick a ninety-three-year-old lady out of her house!?"

"They have said that they hope it doesn't come to that. What they *mean* is that they hope she's dead by the time they get around to bulldozing that part of the island."

"Bulldozing! What are they going to do?"

"Exactly what you'd expect of people with buckets of money and zero imagination. Ugly condos, hideous McMansions, a golf course. The real shame is that they are going to ruin hundreds of acres of wildlife habitat, land that's basically untouched by humans. There are foxes, mink, beavers, muskrats, not to mention the *tens of thousands* of birds that nest along the shore and on Cattail Island. Even if they don't destroy it, they're going to disrupt it for years. Swallowtail is going to be a very different place, very soon. The Cheevers are very keen on allowing cars on the island, which would push up the value of the land even more. Their dream is to turn it into a midwestern Nantucket—a place that only really wealthy people can afford."

"Isn't there anything you can do?"

"I'm working on it, but time . . . and just about everything—and everyone—are against me. The locals think it's going to mean lots of jobs for them, and it will—for a while. But then what? It's not like they're going to be able to afford to buy these places. It's all for the summer people. I'm not saying that the Cheevers shouldn't be able to build *anything*, only that there should be some limits in place to protect the island. So far, though, I'm spittin' into the wind."

"There has to be *something* we can do," I say. "Can we back up for a second? Didn't you say that the boat crash had something to do with all this?"

"I'm sure it did—I just can't prove it. Albert Pritchard—my grandfather—was the captain's lawyer and a close friend. The crash happened the *day after* the captain died. Pretty suspicious, wouldn't you say? The two of them dying one day apart? The accounts of the accident just don't add up. Albert grew up boating and had been around the island hundreds of times. Why, suddenly, did he cut that particular corner?" Nadine pokes her index finger at Ada's Reef on the nautical chart.

"That does seem weird," I say.

"There's more. Gilbert Cheever, the captain's brother, was a lawyer, too. He worked for my grandfather, who was several years *younger* than he was. After the crash, though, he conveniently took over all of Albert's clients. Something about it all—the timing, the connections, Albert cutting that corner at Ada's Reef—as Kira would have said, it just doesn't *smell* right." Nadine drifts off for a few seconds, but recovers quickly. "Would you like to see the boat—what's left of it? It's out in one of the sheds."

"It's *here*? Really?"

"They brought it here right after the crash. This was my grandfather's land. He didn't live on it—he had a house in town—but all the barns were here back then. There was an old farmhouse that burned in the twenties, I think, and Albert bought the land for a song. Anyway, the boat. Somebody removed the engine a long time ago, but otherwise it's just like the day they brought it here."

Behind the horse barn is a smaller, decrepit shed with a sagging roof and siding in dire need of painting. "Excuse the condition of this old barn," Nadine says as she slides the wide door open, its rusty hardware screeching in protest. "Haven't gotten around to fixing it up. Everybody says I should knock it down and start over, but I think it still has some life in it. Here, help me fold this tarp back."

Together, we uncover the boat, which is resting on sawhorses, bottom side up. As the picture in the newspaper had shown, much of the bottom is either gone or caved in. Seeing all the damage in person and taking into account the thickness of the wood and all the framing underneath, I get a picture of how violent the crash must have been. "It's kind of scary, seeing it. It must have . . . I mean . . ." I shake my head in awe of what I'm seeing.

Nadine runs her hand along the planking. "I know—I have to keep reminding myself that my grandfather *died* because of this. Left behind a wife and three little kids, all under seven. One of them was my father."

We pull the tarp back over the ruined boat and as we close the barn door behind us, Nadine stops suddenly. "Speaking of my father, I suppose I should warn you about the Wimdits," she says, pointing with her chin at the house.

"The . . . what?"

"A Wimdit is a *who*. There's a separate apartment on the far side of the house. They hardly ever come out. In fact, if you work here all summer, there's a good chance you'll never see them. Most of the time, the only sign of life—if you can call it that—is the TV, which is blaring at all hours, and always the same channel: The Wright News. It's like their religion."

"And you, like, rent out the apartment to them?"

"Sort of. Only I don't charge them rent because they're"—she hangs her head in shame and lowers her voice—"my parents."

"Wait . . . *what*? I thought you said their name was—"

"The Wimdits. Old family joke. When I was a kid, my dad was *crazy*-mad at our neighbor about something stupid, and he was so insanely furious that he was babbling incoherently. At some point, he calls the guy a *wimdit* instead of a dimwit, and I just lost it. And then, of course, he was furious with me, but that's another story. And, well, now the name fits so . . . *perfectly*. They *are* the Wimdits. Herb and Clara."

"So . . . you don't, like, get along?"

"Not from day one," she says, shaking her head. "Let me put it like this. Oh, good golly, this is going to sound incredibly insensitive considering that you actually *are* an orphan—I'm sorry, is it okay to say that?"

I shrug. "Doesn't bother me."

"Oh, good. Do me a favor and let me know if I do say anything that's not, okay? Anyway, from about the time I was your age, I *envied* orphans. I grew up loving *Anne of Green Gables* and *The Secret Garden* because both girls are smart, resilient orphans who totally overcome their lack of parents. I *dreamed* of being one of them." She notes my wide eyes and continues. "See? I told you it was wildly inappropriate. Sorry. All my friends say that I'm too blunt. They'll make excuses for my parents, like, 'They're the product of their environment' or 'They grew up in a different world.' And I say, no, they're just plain old ignorant. And they don't want to learn to live in the world that we have. I believe in telling it like it is. I've always hated euphemisms. You'll never catch me saying that someone *passed on*. Or worse, they were *called home*. Argghh! They're not a kid missing a curfew—they're dead!"

I'm shaking from holding in laughter, but Nadine mistakes it for something else and her hand flies to her mouth.

"Oh, I'm such an idiot! You're never coming back, are you?

What is wrong with me?"

"No, no!" I say. "I love it. You're actually honest. I didn't even know what a euphemism *was* until Mom died. I must have heard a million of them. At her funeral, some guy told me that she'd been carried away by angels. I told him they needed to bring her back—I wasn't done with her yet. I have this rule for when I write in my journal. I call it the GHT. The God's Honest Truth. No baloney."

Nadine smiles, nodding. "The GHT. I like it. So you're not going to run screaming from here?"

"Not yet, anyway."

"Whew. Thank goodness. C'mon in the house and let's get you started. There's something I want you to read," she says as we re-enter the war room. She digs through the stack of documents piled at the far end of the table until she finds what she's looking for—a half-inch-thick stack of paper held together with a binder clip. "Ah, here it is. I finally got this yesterday. Been waiting for it for a while. It was in an archive in a courthouse somewhere on the mainland."

"What is it?"

"The report from the coroner's inquest after Albert's death."

"Inquest?"

"Basically, whenever anyone dies suddenly or unexpectedly, the coroner investigates and determines the cause of death. It's kind of like a trial—there's usually witnesses, but it's not to decide if somebody's guilty or innocent, only *how* the person died. I've really only skimmed through it so far—you want to give it a try? It's a little hard to read in places. Some of the copies aren't great, but see what you think."

I leaf through a few pages, then flip back to the cover sheet. "How should I . . . I mean, should I take notes, or highlight stuff, or what? And, uh, how do I know what's important?"

"*That's* the real challenge," she says. "Anything that catches your eye or seems fishy. The problem is, we don't *know* what we're looking for. Have to hope we know it when we see it. Highlight whatever you think is important . . . jot your comments or questions in the margin. Here's a notebook if you want to write more. Highlighters and pens are, well, everywhere. Why don't you go sit out on the patio in the back? No sense in being cooped up in here on a nice day. Help yourself to drinks and snacks in the kitchen. One of the perks of working for me is that there's always a jar full of homemade gingersnaps. The only cookie worth eating. My aunt Carol's recipe."

I spend the next three hours curled up in a comfy outdoor sofa, reading and then re-reading every word of that inquest report. Then I go back and highlight these parts:

**NAME OF DECEASED:**

ALBERT MICHAEL PRITCHARD

**CORONER:**

DR. FRANCIS HEWITT, M.D.

WITNESS NO. 1:

**GILBERT A. CHEEVER, ESQ.**

**(SWALLOWTAIL ISLAND)**

---

Q: What was your relationship to the deceased?

GC: He was my law partner. And friend. I've known him since he was a boy.

Q: It was my understanding that Mr. Pritchard was a sole practitioner, that he had no partners. Is that not the case?

GC: Oh, yes, technically, that is true. I suppose I jumped the gun a bit there. We had a, um, well I guess you'd call it an understanding. Nothing in writing, unfortunately, but we had talked about, uh, formalizing our arrangement.

Q: So, it's more accurate to say that you worked for him.

GC: I suppose so. But like I said—

Q: Mr. Pritchard was considerably younger than you, wasn't he?

GC: Well, yes, although I don't know what that has to do with anything.

Q: I'm just establishing the facts, Mr. Cheever. Let's move on. Were you aware of Mr. Pritchard's travel plans on the days preceding his death?

GC: Yes. On the twenty-fifth, he left the office at around ten in the morning. He said he was going to spend a few days with some friends in Leamington, Ontario. Dr. James Wolman and his wife, Sally. They were partners in some business ventures. I've met them a few times here on Swallowtail. Said he would be returning in a week, which would have been August first.

Q:  Why did he return on the twenty-eighth? Do
    you know?

GC: Certainly. Because of my brother's death.
    When I heard the news that evening, I sent
    a telegram right away to Albert, care of
    Dr. Wolman. Edward was an old friend of his,
    as well as a client. I knew he would want to
    know so he could be here to take care of,
    well, whatever needed taking care of as his
    lawyer.

Q:  Did you hear back from him?

GC: I did. I received a telegram from him the
    next morning. He said that he would be
    arriving back at the island at around eleven
    o'clock that night.

Q:  Was that usual for him? That is, to travel
    by boat after dark?

GC: I can't say it was usual, but he had done
    it before. I'll admit that it concerned me,
    traveling from Leamington to Swallowtail
    at night. Big moon, but it was behind thick

clouds most of the time. I don't know the exact distance, but it must be more than thirty miles. Long way in a little boat.

Q: How well did AP know the waters around Swallowtail Island?

GC: Like the back of his hand. Certainly as well as anyone on the island. Sometimes, though, he drove his speedboat in a manner that I—along with some others, I'd wager—would call downright reckless. It was the fastest boat on the lake, and AP was fond of showing off.

Q: Why would AP have cut the corner at Ada's Reef, knowing how dangerous it was?

GC: He must have been tired and in a hurry to get ashore. I hesitate to mention this, because I'm not one for gossip, but I knew Albert to like a drink now and then. It would be understandable if he was upset about my brother's death. They were close friends—closer than I was to Edward. Perhaps he—

At this point, Dr. Hewitt interrupted Gilbert, saying that there was absolutely no sign that Albert had been drinking, and that he had known him all his life and had never known Albert to drink, period. It's hard to tell from just the words, but it seems like he's kind of annoyed that Gilbert said that about Albert Pritchard.

## WITNESS NO. 2:
## MISS DINAH PURDY
## (SWALLOWTAIL ISLAND)

Q: How long have you lived on Swallowtail Island?

DP: I was born here, and grew up on the island, out on Rabbit Ear Point. My father is Elias Purdy. He is, well, was, Captain Cheever's first mate.

Q: So, I assume you knew Captain Edward Cheever. Did you know the deceased, Albert Pritchard?

DP: Not well, but I met him a few times at the Cheevers' house. He was nice. He knew of my plan to go to law school and he, well, I guess you could say that he encouraged me.

Q: Let's move on to the night of the accident, July twenty-ninth. Can you describe exactly what you witnessed on the night of the crash?

DP: It was a beautiful night. Some clouds, but the air was perfectly clear. I was sitting on the porch swing and I remember a nice breeze blowing straight in at me. Dad had gone to bed already, but I stayed up. Must have been around eleven o'clock that I heard a boat approaching from the north. It was moving right along. It's funny, I thought it might be Mr. Pritchard, because he always had fast boats. When I was a little girl, I watched him fly past the point lots of times.

Q: How far offshore was this boat when it passed by your house, and could you be a bit more specific as to its speed?

DP: Less than a mile, I'd say. As for speed . . . fast. There were some waves from the northwest and he was really bouncing over them—the lights on the boat were going up and down. I can't tell you in miles per hour, but I can say this: The engine was very loud, as if the throttle was wide open.

Q: Did you see or hear the crash?

DP: Both. Because it was such a clear night, I could see the flashing light of the buoy, and I followed the stern light as it got closer, and then suddenly there was a loud crash and a bright flash—I don't know what caused it. An explosion from the boat hitting the rocks, I suppose. And then, nothing. No noise from the engine. The light on the buoy was still flashing. There was no moonlight and no lights left on the boat, so I couldn't see it anymore. I couldn't be sure what happened, but I didn't have a good feeling about it. I would have called the police, but we don't have a phone. They haven't run the wires out to the point yet. It wasn't much longer before I saw other boats out there.

Q: From where you were that night, could you tell if the boat you saw went inside or outside of the buoy at Ada's Reef?

DP: I can't be a hundred percent positive one way or the other. It all happened very fast. I've been watching boats go up and down the shore and around the rocks and that buoy all my life. I know where they're supposed to be, and nothing seemed out of the ordinary. But obviously, he must have been on the wrong side of the light, right? What other explanation can there be?

## WITNESS NO. 3:
### SIMON STANFORD
### (SWALLOWTAIL ISLAND)

---

Q: Where were you on the night of July twenty-ninth, at approximately eleven o'clock?

SS: Sitting on the rocks near the end of the breakwater at the little harbor.

Q: At eleven o'clock! Aren't you a little young to be out alone so late?

SS: I'm eighteen, almost nineteen. I've had some . . . personal . . . things to work out in my head, and I like it there. I'd walked out to the end at about ten, maybe a few minutes before. It's peaceful. I go there when I need to think.

Q: From your vantage point on the breakwater, is the Ada's Reef buoy visible?

SS: Oh, yes. It's less than a mile away. And that was a very clear night.

Q: Tell us what you saw from the moment you arrived at the breakwater.

SS: Sure. Right when I sat down, I noticed a small boat out by the buoy. It wasn't moving, so I assumed it was a fisherman. I've heard people say that there's good fishing all around there, because of the rocks. The strange thing was that he didn't have any lights on. Didn't seem very safe. It was a dark night and it would have been hard for other boats to see him. The only reason I saw him was that every time the buoy light flashed, it shined on his boat.

Q: Were you able to identify the boat? Was it familiar to you?

SS: No, it seemed to me to be an ordinary fishing boat, under twenty feet, I'd say. But that's . . . all I can say about it. A few minutes later, I heard a small outboard motor running, and the boat disappeared. I don't know where it went. Further up the coast, chasing perch or walleye, I suppose.

Q: Then what happened?

SS: Well, nothing . . . for a while . . . then I heard another boat approaching from the north. After eleven. I know because I had checked my watch a few minutes earlier. I saw his port side bow light when he came around the point where the captain's house is. I figured it must be Mr. Pritchard—nobody else has a boat that fast, or that loud. He keeps—kept—the boat at a dock in the little harbor, which was very close by, so I was planning to walk over and help him

tie up. I liked helping him out—he was a
true gentleman. Not many of those around.

Q: But you never got the chance.

SS: No, sir. I saw him start to make
the turn at the buoy and then . . .
there was an awful sound . . . a crunch,
followed by the whine of the engine, and
then . . . nothing. Silence. From the sound
of the crash, I just knew . . .

Q: I'll ask you the same question I asked Miss
Purdy. From your point of view, can you say
with certainty that Mr. Pritchard's boat
passed on the inside or the outside of the
buoy at Ada's Reef?

SS: I . . . no, I don't suppose I can say with
absolute certainty. It's more than a mile
from where I sat, and he was moving so
fast . . . and the dark . . . no, I'm so, so,
sorry.

**CORONER'S CONCLUSION:**

**CAUSE OF DEATH:** ACCIDENTAL (MASSIVE TRAUMA TO BODY AND HEAD RESULTING FROM BOATING ACCIDENT)

Nadine, her brow deeply furrowed, is standing over a pile of yellowed newspaper clippings, sorting them into two piles when I knock on the half-open door to the war room.

"Come in, come in," she says without looking up from her piles. "You don't have to knock." Behind us, the clock in her foyer starts to strike the hour. "Good golly. How did it get to be four o'clock? I'm sorry—I didn't mean to ignore you on your first day like that. I guess I got . . . how are you coming along?"

"Um, good, I think. I'm done." I hold out my copy of the inquest report.

"Done! Wow—I think I chose my assistant wisely. You're a fast reader."

"I guess," I say with a shrug. "I think I always have been. I highlighted some sections that I think . . ."

Nadine flips through the pages of the document. When she reaches the bright yellow highlighting, she takes a pair of tortoiseshell reading glasses from her blouse pocket and puts them on. Without taking her eye from the page, she pulls out a chair and slowly sinks into it. "Hmm. *That's* interesting. Gilbert managed to get caught in *two* lies. He's such a . . . twerp! And you can tell that the coroner thinks so, too. Now we know where the rest of the family gets it. Okay, good . . . Dinah's testimony. Nothing really obvious there, but we'll keep looking. Maybe we go see her tomorrow. You need to meet her. Does that work for you?"

"Um, sure. Should I come here first?"

"Let me see . . . I have some things to take her. I help her out with shopping. She still cooks every day, though. I'll get a wagon hitched up—we'll go in style. We'll throw your bike on, too. Then I can drop you at home on the way back. That'll give me a chance to see everyone—and check in with Pip and Tinker. Maybe I can convince Thomas that she's ready to leave the pasture." She turns back to the report. "Simon Stanford. Haven't thought about him in years. *Super* sweet man. I didn't even know he was around when this happened. Whoa! What's this about another boat out by the buoy? This is the first I've heard of that."

"He was eighteen at the inquest, so that would make him . . . ninety—"

"—three, *if* he's still alive. About the same as Dinah. I'll ask around tomorrow morning, find out if he's . . . someone will know what happened to him. Boy, I'd love to talk to him about what he saw that night." Nadine handed the report back to me with a smile. "You did a fantastic job on this, Lark! I don't know about you, but I have a feeling we're onto something here. Now skedaddle before Thomas has to come looking for you."

I'm pretty sure this is the first time anyone has ordered me to skedaddle, and I'm not sure I even know *how* to do it, but I hop on my bike and do my best.

# CHAPTER
# 4

THANKS TO A PATH THAT Nadine told me about that cuts through the two miles of open meadows between our houses, it takes only about ten minutes of skedaddling to get home, where Pogo takes time out of her busy bird-chasing schedule to greet me with enthusiastic wagging and a big kiss. Then she spies a mourning dove in the yard and goes right back to work. Pip, not surprisingly, is in the barn brushing Tinker and talking a blue streak in the pony's ear. Nate and Jack are in the front yard playing catch, and Blake is asleep, stretched out on the couch and drooling on the throw pillow. As I pour some lemonade into a Judy Jetson glass, Thomas pedals into the backyard on a rusty ten-speed bike that he'd coaxed into working order with an oil can and a couple of new inner tubes.

"Hey, you're back!" he says. "How'd it go today? Pip and

the boys seemed to like the soccer camp okay. Where is everybody?"

"You can guess where Pip is," I say, nodding toward the barn and handing him a glass of lemonade.

"Right."

"I just got here. Blake was asleep on the couch when I came in."

Thomas frowns. "He's a big help. He's *supposed* to be keeping an eye on Nate and Jack. Have you seen them?"

"Out front. Playing with knives, I think."

"What!" His eyes go wide and he makes a move toward the front door.

"I'm kidding!" I say, following him out to the yard where Nate throws the ball as high and far as he can, backing poor Jack into the weeds where he trips over a fallen branch, but still makes the catch, holding his glove up in triumph.

"Maybe soccer's the wrong sport for him," Thomas says to me. "Nate, be nice. Not everyone is a daredevil like yourself. And Jack, watch where you're going. I don't want you doing a backflip over that wall."

"That would be *cool*," Jack says.

Thomas shakes his head, then takes a long drink of his lemonade (in the Barney Rubble glass, by the way). "Of all the animals, the boy is the most unmanageable. Plato said that." He ignores my grunt and eye roll and adds, "So, all good with Nadine?"

"Yeah."

"What'd you do?"

"Mostly reading." I hear Mom's voice in my head: *Would it kill you to talk to him like a real person?* "I saw something cool, though. You know that speedboat that was in the paper? It's in one of the barns at Nadine's."

"Oh yeah? Is that what you were reading about?"

"Uh-huh. After the crash, I guess there was this . . . inquest, they call it."

"Right. The coroner."

"Uh-huh. I read the report, all the witnesses, that kind of stuff," I say. "Nadine just got it, so I was the first one to read it."

"And? Did you uncover the long-lost secret?"

"I . . . I don't know. Not yet. We're going out tomorrow to talk to that old woman who lives way out on the point. Dinah Purdy. She was one of the witnesses."

"Really? Lucky you, getting to meet her. Well, I can't wait to hear all about it. I have some news, too. I told you that I had talked to the museum here about some restoration work, right? Well, that's turned out even better than I'd hoped. They have *six* paintings that they want me to work on now, and if they like my work, another six later. Two really aren't worth restoring, but they want me to do them anyway. I'm setting up shop over there tomorrow. The best part of all? They didn't bat an eye when I gave them my estimate for what it would cost. Wrote me a check on the spot for part of it."

"Does that mean we're going out for pizza tonight?"

"Would that make you happy?"

"Let's not get carried away," I say.

When I walk off the soccer field at noon the next day, I am really steamed. During the last drill of the day, I handle a slightly-behind-me cross from a teammate perfectly, getting the ball under control and breaking for the goal. Only the goal-tender stands between me and my moment of glory, and sorry, but the poor kid doesn't have a chance against me. And then it happens: Owen Cheever, with his stupid boy-bun and his pink polo shirt and his two-hundred-dollar cleats, slides in out of *nowhere*, steals the ball from me, and dribbles it untouched the length of the pitch where he nonchalantly chips it over the head of my side's goalkeeper and into the net.

"That's Owen A. Cheever," he says, jabbing his chest with both thumbs. "C-H-E-E-V-E-R. And *that's* how we do it on Swallowtail Island."

When he looks back over his shoulder at me, I am reminded of a certain palomino that threw me off his back. Even the teeth look familiar. I feel the blood rising to my face, but I grit my teeth and turn away as his teammates mob him.

"That was *awesome*, dude," one says.

"Did you see the look on her face?" another asks. "She was, like, what the . . . ?"

And then, from Owen himself: "She's actually not bad . . . you know, for a girl. She's probably never had to play against somebody with actual *skills*. Girls usually just stand around and wait for the ball to come to them."

"Keep walking," I tell myself as steam pours from my ears.

*"Not bad for a girl"?*

*"Girls usually just stand around and wait for the ball to come to them"?*

I'm clenching my fists and imagining a sequel to the ISF when I hear Pip's voice.

"Lark! Wait for me!" She's sprinting across the field to join me, backpack in her hand. She knows something is up from the look on my face. "What's wrong? What happened?"

"Nothing. Let's go."

"Who is that boy—the one with the long hair? In the pink shirt?"

"Why?"

"I think he likes you. He's always looking at you. He was, just now."

I stop in my tracks. "What are you talking about?"

*"That* boy."

"Don't *point. Geez.*"

"He didn't see me. He's going the other way."

I kneel down, pretending to tie my shoe, and peek behind

me. "Are you messing with me?"

"No! I swear. It's so *obvious*. What's wrong—do you like him or something?"

"Eww! No! And don't you say *anything* . . . to *anybody*."

Pip slides a make-believe zipper across her lips. She then spots Nate and Jack and calls to them.

"Be careful going home," I say. "Nadine's going to drop me off later. She wants to see you and Tinker again."

"I like her," Pip says. "Nadine, I mean. *Obviously* I like Tinker."

"Yeah, she's great," I say.

"Do you think . . . she and . . . do you think Thomas will ever . . . you know?"

"Get married again? I don't know. The poor guy has already had two women die on him. Maybe he should take a break. People will start to be suspicious if something happens to a third one. Why are you . . . NO! Don't even think about it, Pip. That is *not* going to happen. And you are not going to try—in *any* way—to make it happen. Mom's only been . . . for a few months. And besides, I'm pretty sure that Nadine is . . . never mind. Leave it alone."

"Nadine is *what*?"

"Er, not interested. They're *friends*, that's all. They hardly know each other. Now, promise that you are not going to say anything. To anyone. About anything."

"You think I'm going to blab *everything*, don't you?"

I pull her baseball cap down over her eyes. "Nope. Because I keep reminding you not to. Now go home so I can get to work."

Dinah Purdy's cottage stands on a very narrow spit of land called Rabbit Ear Point for reasons you can probably guess. Because the point itself is only a couple of hundred feet wide, she has a clear view of the north end of Cattail Island, a state-protected refuge for thousands and thousands of birds and other wildlife, *and*, from her front porch, a wide-open view of the west end of the lake.

"Million-dollar views," Nadine says as she knocks on the screen door to the porch of what is, without a doubt, the smallest house I've ever seen. "Dinah? It's me—Nadine."

"Come, join me," replies a voice that is stronger and younger-sounding than I expect. "No need to knock."

"Sorry we're late," Nadine says. "I got a call from my editor as we were getting ready to leave. I brought someone I'd like you to meet. Dinah Purdy, Lark Heron-Finch."

"Come closer," Dinah says. "Let me get a better look at you."

I climb the steps to the porch and approach her. "It–It's nice to meet you, Ms. Purdy."

"The pleasure's all mine," she says. "But do call me Dinah. It's so much easier. My, you are a tall, cool glass of water, aren't you?" Her voice ripples with age, but every word is enunciated perfectly. My mind flashes back to my mom, who cringed every time a "gonna" or "kinda" came out of my mouth.

GHT? Dinah looks every day of ninety-three years old—except for her eyes, which are bright and clear, the color of the seventy-percent dark chocolate I love so much. Her face is deeply wrinkled, the lines a road map from hairline to chin. As she looks me over, I get the immediate impression that her mind is still razor-sharp. She's barely over five feet tall, and the skin on the back of her hands and arms is as thin and transparent as wax paper, her long, bony fingers crooked with arthritis. Her long hair is pulled back into a steel-gray bun, and she is wearing a long, loose-fitting summer dress in a bright floral print.

Over glasses of iced tea and homemade sugar cookies, Dinah conducts a thorough interrogation of me, nodding knowingly when I get to the part about Mom leaving the house on Swallowtail to Pip and me.

"The Roost. I *know* that house," she says. "When I was a girl, it was owned by a family named Bradford."

"That was my grandmother's name," I say. "Before she got married. Lillian Bradford. My grandfather was Patrick Heron."

Dinah's eyes light up. "Lillian Bradford was your grandmother! I remember her so well. She was a beautiful little girl, and sharp as a tack—a lot like her granddaughter. But if I'm remembering correctly, she lost her father in the war not long after they came to Swallowtail."

"That's right," I say. "He was on a ship that got torpedoed."

"How sad," Dinah says, nodding. "After that, Captain Cheever and my father used to help out Mrs. Bradford. Little things, because she wouldn't accept charity, but a bushel of apples here, a pound of sugar there. You see, all three had all lost their spouses, so they were like an exclusive club. In a way, I felt as if I belonged to the club, too. I had lost my best friend to the flu in nineteen forty. Ada Cheever, the captain's daughter. The two of us were thick as thieves, and we spent hours and hours exploring the coastline. We always said we were going to walk all the way around the island, but we never made it, and then . . ." She drifts off momentarily, smiling sadly at the memory of a long-lost companion. "Ada was the first of many friends to go. That's the way of life. One day soon, it will be my turn to be thought of fondly."

"Nonsense. We still have too much work to do on the book. It would be a *terrible* inconvenience for me," Nadine said, winking at me.

Dinah laughs out loud, a tinkling *he-he-he-he-he*. "Well, I wouldn't want to make your job any more difficult, my dear. Before I forget, thank you for the grocery delivery. I don't know what I'd do without you. Starve to death, I suppose."

Nadine scoffs. "I doubt that very much. You'd be catching perch or shooting ducks. Even the deer would start to get nervous coming out this far." She opens a portfolio and takes out the coroner's report that I had highlighted. "Ready to go back in time a few years? Like, seventy-five?"

"Is that the inquest report? You found it! That was the summer I left the island for college. It's like it was yesterday. I was sitting here, on this very swing, when he went past." She points out at the lake, sweeping her arm from right to left to show the path of the boat.

"I'm curious about some of the things that were said at the inquest," Nadine says, flipping to the highlighted pages. "I'm guessing that you weren't in the room when the other witnesses testified—is that right?"

"That certainly sounds correct. That's the way it should have been done, certainly. Remind me who the other witnesses were."

"The first was Gilbert Cheever," Nadine says.

Pursing her lips as if she's taken a bite of something bitter, Dinah says, "*Unpleasant* man. Not fit to carry his brother's shoes. Treated my father like . . . well, as if he were some inferior creature. At the time, he worked for Albert, no?"

"That's right. He didn't have much to say—he didn't actually witness the crash."

"He tried to make it sound like Albert Pritchard had been drinking," I say. "And that's why he cut the corner at the buoy."

"The coroner seemed a bit put out by that suggestion," Nadine says.

Dinah shakes her head slowly. "Doesn't surprise me that Gilbert would say something like that without any evidence. It was his modus operandi for years. There's an old saying among lawyers: If the facts are against you, argue the law. If the law's against you, argue the facts. If the facts *and* the law are against you, call the other lawyer names. Gilbert was a great name-caller."

Nadine turns to another page in the report. "The most interesting witness, though, is Simon Stanford. He was eighteen, at the time. Did you know him?"

"Certainly. He was a year ahead of me in school. Smart young man. Thoughtful, kind. His father was mayor for years. We were in a number of classes together in high school. Went off to Yale, I believe. I saw him last summer at a charity event. Returned to Swallowtail when he retired, just like me. Something keeps pulling us back, I guess."

"He testified that he was sitting on the breakwater in the little harbor and that a small fishing boat with no running lights was hanging out right next to the buoy. He's not certain, but thinks it might have headed up the coast a few minutes before the crash. Do you remember seeing another boat that night? Maybe it went past here."

Dinah stares out at the lake, then shakes her head. "There was no other boat. Not out here. I would have seen it. Or heard it at least."

"Hmm. Strange," says Nadine. "Seems like a small boat would stick close to the island at night, especially if he knew his lights weren't working."

"Maybe he didn't *want* the lights on," I say. "Maybe he did something to the buoy. Could . . . someone do that?"

"Sure, they *could*. But *why*?" Nadine asks.

As I'm thinking about that, I pick up a pair of binoculars from the table and look out at some herring gulls floating a short distance offshore. "Wow. These are *nice* binoculars."

"I wanted the best that money could buy," Dinah says. "I spend a lot of time watching the birds."

I spin and look to the south, scanning the surface of the lake. "Hmm."

"What is it?" Nadine asks.

"It's just . . . at the inquest . . . can I see that for a second?" Nadine hands me the transcript and I turn to Dinah's testimony. "Yeah, here it is. You said that it was a clear night, and that you saw the flashing light of the buoy."

"That's right. I saw it blinking, clear as could be."

Nadine sees the confused look on my face. "What's wrong?"

"Well, I'm in the same spot Dinah was that night, and I can't see the buoy from here."

"Are you sure?" Nadine takes the binoculars from me and aims them in the direction of Ada's Reef. "You're right. It must be behind—that's Egbert Island, right? That little rocky one with the trees? Is it possible that the buoy used to be farther out in the lake?"

"I think I can answer that one," Dinah says. "My father explained it to me when I was a child. The buoy is anchored with a long chain, and when the wind is from the south or east, the buoy swings out to the west, and you can see it from here. Today, the wind is from the west, so it's just behind Egbert. That night, the wind must have been from the other direction."

"But . . ." Under usual circumstances, I love nothing more than to point out when adults are wrong about something, but when the adult is ninety-three, it doesn't feel quite the same. Nevertheless, Dinah *is* wrong, and I can't let it go. "See, the thing is, you said at the inquest that there was a strong breeze that night . . . right in your face. So the wind was coming from . . . *there*."

"The northwest," says Dinah, looking at me with increased respect. "Well, I'll be. There's no moss growing on you, is there?" After reading her answers, she hands the transcript back to me. "I'm stumped. You're absolutely right. That buoy shouldn't have been visible that night."

Nadine pats me on the back. "Well done, you. I don't know what this means yet, but I think it could be very important. We may solve this mystery yet. Did I say *we*? I mean *you*. You're like Sherlock Holmes's younger sister."

Sherlock *wishes* he had a sister like me.

When Thomas calls us down to the kitchen for dinner, Jack and Nate straggle in last, swinging heavy-duty cardboard tubes like longswords.

"You won't take my ship, you scurvy pirate!" Nate says. "I'll make you walk the plank!"

"Never!" cries Jack, lunging at Nate. "It's my ship now!"

The cardboard tubes connect solidly, sending the rolled-up papers that had been stored inside one flying across the room and striking Thomas dead center in the chest.

"I'm hit!" he says, staggering backward against the counter. He crumples to the floor in an exaggerated, drawn-out death scene that ends with his last word, "Rose . . . bud."

"Bravo!" Pip shouts, leaping to her feet and clapping with everything she has. Jack and Nate join in; Blake and I look at each other, rolling our eyes in a (rare) shared moment.

Thomas stands and bows deeply. *"Grazie! Grazie mille!"*

"Can we eat now?" Blake asks.

"I don't know," Thomas answers, gesturing toward Jack and Nate. "Was that the finale or is there a second act? Ignore these two philistines—it's clear they don't know real *art* when they see it. That's what happens when you become a . . . *teenager.*"

"I'm not a teenager yet," I say.

"Maybe not chronologically," Thomas says. "But definitely in spirit."

"It's not going to happen to me," says Pip. "I'll always think you're a great artist."

"Thanks, Pip. I think I believe you—that is, about not letting it happen to you. Okay, let's eat before the teens turn on us all."

"Maybe we should make them eat at their own table," says Nate.

"Yeah," says Jack. "Like *we* have to do at Thanksgiving at Aunt Nancy's house."

While this unfortunate display of teen-bashing continues, I pick up the papers that had flown out of the tube and try to unroll them. They are nautical charts—about a dozen of them. They're too big for the table, so I attempt to spread them out on the floor. Because they've been rolled up for so long, they resist my efforts and keep rolling right back into a tight bundle.

"Jack, come here," I say. "Hold this side down so I can see them."

He kneels on one side as I slowly pull the rolled-up part toward me. "That's better. They're all different charts of the lake—here's one of the islands. There's Swallowtail. We're right . . . here. I was out here at Rabbit Ear Point today. That's where Dinah Purdy lives."

"Oh, *right*. What is she like?" Thomas asks.

"*Old*," I say. "But kind of amazing. Lives out there all by herself in this *tiny* cottage."

Thomas sets a platter of sloppy joes and roasted potatoes on the table. "I want to hear all about her, and this big mystery you're working on with Nadine."

Pip raises her hand, as if she's in class.

"Yes, Pip?" Thomas says. "You don't have to raise your hand."

She strokes her chin with a thumb and index finger. "Before Lark starts, I have one question: Who's Rosebud?"

A steady rain falls all evening and into the night, and by nine o'clock, the living room is a sea of sleeping bodies. Jack and Nate crashed and burned in the middle of a video game and are sprawled at crazy angles across the floor. Between them is Pogo, with all four legs and nose twitching, dreams of being in hot pursuit of something—*anything*—with wings. Blake is asleep in a wing chair with his headphones on and mouth open. And stretched out on the couch next to me is Pip, a copy of *Black Beauty* resting on her chest, rising and falling with her breathing. *Her* dreams, I'm sure, involve saving the world with Tinker's help. Meanwhile, my brain is busy replaying my humiliation on the soccer field. Again and again, I picture Owen Cheever's arrogant face mocking me with his idiotic friends cheering him on.

At nine fifteen, curiosity gets the better of Thomas, who has been reading in the bird room. I look up as he pokes his head into the living room.

"Geez, it looks like act three of *Hamlet* in here," he says. "Let's get them up and to bed. C'mon, boys. Pip. Up you go."

It takes a little prodding and pushing, but together we herd their half-asleep bodies up the stairs. When that's done, I realize that *I'm* not at all sleepy, so I wander into Thomas's room and pick out a musty Agatha Christie paperback from the bookcase. Back on my bed, I crack it open and read a few pages, but the GHT is that after twenty minutes or so, the real world creeps in and I find that I can't remember a single detail of what I've read. Annoyed, I toss the book on the table next to the bed and throw the cover over Bedlam's cage.

"'Night, Bedlam."

"Sweet dreams," he says, as always, in Mom's voice.

"Fat chance. I think Pip and Pogo are hogging all the good ones." I turn the light off, and will myself to sleep.

Nope. Not gonna happen.

I turn the light back on and pad down the stairs to the living room, where I had left the rolled-up charts after dinner. The kitchen table is clear, so I find the one with the largest image of Swallowtail Island and unroll it. First with my finger, and then with a pencil and ruler, I draw a line directly from the buoy at Ada's Reef to the exact spot where Dinah's house is out on Rabbit Ear Point. My line runs through—just barely touching, actually—tiny Egbert Island, which is separated from Swallowtail Island by less than a hundred feet of water.

Now that I have seen it laid out on the chart, Dinah's theory about the buoy swinging with the wind and waves makes perfect sense. A few yards in either direction would be all that is needed. Still, I want—*need*—to see it for myself, so I check the weather to find out the expected wind direction. Once this

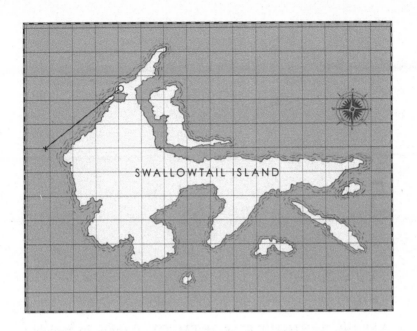

rain moves through, the weather app promises, Swallowtail
will have clear skies and light winds from the south for a couple
of days. If that buoy really is visible from Dinah's I should be
able to see it. And if it's not . . . well, I don't know what that
will mean.

# CHAPTER
# 5

AFTER A NIGHT'S WORTH OF dreams in which I humiliate myself on the soccer field over and over, I leap out of bed in the morning, eager to set things right. I may not win the Swallowtail Summer Soccer Camp award for best player, but I am *not* going down without a fight.

Halfway through my bowl of Cheerios, I feel Jack staring at me.

"Are you all right?" he asks.

"Yeah. Why?"

"You're kind of making a scary face," he says.

"Jack's right," says Pip. "You look like you're mad at your Cheerios.

"I'm just eating," I say.

Nate, usually on my side, makes a face that says *Not really.*

"Fine. I'll eat somewhere else. C'mon, Pogo." I take my bowl and Judy Jetson glass of orange juice into the living room, where Pogo joins me on the couch.

A few minutes later, Thomas finds me. "What's going on? Why are you in here?"

My hands are full and I have a mouthful of cereal, so I point with my chin in the direction of the kitchen. "They're idiots," I mumble.

"Ah. I see. Well, don't forget that you volunteered to make dinner for those idiots tonight. I'll be a little later than usual. Why don't you make tacos? Pretty sure we have everything you need."

"Fine."

"Call me if you need anything, okay?"

"*Okay.*" I down the rest of my orange juice and return to the kitchen with Mom's voice ringing in my ears: "*You're not a little kid anymore, Lark.*"

"Are you guys ready?" I ask, forcing myself to be upbeat.

"Was that . . . a *smile*?" Jack asks.

"A scary-clown smile, maybe," says Nate.

"Very funny," I say. "You know, I was going to make tacos tonight, but just for that, I'm going to make your favorite: Mom's tuna casserole."

"Nooo! That's not fair," Nate says. "Jack started it. Make something *he* hates."

"Oh, I think the tuna casserole covers it," I say.

After soccer, I'm watching Pip and the boys pedal off into the distance, still laughing at their lame attempts to talk me out of the dreaded tuna casserole (which, by the way, I have no intention of making—I hate it at least as much as they do), when Nadine surprises me by suddenly appearing beside me on a bike of her own—a very retro cruiser that's the color of cornflowers.

"You scared me! I didn't even hear you ride up. Cool bike."

"What's so funny? You had the biggest smile on your face."

"Nate and Jack. They're going home to hide every can of tuna in the house."

"Thomas threatened them with Kate's tuna casserole, eh?"

"It was me, not Thomas, but yeah. So you know about it."

"Oh, it's *legendary*. She used to make it when we were roommates at Wellesley if we were too broke for pizza."

"Was it any better then?"

"'Fraid not. But I never told her. Anyway, on the topic of food, I was thinking we could swing by Em's for lunch." She aims her bike toward town. "Then we're going to see Simon Stanford. Remember, the witness from the inquest?"

"You found him?"

"It wasn't hard. He's still on the island. Talked to him on the phone, and he sounds great. There's a place out on Pasture Road that's kind of an old folks' home. Swallowtail Meadows.

Was a house, but the previous owners let it go until it wasn't worth much. Somebody bought it for a song and converted it a few years back. Simon's been there about three years."

On the patio outside Em's Docksider, we share a picnic table with a family from Columbus who are looking at houses to buy on the island. Em's is famous (infamous, really) for its "Seagull Special"—a quarter of a scrawny chicken, a foil-wrapped potato, and an ear of corn, all burnt almost beyond recognition on an enormous charcoal grill. I end up on the bench next to a shy boy my age, who undergoes nonstop teasing from the rest of his family.

"Hey, Mikey, maybe Lark will give you a *private* tour of the island," his younger sister says after we've all been introduced. The poor kid's ears turn bright red and he looks like he wants to slip under the table to dig an escape tunnel.

"See, I told you you'd like this place," the father says, elbowing him. "We just got here and you're already sitting next to a pretty girl."

Even the mom joins in: "Mikey's a very talented violinist. Why don't you tell Lark about the time you were on television? He played a *solo* with the Cleveland Symphony. It was on PBS."

Lucky for Mikey (and me), Nadine comes to the rescue. "I'm so sorry, folks," she says, pointing to her phone, "but we have to go. It's George—he got in early and he's waiting for us down at the ferry dock."

We say our goodbyes and make our escape.

"Who's George?" I ask as soon as we're out of hearing range.

Nadine laughs. "Made him up. I had to get us out of there. Boy, that was awkward. That poor kid. I have half a mind to rescue him and bring him along, except I think he'd die of embarrassment."

"I'm used to it," I say. "People act . . . weird around me sometimes."

"I'm not surprised, especially if you mean boys your age. You're the spitting image of your mom, and trust me, she had to fight them off. Most of the time, she'd just start talking about the migratory patterns of tree swallows, or murmurations, and that would send most of them running."

The swallow! With everything else going on in my life, I had completely forgotten about the mysterious silver swallow I'd found hanging in my room.

"Omigosh, that reminds me of something I've been meaning to ask you about," I say. "I found this little bird in my room . . . it's a swallow, and it's made of—"

"Silver? With some *beautiful* blue enamel work on it back?"

"Yeah! Do you know anything about it? Like, where it came from, or . . ."

"Sure, absolutely. I remember the day she found it—seems like yesterday. Hard to believe it was thirty years ago. Don't you hate it when old people say things like that? Anyway, we were twelve, same as you, and it came from a—there used to be a kind of *antique* shop on the island." She air-quotes "antique."

WRECK AT ADA'S REEF

"Today, I'd call it a junk shop. It was the strangest thing. She always said it was more like the swallow found her instead of the other way around. There was a box of books, a real mishmash of things, old and new, but some nice atlases and an oversized volume of Audubon's paintings. And if there's two things your mom loved, it was maps and birds. The guy wouldn't let her pick and choose, though—it was all or nothing, he said. He just wanted to be rid of them."

"Where did they come from?"

"The guy at the shop said they were from Captain Cheever's house. Over the years, one Cheever or another had lived in it, but it was starting to look a little run-down, so the family decided to give it to the town—as long as it would be turned into a museum with their name in big letters. I'm sure they got a big tax break for donating it—probably a lot more than it was really worth at the time. The books were in some boxes of stuff that had been in the attic and were about to be thrown out when the junk-shop guy found out about it. Anyway, your mom straps this heavy box on the back of her bike and lugs it home. That night, she's going through all the books, and when she opens one of them, that swallow was inside. It was remarkable, really. Somebody had cut the pages so that it fit *perfectly*."

"Really? You're not making this up?"

"I swear."

"What was the book? The title, I mean."

Nadine stops, her head tilting to the right. "Huh. *Another* good question. I have no idea. Darn. I should know this. Must have been something fairly thick, though. *War and Peace*, maybe? Where did you find the bird?"

"Hanging from the ceiling in my room with a bunch of others. It must have been there all along, but I never noticed that it was different from the rest. I wonder why Mom never told me about it."

"She probably just forgot. She had . . . a lot to deal with. The five of you. And Thomas."

"Yeah, I guess."

We are standing in front of the Island Diner, tucked between the hardware store and one of the island's many T-shirt shops. "This all right with you? Burgers are okay, and Jessie makes a decent grilled cheese. Come to think of it, I'm not sure why we were at Em's in the first place. The food's terrible."

"I was kind of looking forward to the seagull," I say. "And Mikey *was* kind of cute." I wait a beat, then add, "Kidding!"

"Actually, he *is* a cute kid," she says, dropping into a vinyl booth that's held together with duct tape. "He just needs to get away from his family. He'll be fine when he goes to college. You should get his name so you can look him up in a few years."

"Uh, *yeah*. So, back to this swallow. Did Mom ever find out anything more about it, like why it was hidden in a book?"

Nadine shakes her head. "Not that I know of. She took it with her to Cleveland once, to show it to a friend of your grandfather's, someone who supposedly knew about antiques, but he couldn't help her. He told her that if she liked it, she should hang it up and enjoy it. So that's what she did."

"Huh. Maybe I should do that, too. Right now it's in a drawer, covered by shirts and underwear. I can hang it in Bedlam's cage. He can use the company."

"There you go. Problem solved. Everyone's happy."

The grilled cheese at the diner lives up to Nadine's hype, and they get bonus points for using mayonnaise on the outside instead of butter and for cooking it until it's a deep, beautiful brown. A short time later, we're back on our bikes and heading for Swallowtail Meadows to see Simon Stanford, who is waiting for us out on the porch in an Adirondack chair.

"You must be Miss Pritchard," he says, popping up out of the chair with the energy and enthusiasm of a much younger man. He is wearing a crisp blue button-down oxford with a fashionably narrow tie, and the crease in his slacks is knife-sharp.

"I am," Nadine says, shaking his hand. "Nadine, please. Pleasure to meet you, Mr. Stanford. This is my assistant, Lark Heron-Finch."

He takes my hand and looks me straight in the eyes for a long time. "Lark Heron-Finch. That's quite a name, young lady. Something tells me there's a story there. Do you live here on Swallowtail?"

"Just for the summer," I answer.

"Her grandmother was a Bradford," Nadine says. "The house is called the Roost."

"Of course. Over by the little harbor," says Simon. "I know it well. Come, sit. Do you mind if we sit out here? It's a tad stuffy inside, and fresh air is good for these ancient bones."

"Outside is perfect. And your bones look fine to me," Nadine says. "The way you got out of that chair . . . I don't think I could do it half as fast."

Simon invites me to take the Adirondack; he and Nadine sit on a pair of straight-backed rocking chairs. "So you're Albert Pritchard's granddaughter," he says. "I read your book about your time in Somalia. Heartbreaking. And now you're writing one about Dinah Purdy?"

"That's right," Nadine says. "I'm focusing on some island history that she and her family were part of. Did you see my article in last week's *Citizen*? About the boat crash?"

Simon stiffens at the mention of the crash; the last trace of the smile that had been on his face since we arrived disappeared. "I read it, yes."

There's an awkward pause as we wait for him to expand on his answer, but when it is apparent that he has no plans to do so, Nadine continues: "The thing is, when I did my initial research about the accident, I hadn't seen the coroner's report—the transcript from the inquest."

Another short pause, then Simon nods and a bit of the old smile returns. "You've done your homework. Nobody's asked me about that night in seventy-five years. That day at the inquest—that's the last time I talked about it. Left the island a few days later, took a bus back east to college, and stayed away for a long time. By the time I came back, it was ancient history—not something people were talking about."

Nadine holds out the transcript from the inquest; slowly he lifts a hand to take it from her, and then leafs through the pages until he finds his own testimony.

"Do you mind if I ask you a few questions about . . . some of the things you said?" Nadine asks.

"Fire away," Simon says, not taking his eyes from the paper. "Frank Hewitt. The coroner. Now *there* was a character. Like something from an old movie. I suppose he was doing his job the best way he knew."

"What do you mean?"

Simon points at the first question and answer. "This business about me being out alone at eleven o'clock. Makes it sound like I'm the first young man ever to sit alone and think at night." He turns to me, adding, "Young people have lots to think about. And sometimes you have to get out under the stars and away from your family and friends to do it, isn't that right?"

"Yeah," I say with a smile. "You do."

He smiles and turns back to Nadine. "There. See?"

"What I'm really curious about is this boat that you saw out by the buoy," Nadine says. "You said that it didn't have lights, that you saw it by the reflection of the light from the buoy. Is there anything else? Maybe something you remembered later?"

Simon hands the transcript back to her with a shake of the head. "It was dark, I saw a boat briefly . . . and then I didn't. I may have imagined the whole thing. I'm sorry I can't be more helpful, but I'm not sure why any of this matters now. Your grandfather was a good man, and I'm sorry he died in such a . . . tragic . . . manner, but it was an accident. Probably a moment of confusion on his part, thought he was someplace else. It happens."

Nadine watches him carefully as he speaks, then thinks for a second before digging back in: "You said at the inquest that my grandfather was a true gentleman. What made you say that? The reason I ask is that I never knew him, and my father barely remembers him. He was only seven when all this happened. I'm trying to piece together a picture of the kind of man my grandfather was."

"He . . . he helped out a friend who was in some difficulty," says Simon. "Treated him like a man, like a human being. Everyone else . . ." He drifts off, visibly angry at the memory. "Small-town people can be very narrow-minded."

"So can big-town people," I say.

"Touché," Simon says.

I can't pinpoint the reason for it, but somehow I *know* he's not telling the whole story. I don't think he's lying, but he definitely knows more than he's admitting to. It's something about his eyes, I think. Detectives in books and movies always know just the right question to ask in a moment like this one, but I'm stumped.

Nadine leans forward in her chair. "On the night of the crash, did you call the police?"

"There were no phones out by the little harbor back then. I was starting for town when I heard all the boats. Somebody else must have reported it, and pretty soon there was a whole bunch of boats out there by the light. They towed what was left of your grandfather's boat into the little harbor while I was still there."

"Do you remember who was on those boats?" Nadine asks.

"Sure, there was Pete Jarmond—he was chief of police then—on Len Hopper's boat. They're the ones who towed it in. Then . . . let's see . . . then there was Harold Gullivan, ran the boatyard. Had a couple people on board with him. Harry Fineman. And Ronnie Barker—yeah, that's right. They said they'd been fishing not far away when they heard the crash. Oh, almost forgot. The third boat. Gilbert Cheever, of course."

"*Gilbert Cheever*?" Nadine says. "Did I miss something?"

"He was a lawyer, worked for your grandfather. You must have read his testimony in there," he says, pointing at the papers on Nadine's lap.

"Yes, but there's no mention of him being out on the water himself that night. Was he alone?" Nadine asks.

Simon nods.

"What kind of boat did he have?" I ask.

"Nothing special," Simon says. "Ordinary fishing boat, seventeen, eighteen feet."

Nadine stands and shakes Simon's hand. "Thank you, Mr. Stanford. You've been very helpful." She gives him a business card and says, "Please call me if you remember anything at all about that night."

"I-I will," he says. "Good luck with your writing. I look forward to your book about Dinah Purdy. She's a true hero of mine. Standing up for people, for all people. That takes courage . . . courage that we don't all have." He has turned wistful as he says those last words, and drifts off into his own world as we say our goodbyes.

Thanks to the threat of the tuna casserole hanging in the air, my tacos are a bigger hit than usual. When the table is cleared and the dishes put away, the sun is still high above the horizon, so Pip leads us out to the barn, where, for the first time, she lets Nate and Jack ride Tinker. Each takes a few gentle turns around the paddock while Pip watches like a hawk and offers encouragement.

After applauding Nate's success, Thomas nudges me with his elbow. "How about it, Lark?"

"How about what?" Like I don't know what he's suggesting.

"You. Tinker." He makes a circling motion with his finger. "Why don't you take a few laps?"

"I'm good," I say.

"C'mon, Lark, it's *fun*," Jack says.

I nod in agreement. "Yeah, looks like a *blast*."

Pip looks at me with a hopeful expression. "She's the sweetest, most gentlest horse ever. She's *nothing* like that horse at camp."

"Is *that* why you don't ride anymore?" Thomas asks. "Because you fell off one horse?"

"I didn't *fall*," I say. "That horse was *evil*. You could totally see it in his eyes."

Thomas almost falls off the fence laughing. "Well, you know what they say. When you get thrown by an evil horse, you have to get right back on."

That's the cue for the other four of them to join the fun, but I dig my heels in (and maintain a firm grasp on the fence). "You're not going to shame me into it. When I'm ready to ride the stupid horse—sorry, Pip, Tinker is *not* stupid—I'll do it. I'm not *afraid* to ride her."

And you know what? I *almost* believe it.

Once again I'm the last one still awake, and I use the quiet time to look for the carved-out book that supposedly held Mom's swallow. A search of every book in Pip's and my room turned up a dozen pressed leaves and flowers, a shopping list, a sheet of nine-cent stamps, and a birthday card from my grandparents to Mom with a twenty-five-dollar savings bond inside (sweet!)—but no swallow-shaped holes. So I head down to the bird room. Naturally, all the most promising books are on the high shelves, reachable only with the help of a ladder that runs all the way around the room along a steel track attached (solidly, I hope) to the wall. It creaks more than I like as I climb to the top but feels solid beneath my feet, and I start pulling books out for inspection. If there's a plan of organization, it's beyond my comprehension. There's a little bit—actually, a *lot*—of everything, all of it shelved willy-nilly (so NOT like Mom that I *know* someone else was responsible): fiction and nonfiction, old and new, thick and thin, hardcover and paperback, leather and cloth, classics and never-heard-of-its.

Two-thirds of the way down the next-to-last shelf, I spot a thick volume with a faded leather binding. Resisting the temptation to pass by the other books on the shelf and go straight to it, I maintain my routine, opening each and leafing through its pages. When I finally reach it, I try to read the worn lettering on the spine; I'm able to make out only this: *Th Pi wi k ape s har s D c ens*. I slide it out from its home of many years and flip open the cover. The title page is still intact, revealing the full title and author: *The Posthumous Papers of the Pickwick Club* by Charles Dickens. I flip a few more pages and then my heart leaps, because suddenly there are holes cut out of every one. I suppose that I expected the cutouts to be swallow-shaped, but it turns out that only the ones near the center are like that. I find page 433, the exact center of the book, and suddenly it all makes sense. Whoever did this took his time. He—or she—wanted a *perfect* fit.

In my excitement, I almost lose my balance on the ladder, and have to reach out to grab the shelf so I don't fall backward. Once I'm back on solid ground, I set the book, still open to page 433, on a table and race up the stairs to retrieve the swallow. I don't want to wake Pip by turning on a light, so I fumble around in the dark until I feel it in my dresser drawer. Back in the bird room, I wiggle the swallow into the bottom half of its "nest." Satisfied with the fit, I gently close

the top half. With the swallow in place and the book shut, there is nothing unusual or noticeable about it. Even more amazing, it's possible to leaf through the first few pages (the way you might if you were browsing casually in a bookstore) without noticing a thing, which explains how it ended up in a box of books in a junk shop.

Some obvious questions about the silver swallow (I'm starting to think it requires capitalization) and the book come to my wannabe-scientist mind: Who made the swallow? The "nest"? When? Why? Is it valuable? Like, new-bike valuable . . . or college-tuition valuable?

The book itself seems like a good place to start. There's no envelope containing all the answers to my questions inside, but there is *something*. Two things, actually. Stamped in green ink at the top of the inside cover is this:

CRACKENTHORP BOOKS
59 DOVER STREET
MAYFAIR, LONDON

And below that, in elegant cursive:

*ex libris*
*T. P. & P. C.*

Not a lot to go on, but what's one more challenge to me? I've got nothing but time. Tucking *The Pickwick Papers* under my arm, I head upstairs to bed. Bedlam whispers his usual, "What are you doing?" when I lift his cage cover.

"Hi, Beddie. Got a little friend for you." From my pocket, I take out the length of line I borrowed from Jack's fishing pole. One end goes around the loop on the back of the swallow and the other is attached to a bar at the top of Bedlam's cage. Before closing the cage door, I give the swallow a push so he swings back and forth in front of Bedlam, who seems unimpressed.

"Out-raaageous!" he says as I drop the cover over him.

# CHAPTER
# 6

A LITTLE AFTER MIDNIGHT I sit up straight in bed, wondering who and *why* someone is shining a flashlight in my face. Only it's not a flashlight—it's the biggest, brightest moon I've ever seen, practically filling the top half of the French doors across the room. I throw off the covers and go out onto the balcony, where a light northwest breeze chills me enough to make me go back for a blanket to wrap around my shoulders. Below the moon, the lake shimmers as if sprinkled with glitter, and to my right, the buoy marking Ada's Reef flashes its warning again and again. All around it are the red and green running lights of a number of small fishing boats taking advantage of the clear night and calm water.

Behind me, Pip stirs in her bed, then sits up, shielding her

eyes from the glare. "What's going on?" she asks.

"Come here. The moon is a-maaazing." She stumbles onto the balcony where I wrap my arms and the blanket snugly around her.

For a good thirty seconds, neither of us talk. I don't know about Pip, but my brain is full of Mom, and of nights like this back in Connecticut, before she got sick. When everyone else had gone to bed, she and I used to walk down to the water's edge in Essex to sit and look at the moon. It was her way of winding down, of putting the day's events in perspective. For me, it was an excuse to stay up late, to have some alone time with Mom, and yeah, I suppose, to try to figure out my own life. On the night she died, I fell asleep in a chair in her room;

when I woke at two o'clock, moonlight shone through a gap in the window shade, casting its light across her face as she lay there, her breathing getting shallower by the minute. I opened the shade and stared at the moon for a long time, until Thomas came in and shooed me off to bed. When I woke up, the moon was gone—and so was Mom.

Pip breaks the silence: "What are all those boats doing out there?"

"Fishing, I guess. It's probably something to do with the moon and the fish biting better. Feel like going for a bike ride?"

"Now?"

"Sure. It's bright as day out there."

"Where d'you want to go?"

"Up there." I point in the direction of Dinah's house. "I want to check something out for myself. C'mon, get dressed."

Pip, still half-asleep, pulls on some clothes and we tiptoe down the stairs and out to the barn to get our bikes.

"Do you know how to get there?" she asks.

"I've been there, remember?" I say. "It's easy. There's only one road. And she has a mailbox that's painted with birds."

Although the road out to Rabbit Ear Point is unpaved, the moon provides more than enough light for us to see where we're going, and in no time at all, we have dropped our bikes alongside Dinah's driveway and walked out to the edge of the small rocky mound, maybe ten or fifteen feet above the lake, where her house sits.

"Is that her house?" Pip whispers. "It's so *cute*. Omigosh—she has a porch swing. I *love* those!"

I sneak a little closer to the house so that when I look south toward the Ada's Reef light, I am seeing exactly what I'd be seeing if I were sitting on Dinah's swing. The wind, still steady from the northwest, is cool on the right side of my face as I scan the shoreline, searching for the blinking light of the buoy. The fleet of fishing boats I'd seen from my room circle the area like sharks, disappearing behind the point of land just to the south of where I stood. Evidently, Dinah is right about the position of the buoy depending on the direction of the wind, because it is definitely *not* visible. But then I notice something interesting when I look to the *left* of Egbert Island: Where I'm standing is high enough that I can see all the way to where the fishing boats are circling the buoy.

"I wonder . . ."

"What?" says Pip.

"I'll explain it later," I say. "It'll be easier to show you on the chart. I have a theory about something. C'mon, let's go home."

The ride back is a little trickier because the moon is hiding behind some clouds, making the narrow, twisty road harder to see. We're about halfway there when we almost crash head-on into a golf cart. At the last possible moment before the collision, I see the glowing end of a cigarette and veer off into the weeds alongside the road, with Pip right behind me.

"Hey!" I shout. "Watch where you're going. Jerk."

The golf cart skids to a stop and the driver aims a flashlight into our faces, blinding us.

"Turn it off!" I demand, moving so that I'm between whoever he is and Pip. When he lowers it from my face I see his uniform and the words Swallowtail Police painted across the hood of the golf cart.

"What are you kids doing out here?" a man's voice asks. "It's after one o'clock."

"So?" I straighten my back and stick out my chin. "We're allowed."

"Actually, you're not. There's a curfew. Kids under sixteen have to be home by eleven."

"I'm seventeen," I say. "And my sister's with me."

He returns the light to my face, then down the length of me stretched to maximum height. "Yeah. And I'm Batman. C'mon, where do you kids live? I'm not going to write you up—this time. Just need to get you home."

"How do we even know you're a *real* cop?" I say. "I need to see your ID."

From his back pocket he pulls out an overstuffed wallet and flips it open so that his badge shows. "Real enough for you? Now let's go. Your mom and dad home?"

"Nope."

Pip pokes me in the back. "Lark."

"What? They're *not*."

"I know, but . . ."

"All right, are there any *adults* home right now?" the cop asks. This time he points his light at Pip.

She nods. "Our stepfather."

"Great. And where do you live?" Once again, he ignores me and asks Pip directly.

"The Roost," she says. "It's not far."

"I know it," he says. "Do you want to ride the bikes or throw them on the back of the cart?"

"We'll ride," I say.

The cop walks a few steps away and calls someone on his radio.

"Petey, come in," he says.

The radio crackles with what I assume to be Petey's reply: "What's up? Where are you?"

"I'm up the road a quarter mile from where I left you. Found a couple of kids snoopin' around. I need to run 'em home, but"—he lowers his voice—"nobody's s'posed to know you guys are out here already. You need to get off the road, far enough so we can't see you."

Petey swears. "Fine. Give us five minutes."

"Roger." The cop turns back to Pip and me. "What are youse doing out here anyway?"

I know he's stalling for time, so I get on my bike and set off down the road. "C'mon, Pip."

"Hey! Wait! You gotta wait for me."

"It's all right. We know the way," I say, pedaling faster.

Unfortunately, the police golf carts are, like, turbocharged, and he catches up, going into the weeds to get around us and then grabbing my handlebars to stop me.

"I thought you wanted us to go home," I say.

"I do—when *I* say so."

His radio crackles again. "All clear," the voice says.

"Ten-four," says the cop, returning the radio to its holster. "Okay, *now* we're going to get you home. Nice and slow this time. Stay right in front of me."

When we get a couple of hundred yards down the road, I whisper to Pip, "Keep your eyes open. Don't turn your head, but look over to your left."

"What are we looking for?" she asks.

"I don't know yet."

"Over there!" she says. "Someone just lit a cigarette."

"Okay. Hold on!" I turn my bike into the weeds and wipe out on purpose.

"Lark!" cries Pip, slamming on her brakes. "Are you okay? What happened?"

"I got caught in a rut," I say, climbing to my feet.

"If you're okay, let's go," the cop says.

"Just a second," I say. I scan the weeds and low shrubs where the orange glow of the cigarette appears and disappears, as if a branch is moving back and forth in front of it. The moon, which would be really helpful right now, is playing hide-and-seek behind a bank of thick clouds. I make a mental note of where we are and pull my bike from the weeds.

When we get to the house, the cop bangs on the back door and Thomas comes down in his pajamas a few seconds later. He looks more befuddled than usual when he sees Pip and me. "Lark. Pip. What's going on?"

"'Evening, sir. Found these girls on their bikes out by Rabbit Ear Point. I'm Officer Pawlowski. Youse are prolly on vacation and all, and maybe not aware of it, but there's a curfew here on Swallowtail."

Thomas runs his hand through his hair, shaking his head. "I-I thought they were upstairs. In bed. I *saw* them go up. When did you . . . where . . ."

"The moon woke us up," Pip says. "It was so bright. And then Lark wanted to show me something . . ."

"At . . . one o'clock in the morning?" Thomas says, stepping out on the porch to look up at the sky, where heavy clouds still obscure the moon. "What moon? Thank you, officer. I'll take it from here."

"Yes, sir. You have a good night."

Thomas closes and locks the door, then turns slowly to deal with us. He takes a deep breath, closing his eyes for a long while. "It's late and I don't want to get into this now, but . . . what were you *thinking*, Lark?"

I stare at my shoes for several seconds before lifting my eyes defiantly. GHT? I'm not crazy about myself for what I'm doing, but that doesn't stop me from basically *daring* him to punish me so I can really lash out and say all the mean things that have been building up inside.

"We're sorry, Thomas," Pip says, running to him and throwing her arms around his waist. "We won't do it again. It was just such a beautiful night."

I glare at Pip. "I'm not sorry. I'm glad I did it. It was *important* to me. Mom and I used to—"

"Pip, honey, why don't you go back up to bed," Thomas says. "Lark and I need a few minutes."

Pip climbs the stairs, stopping halfway to look back at me. I turn away as if she's betrayed me.

"Let's go into the kitchen," Thomas says, and I reluctantly follow him. He pulls out a chair for me, but I refuse it and lean against the counter, arms folded tightly across my chest.

"What?" I say.

Thomas takes a deep breath and presses his palms together. "You know, I'm trying, Lark. I'm doing the best I can. I know it hasn't been easy for you. I know you miss your mom."

"And my *dad*," I add, cruelly. I'm having an out-of-body experience and see myself becoming a walking, talking adolescent cliché, but am too stubborn to do anything about it except watch myself in horror.

"And your dad. Of course. Look, all I'm asking is that you . . . it's hard enough trying to keep the boys in line as it is, but when they see you . . ."

"Getting away with murder? Is that what you think?"

"I don't think you're getting away with murder, but you make it hard. There was the soccer thing, and now you're out at one in the morning—with Pip, for crying out loud. I want to be fair to everyone, to be a good father to you all—"

"You're not my father."

"I *know* that. I'm not trying to replace him—"

"Good. Because you can't."

Thomas, to his credit, keeps his cool in the face of my Mr. Hyde impression. "When your mom was sick, I made a promise to her. I told her that no matter what, I would—"

"Take care of us? Well, guess what? Pip and me don't need you to take care of us. We're just *fine*."

Someone stop me. Please.

"What I was *going* to say," Thomas says calmly, "was that I promised her that I wouldn't be overprotective, that I would, as your mom put it, 'Let Lark be Lark.' She knew what a fighter you are, and said that the worst thing I could do would be to *not* let you fight your own battles. I understand what she meant, and I really *want* to let you, but do you know how hard that is for me, Lark? I'm a father, and every instinct I have tells me to get between my kids and trouble, or danger, or *anything*. And so, when you put yourself—and Pip—in danger by sneaking out of the house in the middle of the night, I have to get involved."

"You didn't even ask what we were doing. Like, maybe it was important to me."

"C'mon, Lark. You're twelve years old. And Pip is *ten*. It really doesn't matter why you were out. Unless it was an actual emergency and I was incapacitated, which I'm not, it could have waited till morning. There have to be consequences. I can't take away your phone or your bike, because you need them for work, I'm sure. Maybe soccer camp—"

"You can't! It was your idea in the first place!"

"And probably not one of my best. I'll sleep on it and we'll talk about it in the morning."

I run up the stairs and slam the bedroom door behind me.

I'm up and out of the house before anyone else wakes up. I can't face another confrontation with Thomas, and since it's probably best for everyone if I'm not around people for a while, I hop on my bike and start down the road that follows the shoreline of the little harbor—the spot where Albert Pritchard's boat was brought ashore seventy-five years ago. A handful of boats are moored there, mostly small sailboats, with the long stone breakwater providing protection. Wheeling past a broken-down shack that had once been a hot dog stand, I notice someone sitting on one of the park benches along the shoreline. I would have kept right on pedaling, but when I realize that it is Simon Stanford, I make a sharp turn into the gravel parking area. The crisp creases in his shirt and pants are visible from across the lot, and when he turns to see who's approaching, I catch a glimpse of a summery plaid tie.

I wave. He nods and lifts his right hand an inch or two from his lap. His gaze returns to the breakwater, and as I pull to a stop, he says quietly, "Good morning, Miss Heron. You're up and about early."

"Soccer camp."

"Mmm."

A long silence. I take a seat at the end of his bench.

"I was thinking about what you said yesterday," I say. "About, you know, having to get away from your family and everybody to think. Today is one of those days. I tried last night but that didn't work out so well."

Another nod, but not even a glance in my direction; he just stares out at the end of the breakwater.

And another long silence.

Then, in a voice barely above a sigh, he says, "David Larsen."

I'm not sure how to react. He seems relieved, as if the simple act of saying the name has lifted the weight of a small car from his shoulders. His eyes narrow, then close for a few seconds before he opens them and turns to me. "I haven't said that name out loud in . . . a lifetime."

"Who . . . Who is David Larsen?" I ask.

Simon sighs, then slowly inhales. "He was the . . . my . . . he died . . . a long time ago."

"Oh. Sorry."

A great blue heron lands next to the breakwater, its long bill immediately starting to stab repeatedly at the water for minnows and insects.

"Miss Heron . . . it's Lark, right?"

"Mm-hmm."

"I do like that. Well, Lark, I'm going to tell you a story. About what really happened—right out *there*—on a warm July night, a long time ago."

"I had just finished my first year at Yale and was on my way home—I grew up here on Swallowtail, my family's been here for generations. My father was elected mayor in nineteen thirty-eight and stayed in the job for twenty-six years. But that's not . . . I met him—David—on the ferry. He was on his way in from Cornell, and he was . . . he was a *god*. Adonis, come to life, on the boat to Swallowtail Island, of all places." Simon pauses, smiling at the memory, then continues: "His parents were friends with the family who owned the marina, and they got him a summer job working on the dock—helping people dock their boats, pumping gas, that kind of thing."

He turns and points to a line of small white cottages across the road from where we sit. "Those were all owned by the marina back then, so he got one for the summer. Well, as I was saying, we met on the ferry, and by the time we reached the island, we were already best friends. At that point in my life, I knew who I was . . . but I'd never . . ." He stops to take a couple of deep breaths. "I'm sorry—I've kept this hidden away for so long . . . it's harder than I thought."

"Hey, it's okay. Don't worry, I know *lots* of gay people," I say, catching him by surprise. "My parents—all of them—have gay friends. One of my best friends is. I mean, he doesn't know it yet, but . . . you know. It's cool. We have all day. Well, until seven forty-five, anyway. Then I have to go to soccer."

"I forget sometimes how much the world has changed," Simon says. "You're a very perceptive young woman."

"Yeah, so I've heard. Okay, so you met David. What does he have to do with the crash?"

"With the crash, nothing. With what happened later, everything. It was the end of the summer; we had only a few days left before we both went back east to college. Normally, we would have been together in the cottage, talking until the small hours about . . . everything, and nothing. Same things young people talk about today, I would imagine. Music, books, movies, but mostly our dreams for the future. And our fears. But he had to be at the marina by five o'clock next morning for a delivery, so we said good night early. When I left him at around ten thirty, I decided to walk down here, to the breakwater, before heading home. It was a lovely night, the stars were out, and I suppose I was a little melancholy at the thought of saying goodbye . . . and the prospect of not seeing David again until the next June. I sat on this very bench for a while, and that's when I saw it—the boat hanging around the buoy. At the inquest, I said that it was there for a while and then it disappeared . . ." He shakes his head. "But that's not what happened, at least not all of it."

"I was right," I say. "When you were talking to Nadine and me, I had a . . . I *knew* there was more to your story."

"Like I said: perceptive," says Simon. "I was curious, so I went out to the end of the breakwater for a better view. Then, something strange happened—the light on the buoy went out, just stopped flashing altogether. I see the boat move away, and then the light starts again, but—here's the thing—it wasn't in the same place."

"What do you mean? They moved the buoy?"

"That's what I thought at first, even though I knew it was impossible. Those buoys have *huge* anchors on them, and this was a very small boat. The Coast Guard uses boats with big cranes to move those things around. So I suppose that I convinced myself that the dark was playing tricks on my eyes, that I was mistaken. Meanwhile, the little boat disappeared up around the point by the captain's house. Still no lights, but it was a quiet night and I heard the outboard motor for a while longer. And I was still sitting right here ten minutes later when I heard something that is to this day *burned* into my memory: Albert Pritchard's boat, throttle wide open, coming from the north. Everyone on the island knew the sound of that engine; there was nothing else like it. I stood up, looking for him, and saw his lights as he made the turn around the buoy—a buoy that he'd been around a thousand times before."

"Omigosh. You *saw* the crash," I say.

Simon's head drops, and he stares at a spot on the ground between his suede wingtips. "I tried waving, but it was no good. He couldn't see me in the dark, and even if he could, he probably would have thought I was doing just that—waving at him. When he hit the rocks, he must have been going fifty or sixty— he never had a chance. The police said he went through the windshield and then . . . there was an eerie silence. I was frantic, looking for a boat to take out, but everything was moored away from shore, so I decided it would be better if I called someone. I'm running down the breakwater when I hear that little outboard motor again, getting closer, heading right for the site of the crash. It's the same boat—the one without lights—and the same thing happens again. The light on the buoy goes out for a few seconds, and when it comes back on, it's in a different place. Next thing I know, the boat is heading right for me, for the end of the wall. As it goes past and into the harbor here, I recognize the man at the wheel: it's Gilbert Cheever."

"No. Way. Why would he . . . why didn't you—"

Simon holds up his hand. "Let me finish. He pulled the boat up on the beach and I ran over there, frantic, shouting that we have to go help Mr. Pritchard. At that point I didn't know if he was even alive, but I knew we had to do *something*. When I'm a few yards away, though, Gilbert puffs himself up big as he can, and says, 'Stop right there if you know what's good for you.' I'm close enough to see inside the boat, where there's a heavy tarp covering something. At first I think it's Mr. Pritchard's body, but then I get a better look. Sticking out from both ends is some kind of a contraption. It's a wooden post with a flashing red light at the top, and it's weighted at the bottom with a car battery and a heavy chain so it'll float standing up—"

"Like a buoy!" I say. "He built a fake buoy and anchored it . . . and I'll bet he used the tarp to cover up the light on the real one! It's . . ."

"It's *genius* is what it was," says Simon. "Evil genius, but genius nonetheless. I tell him to get back in the boat, that we need to get out there, but he just smiles. 'I'm not going anywhere, Daisy. And neither are you.' That's when I see the gun in his hand. 'I'd hate to have to use this, but I will,' he says, cool as a cucumber. 'Listen closely, 'cause here's what's going to happen. When the time comes, and the police ask you what you saw, you're going to leave me out—understand? You heard the boat coming from the north and you saw the crash. You never saw me. Or'—he pointed to the inside of his boat—'anything else. End of story. Is that clear enough for you?'"

"Man," I say. "I can't believe how he could be so calm . . . I mean, he just *killed* a guy."

Simon continues: "He keeps the gun pointed at me until I say

WRECK AT ADA'S REEF

that I understand. My mind is already going a mile a minute. All I'm thinking about is how I'm going to turn him in the first chance I get, when he puts the gun in his pocket and smiles at me. If I live to be *two* hundred, I'll never forget that horrible smile. 'Simon Stanford. Oh, I know all about you, Simon. You and your little boyfriend Davey.' Then he points over at the cottage. 'Sweet little love nest you two have there. Shame if your parents were to find out. Your father being the mayor and all, your mother, head of all those committees. Of course, your secret's safe with me . . . long as you return the favor.'

"And that was that. You have to understand, things were different. My parents, my friends, college, *everything*—I would have lost it all. I just couldn't . . ."

"But . . . Mr. Pritchard . . ."

"It wasn't going to bring him back. I know, that's no excuse for what I did. If it makes you feel better, not a day goes by that I don't think about it. A man literally got away with murder because I was afraid to stand up . . . to have to admit to who I really was. When Gilbert finally died, back in the eighties, I slept a little easier, but by then . . . I didn't see the point in digging it all up again and having to explain why I didn't say anything at the time."

"How many people know about . . . what you saw?" I ask.

"They're both on this bench," Simon answers. "At least that's what I thought . . . until yesterday."

"What do you mean, until yesterday?"

"After you and Nadine left, I had another visitor. Not five minutes later. He knew I'd met with you and Nadine."

"Who's *he*?"

"Reginald Cheever. Gilbert's grandson."

"Geez, how many Cheevers *are* there?"

"Too many to count, I'm afraid."

"What did he want?"

"He knows what Nadine is up to, and I can tell he's a little nervous. Mostly he was snooping around to find out what we had talked about. 'The old days on the island,' I told him. I mentioned that Nadine was interested in stories about Dinah Purdy for a book she's writing. I didn't say anything about the crash, or Gilbert. At first I thought he was satisfied, but then, well, he couldn't leave it at that. He is a Cheever, after all. He had to threaten me, just a little."

"He *threatened* you?"

"In his own way. He asked me if I liked living at Swallowtail Meadows."

"I don't get it. How is that—"

"There are a few apartments reserved for Swallowtail residents like me. We get a special rate on the rent. The fact is, I couldn't afford to live there without it."

Lights flash and bells ring inside my head. "Let me guess. The Cheevers *own* Swallowtail Meadows, right? That is *so* messed up."

"Indeed. Welcome to the real world, as they say. Well, the

second he left, I knew it was time to tell my story. So thank Reggie Cheever, not me. Even if I end up out on the street for the rest of my days, it will have been worth it."

"That's not going to happen," I say. "Look, I have to leave, but is it okay if I tell Nadine? It was her grandfather, after all."

"Cat's out of the bag. Can't see as it'll make a difference, anyway. Everybody's dead. Except me. And Dinah Purdy, but she's going to live forever."

"It must make a difference to the Cheevers, or they wouldn't be coming around trying to scare you."

Oh, they're afraid of something, all right. I just don't know what.

Yet.

# CHAPTER

# 7

I HAVE ONE OF THOSE days I dream about at soccer camp, scoring on Owen Cheever—twice!—in a twenty-minute game. Both times, I steal the ball from him near midfield and scoot away, outrunning him and his teammates until I am close enough to fake out the goalkeeper and dink the ball into the net. After the first, I don't say anything, but when the second one goes in, I can't help myself. I mean, come on. You just don't get that many perfect moments in life.

"Oh, I'm *sorry*," I say. "I forgot—girls are supposed to just stand around and wait for the ball to come to them. I guess you're not used to players with *actual skills*. Instead of Owen, maybe your parents should have named you *Under*. Get it? Under A. Cheever." It's a shame the whole "mic drop" thing has become such a lame cliché, because it would have been an ideal moment for one—if, you know, I had actually been *holding* a microphone in the first place.

Owen fumes, his face turning a shade of red usually reserved for lipstick worn by elderly ladies, especially when one of his teammates chides him for being beaten by a girl (twice!), and the others start calling him Under A. Cheever, but he doesn't say a word. The coaches add to his humiliation at the end of the day when they show everyone video highlights of the game, focusing especially on my two steals from Owen, even calling the second one "a real pro move." By the time the session ends, Owen looks as if he is ready to follow in his great-grandfather's murderous footsteps.

My bike gets a flat tire on the way to Nadine's, but even that can't bring me down. Let's face it, I'm having a flipping *grrr-eat* day and a little puncture isn't going to change that. I push the bike the rest of the way, dropping it on the lawn and then running inside, letting the screen door slam behind me. In the hallway, I nearly collide with Nadine, who's carrying a tray with a pitcher of iced tea and two glasses, on her way out to the front porch.

We both skid to a stop; the pitcher sloshes a little tea, but remains standing. "Whoa! Is there a tiger chasing you?"

"You won't believe the day . . . I've had," I blurt out between breaths. "*Epic.* Everything . . . it's all . . . changed now. It was . . . Gilbert!"

She tilts her head at the mention of Gilbert. "Oh? Come on out on the porch and tell me all about it. But first, drink something. Why are you so out of breath?"

"Bike . . . flat tire . . . pushed it . . . all the . . . way."

Nadine pours tea into the glasses and sets one in front of me. "Now, tell me. What do you mean, *It was Gilbert?*"

"He killed your grandfather. I have *proof.*"

"What!" Nadine sputters, choking on her tea. "How? How did you—?"

"Simon Stanford told me what *really* happened that night. I left the house early because, well, that's another story . . . anyway, I'm on the road by the little harbor, and I see him sitting there on a bench, so I stopped to say hi. And then . . ."

When I finish telling Simon's story, Nadine stands, shaking her head. "Well, you've certainly earned your money this week. Incredible. Seventy-five years, nothing. Then you show up and . . . Bam! You solve the mystery."

"I didn't really *solve* anything," I say. "I was just in the right place at the right time. It was Reginald Cheever who put him over the edge. What a sleazeball. Threatening a nice old man."

"I feel so bad for Simon. Imagine, having to deny who you are . . . choosing to live with the knowledge that a man got away with committing murder, rather than admit to the world that you're gay. Crazy."

"So . . . you're not mad at him? I mean, for not turning in Gilbert?"

Nadine shakes her head. "They were different times. I can't even *imagine* what it must have been like for a gay man back then. It was bad enough in the eighties and nineties when people I knew were deciding whether to come out. He did what he had to do. No, why *Simon* did what he did doesn't bother me. But . . . now that we *know* Gilbert committed the murder and *how* he did it, the question is *why*?"

"Motive," I say, my mind suddenly turning to every detective story I've ever read or seen on TV.

"Exactly. When we were thinking of this as some kind of strange, tragic accident, we were interested only in *how* it happened. But if Simon Stanford is telling the truth—and there's no reason to think he isn't—and Gilbert *murdered* Albert . . . well, there must have been a good reason for it. And by *good*, I mean that it must have benefited *Gilbert* in some way."

"Revenge?"

"Doesn't seem likely," Nadine says. "Not saying I'd discard it out of hand, but Gilbert and Albert worked together, so . . . I guess it's possible that Albert did something that Gilbert took as a slight."

"Like in *The Cask of Amontillado*." I read that story in school, and it has stuck with me. Not that I think any way of dying is great, but there's something about being buried alive that totally freaks me out. "Maybe jealousy?"

"That's more likely. Maybe combined with that other all-time favorite, money. My grandfather was happily married, with three kids. He was an Ivy Leaguer *and* a lot younger and *much* more successful. Other people I've talked to said that Gilbert's legal practice depended entirely on small matters that Albert didn't have time to deal with. That must have driven him crazy. And then there's the timing of Albert's death."

"What do you mean?"

"Doesn't it seem odd that Gilbert commits a murder the *day after* his own brother dies? There must be a connection—the question is, can we figure out what it is, after all these years?"

"We can do it," I say. To say I'm confident—probably *over*confident—after the day I've had is an understatement. "Somebody has to know something."

"I like your attitude, Lark," Nadine says, patting me on the shoulder. "Shall we go see Dinah? I think we can share this news with her. We need to fix your tire first, though. I have a repair kit out in the barn. I can show you how to do it if you've never done it."

"I've done it lots of times," I say. "Piece of cake."

"A girl of many talents. Good for you. How was soccer today, by the way?"

I can't help grinning as I remember my triumph over Owen Cheever.

"What? Why are you smiling?"

"I'll tell you about it on the way. Let's just say that it hasn't been a great day for the Cheever family."

Once we have told Dinah the truth about Albert Pritchard's death, it doesn't take her long to propose a motive for Gilbert Cheever to commit murder.

"Oh, that's easy," Dinah says with a wave of the hand. "There was talk around town that Captain Cheever had written a new will, cutting his brother Gilbert out completely. All it was was talk, though. The judge asked around a little, but nothing ever came of it."

Those words hang in the air for a few seconds before Nadine responds. "Wait . . . do you think that Gilbert killed his own brother, too?"

"No, no. Edward died of natural causes, there's no doubt of that. His housekeeper was with him when he collapsed. She heard his last words—I don't remember them exactly, but he mentioned something about a will. Go to the museum and ask for Louise Tollingham. Do you know her?"

"A little," notes Nadine. "We've been on a few committees together."

"Yes, of course. That makes perfect sense," says Dinah. "She's *very* loyal to the Cheevers, so it may be best not to explain what you're up to, but she can tell you the captain's last words. No, Gilbert didn't kill his brother, but Edward's sudden death would have forced him to act quickly, before that new will was made public. That is, if there *was* a new will."

"Of *course*," Nadine says. "My grandfather knew about the new will, so he had to go."

"No doubt he would have *drafted* it, based on Edward's wishes," Dinah adds. "It's remarkable, really. Tragic. Your grandfather and Captain Cheever. Two best friends dying just a day apart."

"And Gilbert right in the middle of it," I say. "What did he do next?"

"The next stop would have been probate," Nadine explains. "It's a special court where you go when someone dies and there is no will or when the will is in question. The judge works with the executor of the estate, who is like the representative of the deceased person, to make sure everything is on the up-and-up and then determine who gets what."

"Your grandfather *would* have been the executor, but with him dead, the judge had no choice but to give the job to Gilbert," Dinah says. "And as you already know, the will Gilbert presented to the court was one that Edward had written *years* before, when his wife and Ada were still alive. He got that old will past Judge Cavanaugh—no legal scholar, believe me—before anybody had a chance to come forward with any real evidence of a new one."

"And since Captain Cheever's wife and daughter were dead, Gilbert got everything," I say.

"Just for the sake of argument, let's assume that these are the facts," Nadine says, holding up one finger. "One, Edward wrote a new will with my grandfather's help. Two, Gilbert found out about it, which wouldn't have been hard, since he worked in the same office. Three, Edward dies suddenly, prompting Gilbert to hatch and carry out a plot to kill my grandfather, the only other person who knew about the new will. Four, Gilbert finds the will and destroys it, and five, Gilbert acts as executor of his brother's estate, and as the only living heir, inherits everything. I have to admit, it's brilliant."

"The only flaw in the plan was when Simon Stanford saw him switch the buoy," I say. "But he took care of that."

Staring out the window at a sailboat making for Put-in-Bay, Nadine says, "Let's back up a second. Dinah, how many copies of Edward's new will would there have been?"

"Once they were signed and witnessed, one copy would stay in the office file," Dinah says. "And one would have been delivered to Edward."

"Which was almost certainly destroyed by Gilbert as soon as he got in the house," Nadine says. "Is it possible that Edward got more than one copy? Maybe he put one in a safe-deposit box at the bank."

"If he did, Gilbert would have been granted access, as executor," says Dinah.

"And would have destroyed it, too," Nadine adds.

"Okay. I have a question," I say. "Edward makes a new will and doesn't leave anything to Gilbert, right? His wife and daughter have been dead for a long time. So . . . who does he leave everything to? Did he have any other family?"

"No, but he did have friends! Some very good friends, including Dinah's father. Lark, you're brilliant!" Nadine says, leaping to her feet. "Dinah, what if the captain intended to give the land to your father *outright*, instead of the life estate. That would mean that *you* own it—*not* the Cheevers. And that changes *everything*."

"Oh, my," says Dinah.

Nadine musses my hair. "'Oh, my' is *right*. All we have to do is find a copy of a will that may or may not exist, and we have until July twenty-eighth to do it. And *then* we have to convince a judge that it's real. Crazy, isn't it? Seventy-five years, and it all comes down to a matter of weeks."

"Piece of cake," I say.

I'm approaching the Cheever Museum from the north, on my way home from Dinah's, which takes me past the scene of Pip's and my "arrest." Except for an ambulance and a couple of fire trucks, there are no cars or trucks on the island, but I immediately find tire tracks that are too wide and too deep to have been made by a golf cart or a horse-drawn *anything*. I remember something Thomas said to Jack, who wondered aloud how they built anything on the island without the help of backhoes, bulldozers, and cranes. Thomas's answer was that they *don't*. It requires a special permit, but construction equipment *is* allowed on the island for specific projects.

The tracks stop suddenly at a line of scrubby pine trees, where I spot a cigarette butt and an orange plastic cone that must have fallen from whatever was parked there. Stenciled on the underside of its base is *Cheever Construction Co.* I kick it under some brush and walk back to my bike.

"Why are they bringing equipment out here now?" I say, one hundred percent certain that Dinah hasn't given permission to the Cheevers to start construction even one day before the seventy-five years is up.

Farther down the road, Thomas is on his bike, about to make the turn from the Cheever Museum drive out onto the road. He's wearing his favorite sweater, so I know he has started the restoration work on the museum's paintings. Thomas swears that he is able to do his best work only if he is wearing Big Red—an oversized, moth-eaten, paint-covered red ragg wool sweater that he has owned since college. (A few days after the wedding, Mom, unaware of its importance, had tossed it into a bag of clothes that ended up in a thrift shop in Middletown. Luckily, Thomas realized it was missing that evening. The next morning, he waited outside the shop, pounding on the door when they failed to open at exactly nine o'clock. He came home with the sweater and the marriage was saved.) On Thomas's best days, he's a little scruffy—he always looks to be in need of a haircut, even when he leaves the barbershop—but when Big Red goes on, the scruffiness factor increases by ten.

When I see him, instinct tells me to stop where I am and hope he doesn't see me, but suddenly there's Mom's voice in my head, overruling my bratty impulses. *"Be nice,"* she says—her two favorite words—*"and forget about what happened last night."* I speed up to catch him.

"Lark—wasn't expecting to see you." After the initial expression of surprise fades, I can't quite read his face to know whether he's happy to see me or not.

"Uh, yeah. I was out at Dinah's."

"Okay day? You were up pretty early." His face still doesn't give anything away. He's better at this than I would have guessed.

"Yeah, I guess. It's kind of crazy. So . . . Big Red, huh?"

He picks at a bit of dried paint on a ratty sleeve. "A little warm, I guess, but, well, you know. We're a team." Finally, a hint of a smile.

"So . . ."

"Right. Last night. What are we going to do?"

I shrug. "I dunno."

"I have an idea. It's not punishment, exactly, but you'll be helping me out. If I'm going to get everything done at the museum before we leave, I have some long days ahead of me. I could use some help with the grocery shopping and the cooking. This is *not* because you're a girl. It's because I really need the help and frankly, I don't have any better ideas for your penance, at least as long as we're here on the island. Besides, you've already proved yourself in the kitchen. Taco night was a big success. Jack asked me this morning when the next one was. What do you think?"

"Shopping, too?" I say, turning up my nose. I like to cook, but grocery stores are high on the list of my least favorite places in the world.

Thomas nods. "You can stop at the market on your way home from Nadine's. It won't be every day. I'll still do the big shop on the weekends. It's either this or give up soc—"

"No, no, I'll do it," I say.

"Great. You can get started tonight. How about your mom's tuna casserole? Everybody seems to like that."

After dinner (spaghetti with meat sauce that my mom taught me to make), Thomas shows us pictures on his tablet of the six paintings he's restoring. Four of them are of ships captained by

Edward Cheever, including a sailing schooner he started on as a seaman in 1905 at the ripe old age of sixteen. They're all right, I guess, but a ship's a ship to me. The other two are far more interesting despite being in worse condition.

"This is Julia Cheever, Edward's wife," Thomas says, zooming in on her face, which is clouded over with a thick yellowish-brownish haze.

"She looks like a *movie* star," says Jack.

"Yuck. You're *crazy*, Jack. She looks like Mrs. Blanding," Nate says, fake-gagging at the memory of his fourth-grade teacher.

"When was that painted?" I ask.

"There's no date, but probably the late thirties," Thomas answers. He swipes to the next picture, which shows two young girls standing on opposite sides of a small table where a captain's clock, its hands set at exactly five o'clock, rests on a wooden stand. Thomas points to the girl on the left. "This is Ada Cheever, Edward's daughter. And *this*—"

"That's Dinah Purdy!" I say. "She still looks just like that, only older. They were, like, best friends. Ada died when she was twelve."

"Whaaat?" Pip cries, squeezing in between Pogo and me on the couch. "She *died*? How?"

"The flu," I say. "Her mom, too."

Pip takes the tablet away from Thomas for an even closer

look. "That's *terrible*. Didn't they have doctors in olden times?"

"A lot of people used to die from the flu," Thomas says. "For that matter, they still do. But back then, it was even worse. I doubt that there was much in the way of medicine to go around, especially on an isolated island. If she died at twelve, it can't have been too long after this was painted. She's got to be about that here, don't you think?"

"Yeah, probably," I say, taking the tablet from Pip. "It's a little hard to tell 'cause their faces are so dark."

"The museum wants me to start with Edward's wife," Thomas says.

"No," I say firmly. "You have to do Ada and Dinah first. Promise."

Thomas's eyebrows rise; he's surprised by my sudden interest in his work.

"Oh. I, uh, okay, I guess I can do that. I'll probably start work on both, actually. Depending on the . . . yeah, you don't want to hear about how some varnishes dissolve faster than others, do you?"

"Not really," I admit.

"So, that's settled. Now, Saturday," Thomas says. "What's the plan? I was hoping maybe we could do something—all of us together. Maybe a nice quiet day at the beach? We can ride the bikes over. Supposedly, there's a new snack shack with decent burgers and hot dogs for lunch."

Pip, Nate, and Jack all immediately sign on. Blake, who is actually starting to believe that he is too cool for a family outing, waits to see my reaction, a smile-shrug that says *Why not?*

"Looks like we're going to the beach," he says.

Summerson Beach stretches for over a mile at the east end of the island, but if you're picturing acres of pristine white sand and sparkling turquoise water like in some Caribbean paradise, stop. That's not what it looks like. Not even a little bit. First of all, the beach is not very wide, and the sand (where there *is* sand) is muddy brown with lots of sharp rocks sprinkled in. Toss in a little seaweed and a dead fish here and there and you start to get the picture. I'm not complaining, mind you, just telling it the way it is.

We stake out a prime spot at one of the widest points right before eleven, and then spend the next hour and a half in the water, which is surprisingly clear and warm. Thomas is first to retreat to the blanket, where he quickly falls asleep with one of Nadine's books, recently borrowed from the library, on his chest. One by one, the rest of us join him. I'm the last one out of the water, and as I look east toward another sandy spot, I spot a group of boys kicking a soccer ball around in a pickup game. They're a long way off, but I recognize one of them instantly: Owen Cheever.

"Great," I say under my breath.

"What?" Pip says.

"Nothing. I'm hungry."

"Oh, no. It's that kid from soccer camp with the ponytail," Nate says. "Owen something. I *hate* him. He's such a ball hog. I was on his team once and he's like, gimme the ball, *all* the time. He doesn't let any of the little kids even touch it. If they do, he steals it from them. Remember, Jack?"

"What?" Jack says. He's much too busy looking for minnows to care about what happened days ago at soccer camp.

Thomas sits up, shaking off the sleep and the sand that we've kicked onto him. "Okay. Time to eat. Let's see if this snack shack is all it's cracked up to be."

Naturally, the path to the snack bar takes us right through the middle of the soccer game, which comes to a halt as we pass. I feel a little (okay, a lot) self-conscious walking past all those boys in my bathing suit, but I do my best to hide it, and to avoid eye contact with them.

"Hey, isn't that the girl—" one starts to say. Out of the corner of my eye, I recognize him as one of the boys who had teased Owen after I scored on him. Twice.

"Shut up," says Owen.

"Sorry, boys," Thomas says. "Looks like we're interrupting your game."

"No problem," the first boy answers. "Hi, Lark."

I nod hello and my eyes drift left to Owen, who's staring

at me. His eyes dart away.

The first boy, whose name I now remember is Matt, says, "Hey, do you guys want to play? We could use a few more. Are these *all* your brothers? I've seen these two—"

"Look, we would, but we're on our way to get lunch," I say. "But thanks."

"Sure. Cool," Matt says.

We're about to make our escape when Thomas opens his big mouth. "You kids stay and play for a while. I'll get lunch and bring it back." He takes off without a look back before I have a chance to argue with him.

"I call Lark," says the boy holding the ball. "Me and Owen are captains. I'm Paul."

"Pip has to be on my team," I say. "Or I don't play."

"Fine," says Owen. "Whatever. I get the brothers."

Nate looks up at me, open-mouthed at my betrayal.

"It's only for a little while," I say. "You'll survive."

As we split up into two teams, I suddenly feel very bad for Blake, who, let's face it, is *not* a gifted athlete. He takes after his dad: He's artistic, plays piano, and, according to my friends, is cute in that nineties-boy-band kind of way—but when it comes to sports, he's *hopeless*. The thing is, he has this lanky, athletic look about him that is totally deceptive. It's only when he starts moving that you realize something's wrong. When he runs, his arms and legs seem to have lives of their own—very *separate* lives.

For a few minutes, I forget the reasons I had for not wanting to play and actually enjoy myself. Playing on the beach has its own challenges; for one thing, it takes a *huge* amount of energy to run in the sand, so lots of passing is encouraged. Our side takes the lead after I loft a long pass across the field to Pip, who taps it to our captain, Paul, streaking toward the goal. He boots it past the goalkeeper, and then does a cartwheel right in front of Owen.

I score another goal five minutes later, and the game starts to turn ugly. The first thing I notice is Owen and some of his buddies making fun of the way Blake runs. They pass him the ball and then literally stop and watch, smirking and laughing as if it's the funniest thing they've ever seen. Poor Blake is oblivious to it, but Pip, Nate, and Jack have all caught on, and are looking at me, so I make a point of bumping hard into Owen and saying, "Leave him alone. I mean it."

Owen snorts. "What?"

"You know what." I stretch to my full five-eight-and-a-half and narrow my eyes. "Cut it out."

He walks away, shaking his head and muttering to his friends. "Like I expected. His sister fights his battles for him."

"Let's just go," Pip says, the memory of the ISF still fresh in her mind. "Thomas will be back in a minute anyway."

She's right, I know. Sometimes it's best to walk away. But this is not one of those times.

"Not yet," I say. I am hoping that my message is crystal

clear, but just like the other night with Thomas, there's a part of me that is *daring* Owen to defy me. This time is different, though. With Thomas it was about me, and this time it's about standing up for somebody else. Blake and I have had our problems, but there's no way I'm going to just let this go. "Keep playing."

Owen's team quickly gets one goal back, thanks to an unintentional deflection that caroms off the back of Nate's head, catching our goalkeeper going the wrong direction. And a minute later, Owen ignores his teammates' calls for him to pass and he threads his way through our defense and scores, making it a 2–2 game.

"Yes!" he cries, puffing up his chest in Paul's face.

"Next goal wins," Paul says.

We are all tired, and the game has stopped being fun, but neither team wants to be the one to call it quits, so we play on. Back and forth, up and down the beach, but the ball gets nowhere near either goal.

Until, that is, I finally break through and find myself with only Blake standing between me and the winning goal. But, in a truly bizarro-world moment, he somehow manages to get a leg in and actually steals the ball away from me! For that one brief, shining moment—a few seconds, really—he's a hero.

And then, not.

In his excitement (and, no doubt, shock at having beaten me), he attempts to pass the ball off to Owen, who is standing near the goal, but instead, like a nervous golfer with all the world watching, hooks it firmly and directly toward his own goal. The goalkeeper and Owen both dive for it, sending sand flying in all directions, but they're too late and the ball trickles past them and over the goal line for my team's win.

Game over.

Owen picks himself up from the sand, looking for Blake. "You . . . stupid . . ."

I step in between them, facing Owen, whose face is closer to the color of an eggplant than the old-lady-lipstick-red he turns when he's embarrassed. "I told you. Leave him alone," I say. At my sides, my hands clench and unclench.

"What are you going to do—hit me?" he says.

"If I have to." (Mom's voice: *Lark—you made your point. Now count to three and walk away.*)

Owen laughs at me and continues to try to provoke the decidedly *non*violent Blake into a fight. I could have let a little name-calling slide, but then he makes the mistake of using a word that no one should *ever* use, so I do what I have to do—what I have *promised* to do. And I always keep my promises.

I slug him.

His knees buckle and he drops to the ground like an apple from a tree, one hand going to his nose, which begins to bleed in an impressive way.

For the next few seconds, I hear nothing; it's as if a grenade has gone off and the concussion has deafened me. I feel my heart pounding against my ribs, and then Pip, Nate, and Jack taking me by the arms, pulling me away from the scene of the crime.

And then, Thomas, standing in front of me, a confused/worried/disappointed look on his face.

"Lark punched that Owen kid," Nate says. "Right on the *nose*. It was *cool*."

"*What!?*" Thomas looks past us to the circle of boys huddled around Owen, who has made it back to his feet. "Oh, Lark." He momentarily closes his eyes as if trying to block out the reality that has intruded on his perfect beach day, then says, "Okay. First off, are *you* all okay? Nobody's hurt?"

"We're fine," Pip says. "It wasn't her fault. He called Blake a *really* bad word."

"Stay *here*," Thomas orders us. "Don't move. Where *is* Blake, by the way?"

"There," Jack says, pointing down the beach toward our blanket, where Blake lies, staring up into space.

"Okay, just . . . just stay here," Thomas repeats before heading toward Owen and the other boys.

As soon as Thomas is out of earshot, Nate says, "That was *awesome*. Did you see him go down? It was, like, BAM! I think you broke his nose." He's looking at me with even more admiration than usual.

"I didn't break his nose. I would have felt it." I'm *hoping* that's true. A bloody nose is one thing, but if it's actually broken? That sounds much more serious. "Shoot. I'm an idiot."

"What do you think is going to happen?" Pip asks.

"We'll stick up for you," Nate says. "Owen is a *jerk*, everybody knows it. And besides, Dad *wanted* us to play with them."

Thomas returns, his expression revealing nothing. "Let's go." He picks up the giant bag containing our lunch and starts walking toward our blanket and Blake. Without looking at me, he says, "This isn't good, Lark. His father and grandfather are on the board of the museum. I could lose . . . *why?*"

I kick some sand with my bare feet, fighting back tears. "Because . . . he made fun of my *brother*. I couldn't . . ."

And right then, I know everything is going to be all right, because through all of his anger and disappointment and the possibility of losing his gig at the museum, Thomas *smiles*. Then he puts his arm around my shoulders, pulling me close. "You are *such* a pain in the neck."

"I don't get it," I say. "Why are you . . . happy?"

"Because not only did you stick up for Blake—not that I'm condoning *how* you did it and that is something that is going to have some *serious* consequences for you—but you called him your . . . *brother*. It's the first time you didn't say *step*brother."

# 8

I'M IN BED PRETENDING TO read when there's a quiet tap on the door. I glance across the room at Pip, who's fast asleep with Pogo curled up next to her.

"Lark, you awake?" It's Blake, whispering.

"Yeah."

"Is Pip?"

"No." I hop down from the bed and tiptoe to the door. "What do you want?" I whisper to the dark wood.

"I-I didn't want to say anything in front of everybody, but . . . thanks. You know, for sticking up for me. I don't want you to get in trouble."

"I think it's too late for that. Thomas says I can't go to soccer Monday, until he talks to the camp counselors, I guess. He says it's for my own good. He's afraid those guys will go after me."

"He's probably right." Blake doesn't say anything for a long time, but I know he's still out there.

"You okay?" I say.

"Mm-hmm. Yeah. I, uh, I'm sorry I'm so bad at sports."

"I could help you."

"I doubt it."

GHT? He's probably right. And while it's on the tip of my tongue to tell him I'm no miracle worker, the new, *evolved* me says, "I'm not saying I can turn you into Lionel Messi, or even be as good as me, but maybe I can teach you enough to be, uh . . ."

"*Not* so uncoordinated?" he offers.

"Something like that."

"Maybe. We'll see. Anyway . . . look, I . . . I'm really glad you're my sister."

"Yeah. Me, too." GHT, again: I'm glad the door is still closed between us. He might want to hug it out or something, and I'm *definitely* not ready for that.

I take advantage of my mini-break from soccer camp by sleeping in a half hour later than usual.

By the time I stroll into the kitchen, the younger kids are already gone and the screen door has just slammed shut as

Blake picks up his bike from the yard.

"Where's Thomas?" I call out to him.

He shrugs. "I dunno. He was gone when I got up." He climbs aboard his bike and pedals down the road.

I help myself to some juice and a giant bowl of cereal while leafing through the latest issue of the *Citizen*. "Wow. *Slow news week*," I say in response to a front-page story about an eighteenth birthday party for a cat. My ears perk up at the sound of bicycle tires crunching on gravel, followed by two voices: Thomas, I am fully expecting. The other, though, is Nadine, and I'm not at all sure what to make of *that*.

"Oh, good, you're up," Thomas says.

From the tone of his voice, I can't tell what kind of mood he's in, so I nod.

"G'morning, Lark," says Nadine.

"What's going on?" I ask.

Thomas hands Nadine a mug of coffee. "We've been visiting a friend of yours," he says. "Dinah Purdy. I've been consulting with her and Nadine."

"Thomas told me what happened yesterday. And the night before," Nadine says.

"And about the ISF," Thomas adds, making me cringe.

I can't look Nadine in the eyes. "You must think I'm some kind of juvenile delinquent."

"Not at all. I think you're a bright, talented, amazing, wonderful twelve-year-old girl who is doing her best to navigate a complicated world that hasn't exactly been kind to her."

"But I keep screwing things up. There's something wrong with me."

"No," says Thomas. "There's not. You follow your instincts. Yesterday, your instincts told you that Owen Cheever had to be dealt with, and they were right. Pip and the boys told me everything that happened, and this kid sounds like . . . well, I don't want to say he had it coming, but somebody needed to do *something*."

"The hard part is figuring out what that something is," Nadine says. "But I know someone who can help."

"I've already talked to a shrink," I say. "It didn't do any good. Maybe I can't be helped."

"It's not a shrink. It's Dinah," says Nadine.

"Dinah. I don't get it."

Nadine says, "For her entire career, her entire *life*, Dinah has dealt with injustices big and small and racism and prejudice that we couldn't imagine if we tried. She knows more about hitting back without actually *hitting* than anybody in the country. When it comes to nonviolent protest, she's a Jedi Master. She's like Yoda."

"And she has agreed to be your mentor," Thomas informs me. "Think of it as character building. With a side of rehabilitation."

"I think it'll be good for you both," Nadine says. She turns to Thomas, smiling. "We . . . took the liberty of making some suggestions for reading material. Some things that should give the two of you lots to talk about."

"Starting with a little Gandhi," Thomas says.

"Who?"

"Don't worry. You're going to love him," Nadine says. "And lots of others. Martin Luther King, Nelson Mandela, Lech Walesa."

"What about my job?" I ask. "The will? There's not much time . . . how can I . . . I mean, we *have* to solve it. How can I help if I'm . . . and what about cooking?"

"Nadine's filled me in about what you two have been up to, and I want you to see it through to the end, so you'll still go to her place right after soccer, in place of working at Dinah's," says Thomas. "You don't need to be at Dinah's till three thirty or four, and it won't be every day. She thinks a couple of weekdays, and maybe Saturday mornings. The other kids are going to help with the cooking and shopping for now. So you're not off the hook for that—not completely, anyway."

"Don't worry, you'll have time to do everything," Nadine says. "I'm still counting on you as much as ever. More, even, now that you've shown me what you're capable of."

"So . . . I'm not kicked out of soccer?"

Thomas shakes his head. "I called the program director and told him what happened, that it was all on you—"

"But Owen was acting like a—"

WRECK AT ADA'S REEF

Thomas holds up a hand to stop me. "Doesn't matter. You can't go through life *punching* everybody you disagree with, Lark. Hopefully, Dinah will help you understand that. And teach you a better way. Marcus Aurelius said that it is a man's duty to love even those who wrong him."

"I am *not* gonna love Owen Cheever," I say.

"You know what I mean," Thomas says. "Regardless, the short answer is no, you're not kicked out of soccer. But that will change in a hurry if you're involved in *anything*. . . . Understood?"

"Fine. But what if he—"

"If Owen Cheever, or any of his friends, says or does *anything* to you, you are to tell the coaches, tell me, tell Nadine, and *we* will deal with it. You are *not* to take matters into your own hands. Your hands have caused enough trouble for a lifetime. Is that clear?"

"Crystal."

The only trees on the rugged land surrounding Dinah's house are some scrubby pines, bent and bowed by years of steady breezes, the kind that look like they're holding on for dear life. As I make the turn at the familiar painted mailbox, the trees are also gorged with birds—thousands of them,

151

chattering at the top of their tiny lungs. I've seen enough old movies to be wary, and as I make my way to the door, I don't turn my back to them.

Dinah calls to me to come in when I knock; she's in the kitchen making a pot of tea and opening a packet of Lorna Doones, and smiles at me as I come inside. "Your timing is impeccable," she says. "I'm so glad you're here. Thomas told me about both of your . . . indiscretions. Can you keep a secret?"

"Um, sure," I say.

She leans in close to me, those chocolate eyes twinkling. "Strictly between you and me, sounds like they both had it coming. But I know that's not the right answer. And I think you know it, too. When I started working with Thurgood Marshall, I was of the belief that sometimes a punch in the nose is the only way to get some people's attention. He—and lots of others—convinced me over the years that there was almost always a better way."

*"Almost?"*

Dinah laughs quietly. "Well, you know what they say: Never say never. In any event, we're going to have fun, you and I. And we're going to get to know one another properly. I'm sure there's much I can learn from you, too."

"I'm not so sure about that," I say. "I haven't exactly . . . lived much yet. I've never traveled anywhere interesting or done anything exciting."

"There are other kinds of life experiences besides travel. Your own journey, for instance, has hardly been typical. Losing your parents at such a young age is difficult. It's difficult at *any* age, truth be known. But you've survived. Thrived, even, based on what I've seen. Here, sit and have some tea. I have a surprise for you."

She takes a yellowed envelope from a cubbyhole in her desk and hands it to me. It is addressed to "Miss Dinah Purdy on Guynes Street in Jackson, Mississippi"; the return address is simply: "Elias Purdy, Swallowtail Island."

Dinah says, "After we spoke about Edward Cheever's last words, I remembered something that my father had written. I have every letter he ever wrote me. This one is from a few weeks after I had left the island for college."

The letter, four pages long with practically nonexistent margins, is written in narrow, slanting handwriting that takes me a while to get used to. Two paragraphs on the last page make me sit up straight:

> *Despite that lunkhead Gilbert's best efforts to keep*
> *me away from Edward's house, today I finally had*
> *occasion to speak with Mrs. Abbington. I waited outside*
> *the house in the boxwoods until he left for town. I heard*
> *him warning her not to answer the door or talk to anyone,*
> *but when she saw it was a familiar face, she let me in.*

*She kept house for Edward for a good many years, and he was always very good to her. Her circumstances are much changed under Gilbert's dominion. As with so many aspects of their lives, Gilbert has not lived up to his brother's example. He treats her quite ill indeed.*

*Though I was forced to keep our conversation brief, I learned a great deal. On the day he died, Edward had collapsed in his study and was discovered by Mrs. Abbington. He was quite agitated and according to her, these were his final words: "Will . . . safe . . . two bells . . . Ada holds the key." She admired him greatly, as did I, and wrote them down immediately so that they might be saved for posterity.*

I read Captain Cheever's final words a second time, aloud: "Will. Safe. Two bells. Ada holds the key."

"I got chills up and down my spine when I read it," Dinah says. "His dying breath, and he's thinking of his daughter."

"What do you think he means, 'Ada holds the key'?"

"Maybe for him, she holds the key to understanding life itself."

"Sounds like a clue. Will. Safe. Two bells. Maybe he was trying to tell his housekeeper where his new will was hidden. I think it's time for me to finally take a tour of the Cheever Museum."

Thomas, naturally, has questions for me during dinner, starting with, "So, how was soccer today? Any . . . *fallout* from the other day?"

"Nope. All good."

"Owen and his friends didn't say anything, or . . ."

"Nope."

"Huh. Well, that's good, I guess." He looks to Pip to confirm my story.

"I didn't see anything," she says. "But I wasn't on the same field as her. You should ask Nate."

Nate's mouth is open, ready to speak when I jump in. "You don't need to ask Nate," I say. "Or Jack. Nothing happened. End of story." That's a *mostly* true statement. GHT? I did have one teeny-tiny run-in with Owen. After the way he acted around Blake, I didn't think it was possible for me to like him less, but leave it to him to find a way. During a corner kick drill, we both went after the same ball. And here's the thing: He let me beat him. There was no doubt that we were going to collide. I was fully braced for it to happen and then . . . *nothing* as he drifted off toward the goal, his back to me.

"What are you doing?" I demanded.

"What?"

"You let me have that ball."

He shook his head, and for a microsecond I thought he might cry. Instead, he threw up his hands and said, "What is your *problem*?"

"I don't have a problem. I'm not the one who's quitting on balls."

As he joined one of his friends, I heard the friend say, "Geez, could she *be* more intense?"

The answer is simple, little man: Yes. Yes I can.

It's Blake's turn to choose the movie for Family Movie Night, but he hands off the option to me. Immediately, everyone has a suggestion. Jack wants animated. Nate, superheroes. And Pip, naturally, goes with something horse related, making the others groan.

"No horses," says Thomas. "This family needs a comedy, *stat*. Something light."

"What was Mom's favorite movie?" I ask.

"*Seabiscuit!*" cries Pip.

"Nice try," I say. "Seriously, Thomas, what was it?"

He chews on his bottom lip, staring into space for a few seconds. "*The Ghost and Mrs. Muir*," he says. "She watched it with her mom when she was a kid, probably sitting on this couch. The house in the movie is called Gull Cottage, and she used to pretend that it was this house."

"Is the house haunted?" Pip asks.

"It is. And the woman who lives there falls in love with the ghost," Thomas explains.

"Yuck. It's a love story," says Jack, disappointed.

"Let's watch it," I say.

"It's not exactly a comedy," says Thomas.

"Blake gave me his pick, and that's my choice," I say.

As the opening credits are rolling, Nate says, "Why does it look funny?"

"What do you mean?" I ask.

"There's no . . . colors."

"That's because it's a . . . *black-and-white* movie," I say.

"You mean the whole thing is gonna look like this?"

Thomas musses Nate's hair. "I can't believe you've never seen a black-and-white movie. You don't know what you're missing."

"Yeah I do. The *colors*," says Nate.

Thomas, Blake, and I are the only ones still awake when the movie ends, and all three of us try to hide the fact that we're crying. The others are sound asleep, the boys on either side of Thomas, and Pip with her head on my lap.

"I'm not sure we made converts out of them," Thomas says. "What did *you* think? Did you like it?"

Blake and I nod.

"It was sadder than I thought it'd be," Blake admits. "But it was sad in a good way, you know what I mean?"

"Yeah," I say. "I'm just glad she didn't marry that writer guy. He was ca-reeee-py. I can see why Mom liked it, though. She was just like Anna." As Thomas hoists Jack into his arms, I try lifting Pip, but she's making herself heavy and sinking deeper into the cushion. "Blake, can you give me a hand with her?"

Together, we carry her up the stairs and set her on the bed.

"Thanks," I say.

"Sure," he says, stopping to look at Bedlam. "What's *that*?" He's pointing at the silver swallow hanging in the cage, spinning slowly in the breeze coming off the lake.

"Oh. I found it. It was Mom's. I can't believe you saw it. Pip still hasn't noticed it."

"Is it . . . I mean, it *looks* expensive."

"You haven't even seen the best part." I take *The Pickwick Papers* from the side table and hold it out to him. "Don't look so disappointed. It's not what you think."

"I think it's an old book. A really *thick* old book."

"Ah, but it's not just *any* thick old book. Close your eyes."

When his eyes are closed, I take the swallow from Bedlam's

cage and slip it into its Pickwickian nest. Then I close the book. "Okay, open the book."

Blake has a puzzled expression as he looks from the book to the cage and back again. He reaches out for the book and I hand it to him with a knowing grin. He opens the cover, turns a few pages, and looks up to me. "I don't get it."

"Turn a few more pages."

"Ohhh." His eyes light up when he sees bits of blue enamel showing. "This is . . . did your mom *make* this?"

"She found it," I say before telling him the story about the box of books at the junk shop. "And, I don't know why, but I just have a feeling that there's something special about it. And I need to find out what."

"How are you gonna do *that*?"

"Well, first I'm going to send a letter. A *real* letter. To England." Once again I open the cover and point out the stamp from the bookstore in London and the handwritten inscription. "I already checked online—they're still in business. I would send an email, but I can't find an address for them. They're probably really old. It's hard to imagine anyone named Crackenthorp being young."

"What are you gonna say?"

"Here, you can read it." I lift the top of the desk that also used to be Mom's and retrieve the letter I've written on stationery I got from Nadine.

Crackenthorp Books
59 Dover St.
Mayfair, London

Dear Mr. or Ms. Crackenthorp,

My name is Lark Heron-Finch, and I live in the
United States. I really hope you can help me. About
thirty years ago, my mom bought a used copy of The
Posthumous Papers of the Pickwick Club by Charles
Dickens in a shop on Swallowtail Island, which is
in Lake Erie. Supposedly, the book came from the
library of a man named Edward Cheever, who lived
here on the island. My mom died a few months ago,
and I just found the book and a big surprise inside.
The pages of the book were cut out to make a secret
compartment to hold a small bird (a tree swallow)
made out of silver. I'm writing to you because the
book is stamped inside with your shop's name and
address, and it also has this, in handwriting:

ex libris T.P. & P.C.

I know it was a long time ago, but I was wondering
if you remember anything at all about the book or the
silver bird or who T.P. and P.C. are. Please write back
to me if you remember anything. It's very important
to me.

Sincerely,
Lark Heron-Finch

# CHAPTER
# 9

NADINE AGREES WITH ME THAT if we're going to get to the bottom of this missing-will business, we need to do some digging at Edward Cheever's old house, now the Cheever Museum, so she texts me, telling me to meet her there after soccer. I've biked and walked past it on the trail along the cliff a few times, but have never been inside. Thomas and Nadine, waiting for me in the first-floor lobby, introduce me to Louise Tollingham, the museum director. She's younger than I expect—early thirties, with hair the color of a new penny, and right away I identify her as somebody who doesn't like kids, and doesn't even know how to fake it. You'd think a museum director would deal with enough school groups to build up some immunity to our kind, but nope, one look at me and "I Hate Kids" is written in purple crayon across her forehead. Not that it bothers me one bit.

Challenge. Accepted.

So, the Cheever Museum. GHT? It's a house. By Ohio standards, it's an old house, but our house in Connecticut is a hundred years older. And yeah, it's big, but up close, there's really nothing special about it. I've been dragged on a tour of some of the mansions in Newport, so I have a decent idea of what a big house is like. Most of the rooms in the Cheever house could use a coat of paint, and the furniture is kind of seedy-looking. Except, that is, for Edward's study on the second floor, which is a-mahhh-zing. Two sets of French doors open onto a large balcony (*much* larger than the one off my bedroom) that over-looks the lake, and impressive-looking bookshelves line the walls behind a desk that would be right at home in the Oval Office. Naturally, since it's a sea captain's room, there's a shiny brass telescope on a tripod and lots of paintings of ships (at the moment, they are reproductions, as Thomas is working on the originals), along with com-passes and other navigation instruments scattered about the room. Centered on the wall opposite the balcony is a fireplace, surrounded by more bookshelves and flanked by a pair of wing chairs upholstered in a fabric that resembles a nautical chart. Finally, to the left of the entrance is a small oval table that I recognize from the painting of Ada Cheever and Dinah Purdy, with a ship's clock mounted on a carved mahogany stand right in the center, just as it is in the painting.

Thomas nudges me. "Not bad, eh? In my dreams, this is what my studio looks like."

"I've always loved this room, too," says Nadine. "I remember the first time I came here as a little girl, probably about Pip's age. My parents had to drag me out. I was ready to spend the night. It reminds me of that old movie *The Ghost and Mrs. Muir.*"

"Omigosh!" I say. "We *just* watched that."

"One of Kate's favorites," Thomas says.

"I remember," says Nadine. "She wanted to change the name of the Roost to Gull Cottage."

Downstairs, a phone rings, and Louise excuses herself to go answer it. "I need to take that," she says. On her way out the door, she looks back just in time to catch me reaching out to touch the ship's clock. "Please don't touch . . . anything."

I pull my hand back.

The ringing phone reminds me of our objective, and my eyes scan the room, landing on a pair of brass ship's bells on a shelf to the left of the fireplace, a few inches above my eye level. "Do you see what I see?" I ask Nadine.

"Two bells?"

"I think I'm missing something," Thomas says, a puzzled expression crossing his face. "What about the bells?"

"The captain's last words," I say. "He mentions *two bells*." I reach into my pocket for my little notebook where I've written the exact words. "Will, safe, two bells, Ada holds the key."

I've been thinking a lot about those eight words and with the help of some pictures on the museum website, have come up with two theories, which I share with Thomas and Nadine. The first is that there is an actual *safe* behind the two bells; the second is that the will was simply placed behind or under the two bells, where the captain hoped it would be *safe* from thieving hands like his brother's. So far, though, I have no ideas about the "Ada holds the key" part.

"I need something to stand on for a better look," I say, scanning the room for something suitable. "How about that?" I point to the heavy wooden chair behind the captain's desk.

"I don't think that's a good idea," Thomas says. "Tell me again what you're—"

"I'll explain it all later," I say. "Give me a boost. All I need is a few seconds to see what's behind there. Hurry, before she comes back."

Thomas shoots a glance at Nadine, who opens the door and listens for footsteps.

"All clear," she says.

Thomas sighs (no doubt remembering, and probably regretting, his "Let Lark be Lark" promise) and then joins his hands to make a step for me. "Here ya go."

With my foot in place, he lifts me up so that I can reach back to the wood paneling behind the two bells, which are mounted on thick slabs of wood with brass plaques identifying the ship and the date it was launched. The bells themselves are solid brass, about nine inches in diameter, and so heavy that it takes all my strength to slide them down the shelf out of the way.

"No safe," I say. "Unless it's hidden behind the paneling."

"Feel around for a secret hiding place," says Nadine. "Are there any edges that you can get your fingernails under?"

"I don't really have nails."

"She's a biter," Thomas explains.

"Just like Kate," Nadine says, digging into her handbag. "Here, try this. Next best thing." She hands me a nail file.

I slip the point of the file into every crevice I can find ("I *am* being careful, Thomas!"), without success. Next I try knocking on the wood every few inches, listening for anything that might be *something*. "Nothing," I say.

At the same moment Thomas lowers me to the floor, the door opens and Louise scurries inside, followed by a man I've never seen before, but have no doubts about who he is: Owen Cheever's father.

"I thought I heard pounding," Louise says, looking right at me. "Were you—"

"Oh . . . that was me," Nadine says. "I was recounting a story that Dinah Purdy told me, from when she was a little girl. She was friends with Ada Cheever, you know, and the two of them used to dance around in here. Ada took tap lessons and would share what she learned with Dinah. I guess I got a little carried away."

It's clear that Louise doesn't believe her, but she lets it go because she has a guest with her. "Thomas, there's someone I want you to meet," she says. "This is Reginald Cheever, president of the museum board of directors."

Louise Tollingham looks at Thomas, standing there in his ratty sweater, as if she's really seeing him for the first time. "And this is the restorer I told you about. Thomas Emmery."

For his part, Thomas does an admirable job of hiding his emotions when he hears the name "Cheever," but I notice the slight widening of the eyes and the involuntary swallow. "Mr. Cheever," he says. "Nice to meet you."

Cheever nods. "Yes. You, too. Louise tells me that you've undertaken some work for us. You're spending the summer on island?"

"Yes. Some paintings. Cleaning, mostly. A little retouching. Yes, we're here for the summer. My . . . late wife . . . had a place here. She grew up with . . . "

"With me," Nadine says, smiling slyly as she adds, "Hello, Reggie. It's been a while."

He says nothing, but the expression on his chiseled features is perfectly clear: What are *you* doing here?

Meanwhile, I'm trying hard to blend into the wallpaper and praying that the adults in the room have forgotten about me.

Leave it to Thomas, though. Awkward as he is, the guy has impeccable manners. "Oh, this is my, uh, daughter, Lark."

Except for a half nod in my direction, there is no reaction to my name from Mr. Cheever. Either Owen has not shared the details of our recent run-in, or my having a last name different from Thomas's is paying off.

"Will the paintings be on display during the gala?" Mr. Cheever asks Louise. "I'm sure our patrons—and more important, our *prospective* patrons—would love to see them, to see the work in progress."

Louise hems and haws; it's clear she hasn't planned for this. "I, uh, Thomas . . . what do you think? Could we show the paintings?" She's gathering confidence as she plows ahead. "It might be interesting for our patrons to see where their money goes. Perhaps a . . . before-and-after kind of thing? And you would, of course, be here to talk about the process. Maybe even give a little talk."

Thomas? Give a talk? This I have to see.

He actually blushes just thinking about it. "I . . . I . . . hadn't planned on anything like—"

"Oh, nothing too long," Louise says.

"Or too technical," adds Mr. Cheever. "No need to bore us with all that scientific mumbo jumbo."

Louise nods in agreement. "Right. Right. Talk about the importance of preservation. A basic overview of what you do. Leave the rest to us."

"Getting them to open their checkbooks," Mr. Cheever says. "That's the *real* hard work."

"Remind me, when is this . . . gala?" Thomas asks.

"A week from Saturday," answers Louise. "Plenty of time to prepare. Will you do it? You really must."

Thomas's mind, I know, is racing, looking for a way out, but none comes to him. "If you're really sure you want me. I'm *not* a gifted speaker."

"You'll be great," Nadine says. "I'll help you put something together if you want. And you have a captive audience at home to practice on. Right, Lark?"

"Uh, yeah. Sure," I say.

"Why don't *you* join us as well?" Mr. Cheever says to me.

"We have a small army of young people who volunteer as docents, helping the caterers, whatever is needed."

"Me? This is my first time in this place. I don't know anything about . . . anything."

Louise clearly isn't thrilled by the idea either, but she's not about to disagree with anything Mr. Cheever says. She gives me a fake-as-her-hair-color smile. "That's not a problem. We'll pair you up with someone who does."

"You're about the same age as my son Owen," Cheever says. "He'll be here."

Thomas sticks the knife in my back. "I think it's a wonderful idea. It'll be a good way for you to make some friends here on the island. Maybe Blake should come, too. Do you have room for one more? My son is thirteen."

"Sure," Mr. Cheever says before Louise has a chance to speak. "The more the merrier."

Grrr. I grit my teeth, resigned to my fate.

When Cheever and Louise finally make their exit, I punch Thomas on the arm. "Thanks a lot, Thomas. No way am I going to that stupid . . . *gala*."

"I really think you should," he says. "It'll be good for you."

"No, it won't. How is it going to be *good* for me? Nadine, tell him. I shouldn't have to go, right?"

Nadine holds up her hands in surrender. "I'm staying out of this. How about we get a look at these paintings, up close and personal."

"We'll talk about it later," Thomas says.

"Or not," I say.

Thomas leads us to his temporary studio where the four paintings of ships, no longer in their frames, are lined up on a long table against the wall. In the center of the room, where Thomas can take full advantage of the natural light from the windows while he works, are two large studio easels. On one is the full-length portrait of Edward Cheever's wife, Julia, and on the other, the dual portrait of Ada and Dinah.

Thomas's work has already made a startling difference. In her portrait, Julia Cheever is standing next to a large floral arrangement, and some of the flowers and the vase are noticeably cleaner and brighter than the areas around them.

"Look at that," Nadine says. "Like there's a spotlight on the flowers."

"That one had a really thick layer of old varnish on it," Thomas says. "Judging by the way it was kind of slopped on, there's no way it was done by the artist. Luckily, it's coming off pretty easily, and it's not lifting any pigment. It's going to look like new when I finish. People are going to think I repainted it." He moves over to the painting of Ada and Dinah. "This was done by a different artist, James Liggett-Smith. You can see where he's signed down on the bottom left. This is the better of the two by far. His technique—the brushstrokes, the palette, the composition—reminds me of Sargent. Higher-quality varnish, too, which is making it a little trickier. Have to go a little slower. Already finding some surprises, though. Take a look at the back."

He lifts the painting out of the easel and turns it around so we can see the backside of the canvas. "There was a paper label stuck on right here," he says, pointing at a rectangular area that is a shade lighter than the rest of the canvas. "It was nothing important, an inventory label. But when I looked closer underneath, I was able to make out some writing. It looks like Liggett-Smith wrote the title in pencil, or maybe charcoal."

Nadine and I lean in at the same moment for a closer look, bumping heads and then laughing.

"You go first," Nadine says. "Your eyes are probably better than mine anyway."

"Here, let me shine a light on it," says Thomas, unclipping a light from the easel and pointing it at the spot in question.

"What is that, French?" I ask. "De-ux bell-es je-unes fill-es. What does that mean?"

Nadine makes a face as I butcher the pronunciation and squeezes in next to me. "Ah. *Deux Belles Jeunes Filles*." She says it with what sounds to me like perfect French, then adds the translation for my benefit: "Two Beautiful Young Girls."

I take another look. "Say that again. The French part."

"*Deux Belles Jeunes Filles.*"

"It sounds so much more . . . mysterious that way. You speak French?"

"*Oui.* I spent a lot of time in Western Africa. Benin, Côte d'Ivoire, Togo. And, well, France."

"That's so cool. I want to learn French. Thomas thinks I should take Spanish."

"I think you should take what you want," Thomas says. "All I said is that Spanish is probably more *useful* these days. Anyway, it's pretty cool, no? Louise says that *nobody* knew about this. It was always just the portrait of Ada and Dinah. Now it has a real title. You can't tell anyone, though. She wants to keep it secret until the night of the gala."

"What's the big deal?" I ask.

"People love surprises," Nadine answers. "The people who give to museums feel good because it was their money that made it possible for Thomas to do his thing. Now, speaking of doing *my* thing, I need to scoot. I have a call with my editor and her boss later, and she'll have my head if I'm not ready for it. See you tomorrow?"

"Sure. Right after soccer," I say. "I'm on my way to Dinah's for . . . you know. Reading and stuff."

"Perfect. Hi to Dinah for me. Thank you, Thomas, for sharing the secret about the painting. And don't worry about the gala. You'll do fine."

We walk Nadine out to her bike and when she rides away,

Thomas says to me, "I mean it about this museum thing. I love that you spend so much time with Pip and the boys and me, and I'm glad you've really connected with Nadine, but you need to make some friends your own age."

"I have lots of friends," I argue. "Just because I'm not going on sleepovers doesn't mean—"

"The only name I've even heard you *mention* from soccer camp is this Owen Cheever, and you punched *him* in the nose. There must be *somebody* that you like. It sounds like they get lots of kids to volunteer for this party, so I'll bet if you ask around, you'll see that you're going to be the only one from camp who's not going. It'll be a good opportunity to . . . *bond* with kids that you already have something in common with."

I say nothing for a good ten seconds and walk slowly toward the stone patio on the lake side of the museum. The thing is, I hate all that fake drama that most of my friends *live* for. In fact, I hate the *word* "drama," period. I'm focused on two things: soccer and my grades. Middle school is, to me, an obstacle to get over (or past, or around) on the way to high school and college. Finally, I tell Thomas, "Fine. I'll go. But for the record, I'm going because I need to get used to volunteering. Public service. Colleges *love* that."

Thomas shakes his head. "Well, just be sure not to have any *fun*."

Ouch. I think I'm bleeding.

The next few days are a blur of dashing from place to place on my bike. I am putting some serious miles in. If nothing else, I'm going to be in *awesome* shape for soccer season back in Connecticut—assuming that they let me play. Sometimes the order changes slightly, but a typical day looks like this: Home. Soccer. Nadine. Dinah. Home. Repeat. When I show up at Dinah's on Friday afternoon, though, she doesn't have her usual fizz. Most days, I can barely keep up with her while she scurries into the kitchen to make me an Arnold Palmer and ransacks the cupboards in search of cookies, but today she doesn't move from the porch swing when I arrive, and worse, she's wrapped in a blanket—on a 90-degree day.

"Are you all right?"

"I have a little summer cold, that's all. Nothing to worry about," she says. "You could pour me another cup of tea, though. And please help yourself."

"You're sure? Do you want me to call anyone?"

"Pish. I'll be right as rain in a few hours. Serves me right for going to the doctor the other day. *That's* where I picked it up—you can count on it. A doctor's office is like a petri dish."

I'm not so sure that it is nothing, but I refill her tea and make myself a lemonade-heavy Arnold Palmer. "What are we reading today?" I ask as I set our drinks on the table in front of the swing. "More Thurgood Marshall? I like him. He's a little easier to understand than some of the others."

"I'm not sure I'm up to concentrating that hard today. Let's chat a while, and then . . ." Her voice fades into the background, mingling with the sounds of the waves lapping against the shore and the leaves rustling overhead.

"Do you want to sleep for a while?" I ask. "Can I get you anything else?"

"Not a thing. Tell me about *our* case. You haven't mentioned it in a while. Do you have anything to report?"

"Oh! I do. I mean, we haven't found the will yet, but we're going to—I just know it. We still have time. But I forgot to tell you. You know that painting of you and Ada? My stepdad found a clue, something on the back, the original title." Reading from my notebook, I give the French pronunciation my best shot: "*Deux Belles Jeunes Filles.*"

Dinah closes her eyes for a couple of seconds and the corners of her mouth turn up in a barely perceptible smile. "His two *belles*," she says. "That's what Captain Cheever used to call us. Ada pointed out that his translation didn't quite make sense, but he didn't care."

Something clicks in my brain and I flip back a few pages in my notebook. *Will, safe, two bells.* Two bells. Two . . . *belles*! "It's not *bells*. It's *belles*!" I say.

"I'm afraid you've lost me. I'm sorry, dear. I guess I'm more tired than I thought," she says, struggling to keep her eyes open. "Please explain what you mean."

"Well, I thought his last words meant that the will was safe or was in a safe by those two brass bells up on the shelf. But he didn't mean *those* bells. He was talking about you and Ada. The painting. His two *belles*, with an *E*. It has to be it."

"Oh. I see," she says through closed eyes. The air on the porch is perfectly still, but her head looks as if it is swaying in the wind.

"Maybe you ought to lay down," I say.

She doesn't respond, and sits there quietly for a minute before saying, "I'm going to lie down on my bed and sleep this cold away. You should go. I don't need a thing, except some rest. I hope to see you tomorrow."

"What do you mean, you *hope*? You *will* see me. I'll be here first thing."

She holds out a hand for me to help her down from the porch swing. I shiver when I feel how cold her hand is. "You're a dear for worrying about me. I'm so glad that we've become friends."

"Me too," I say. "I'm gonna hang around for a while, just in case you . . . change your mind or something."

"Do me a favor and turn on the kitchen light on your way out. If I wake up in the middle of the night, I like to be able to see where I'm going. You go on home. You have clues to follow. If you and Nadine are right, and all this land is mine, maybe I'll put in that swimming pool I've always dreamed about. If I was ten years younger, I'd be leading the way to the Cheevers' door." She winks at me, and attempts a smile, but she looks older, and more frail than I've ever seen her. My heart sinks as she steps out of the light and into the dark bedroom.

I pace around the tiny living room and the porch for a few minutes while I try to reach Nadine on her phone. She doesn't pick up, so I send a text about Dinah and ask her what I should do.

A minute later, she texts back: there in 20 min.

Not quite fifteen minutes later, I hear the beat of a horse galloping up the dirt road outside the house and meet Nadine outside.

"How's she doing?" she asks, jumping down from Lulu's saddle.

"She's sleeping," I answer. "But she's . . . restless. Moving around a lot, like she's having trouble getting comfortable. I'm really sorry. I know you're busy. I just—"

"No, no. You did the right thing." She leads Lulu to a shady spot and ties her to a post near the back door. "Could you fill a bucket with water for her while I check on Dinah? Thanks."

I'm rubbing Lulu's face when Nadine comes back outside. "She's okay, I think. She woke up when I went in. She's probably right, that it's just a cold, but when you're her age, a cold can be . . . Someone needs to keep an eye on her, that's all. I rode Lulu over because I had the trainer out and she was already saddled, but maybe I'll take her home and come back in the golf cart and stay the night."

"You . . . really think she's all right? She said she hoped she'd see me tomorrow, but the *way* she said it . . . kind of freaked me out. It was like she didn't really expect to."

Nadine smiles knowingly. "She does it to me all the time. We all deal with mortality in our own ways. It's one thing to realize and accept that everybody is going to die, but something else entirely when it's you, and you can see the door starting to close."

Suddenly, I'm back in a chair in Mom's room on a moonlit Connecticut night three months ago.

Mom turns her head toward the window, the moon reflecting off her eyes. "Lark," she whispers.

I lean closer, coming out of the chair so I can hear her.

"You're going to be okay, my little Meadowlark," she says. "You can fly. You just don't know it yet."

When I explain the difference between two bells and two *belles* to Nadine she practically pushes me out the door of Dinah's house. "You need to get another look at that painting. She's sleeping peacefully now, so I'll be fine. Go. Call or text me later if you learn anything."

"Call me when she wakes up," I shout over my shoulder as I pedal up the drive.

As I make the final turn toward the museum entrance,

Louise Tollingham is exiting the building. She's on her phone and walking fast toward an electric golf cart with the Cheever Museum logo plastered on its hood, so she doesn't even see me. I breathe a sigh of relief. She's made it clear that she doesn't like me, so I doubt that she's going to let me snoop around the way I'd like to. Thomas, on the other hand . . . well, he *has* to let me.

I wait in the bushes next to the entrance until Louise is out of sight, then I try the door, which is locked.

"What? No." I check my watch; it's 5:05 and the museum closes at 5:00. Pounding on the door, I call out, "Thomas!" several times, but there's no response. I send him a text: at the door let me in.

I sit on a stone planter and wait, aware that Thomas *never* leaves his phone ringer on, and is notorious for ignoring messages even when he sees them. I try again: Hello?

A few minutes go by, and I press my face to the glass in search of signs of life. The lights are all turned off, but then a door opens and Thomas comes out, smiling when he sees me.

"Hey, Lark," he says as he holds the door open for me. "This is a nice surprise."

"Is anybody else here?"

"No. Just us. What's up?"

"I have something big. About the painting. Can I see it?"

"Uh, sure." He leads me to his studio where the easel holding the "two belles" painting is front and center, with the light

179

MICHAEL D. BEIL

from a pair of clip-on lamps reflecting off its surface. Thomas switches them off so I can view the painting in natural light.

"The top layer of varnish is coming off more easily than I thought it would," he says. "Some of the details are starting to pop out. What are you looking for?"

"According to Dinah, Captain Cheever used to call Ada and her his *two belles*."

Thomas is leaning toward me, waiting for me to explain further when it hits him: "Two belles! Right. His last words. . . . I get it."

"What do you get?" A woman's voice. Crap. It's Louise.

"Louise. I-I thought you'd gone. Lark just stopped by to . . ."

"I got almost home when I realized that I'd left my phone here," Louise says. "What's all the excitement about the painting? Whose last words? Did you find something—is there another surprise?"

"No, no. No, I was just showing Lark how the background details are starting to be revealed. Here, on the wall behind the two girls. The books, and knickknacks on the shelves . . . and even the face of the clock. If you look closely, you can even see the *shadow* from the hands. Remarkable."

Louise squeezes in between us for a better look. "Hmm. I see what you mean. Well, do keep me posted if you find anything interesting."

"Of course," Thomas says. "Well, I'm going to call it a day. Back at it tomorrow."

180

Louise walks out with us, locking the door behind her. "Good seeing you again, Lark," she says unconvincingly. "Are you getting ready for the gala?"

"Getting rea—um . . . not really."

"Suppose I need to take you dress shopping," Thomas says. "Maybe Nadine . . . I'll talk to her. Is there anyplace on the island?"

"Not really," Louise says. "At least not for something *nice*. You need to go into Sandusky. Cleveland would be better. Well, have a good night. See you in the morning."

As soon as she's out of earshot, I say, "She's *such* a liar. I saw her leave the first time and she had her phone—she was talking to somebody on it! She came back to spy on you."

"Lark!" he says, laughing out loud. "What *possible* reason could she have for spying on me? I'm an art restorer. This is it. Me and Big Red. And solvent. *Lots* of solvent."

"It's because of me and Nadine. You're connected to us, and she's connected to *them*. She works for the Cheevers—the same people who killed Albert Pritchard . . . and *cheated* Dinah out of her land."

"Whoa, whoa! Slow down. You don't *know* that. Thinking it's true, and creating a story to fit a few details, is *not* the same as being true. You can't go around accusing people of fraud. Or murder."

"You don't believe me. I thought you—"

"It's not a matter of me not *believing* you, Lark. Everything you're saying is based either on pure speculation or the sudden change of heart of a man who testified under oath to a completely different story."

"Like he had a choice! They would have ruined his life if he told the truth. No. You're wrong. Gilbert Cheever killed Albert Pritchard because there was another will, and I'm going to find it."

"Look, Lark, I know how much this means to you, but you need to be prepared for the possibility, the *likelihood*, that the will doesn't exist. I'm not saying it never did, only that . . . it was a long time ago, and a lot of people have . . . well, it just seems like it would have turned up."

"Yeah, but all those people? None of them were looking for a will because they didn't *know* enough to be looking for one," I argue. "Nobody had a *reason* to be looking until now. It's in there. I'm sure of it. You can't stop me from looking, Thomas."

Thomas takes a step toward me, palms out in the "just be cool" position. "Okay, okay. I'm not trying to stop you. I'm not the enemy. I'm *worried* about you. I know you're trying to do a good thing here, but you're becoming obsessed. Is there something else going on? Did something happen that I don't know about?"

I spin away from him because I don't want him to see my eyes. "No. Yes. It's Dinah. She's . . . it was just like when Mom . . . I'm gonna lose her, too. Everybody I love dies."

"Oh, Lark, no. No, no," he says, wrapping his arms around me.

For once, I don't fight it. "It's true," I blubber into Big Red.

"You're wrong. Tell me what's going on. Where is she? Is she with Nadine?"

I manage to pull myself together enough to tell him what had happened out at Rabbit Ear Point. "Nadine said she'll call when Dinah's awake," I sniff.

"There. See? I trust Nadine. If Dinah needed to be in a hospital, she'd be there. Really."

"Yeah, I guess," I admit. "Sorry about your sweater. I got it kinda snotty."

"It's seen worse," says Thomas.

# CHAPTER
# 10

A WEEK GOES BY WITH zero progress in the search for the missing will, but there is some good news: Dinah has made a full recovery. She gives the credit to Nadine, me, and the constant stream of tea and toast that we carried into her room at all hours of the day and night. According to Dinah, if tea and toast don't do it, you can't be cured. By Tuesday, just four days after the scare, she was picking daisies in her yard—until Nadine insisted that she "get out of the sun this instant."

And now, another four days later, it's July 25th, the day of the museum gala. I am no longer Lark, though; I'm a living, breathing cliché, standing on the stairs and waiting for Thomas to take my picture—again. He's already taken a dozen at least. Me, on the balcony outside my room. Pip and me. Blake and me. Pip and all the boys and me. And now me coming down the stairs, like something out of one of those 1980s John Hughes movies.

I have to admit, however, that I *do* love the dress. When Thomas asked Nadine to take me shopping off-island, she jumped at the chance. On Thursday, satisfied that Dinah was out of the woods, we took the ferry to Catawba, where Nadine keeps a car in a garage. Then she drove the two hours to Cleveland, where we had a fancy lunch downtown before embarking on the quest for the perfect dress. In the end, it all came down to two dresses, one black, and one apple green. I was leaning toward the black, but when I tried on the green, Nadine's hand went to her mouth and she dropped onto the nearest bench as if her legs weren't capable of holding her up.

"I just had the most . . . *astonishing* moment of *déjà vu*," she said. "Your mom had a dress exactly that color back when they used to have dances for kids during the summer. We must have been freshmen or sophomores and when we showed up at the school that night—every eye in the place was on her. I suppose I should have been jealous, but I was so happy for her, I was so proud to have a friend like her." She paused, then added, "When you stepped out of that dressing room . . . suddenly I was fifteen again."

"You really like it? It's not too . . . like, princess-y?" If there's anything I *don't* want right now in my life, it's to look like a princess.

"No," she said with a laugh. "It's not princess-y at all. It's perfect."

When we approached the checkout, I reached for Thomas's credit card, but Nadine stopped me.

"Put it away. This one's my treat."

"But Thomas said—"

She held up a hand to stop me. "Don't worry about Thomas. This is for you. And for your mom. She would be so proud of you."

I threw my arms around her and we were both crying by the time I laid the dress on the counter in front of the dumb-founded (and much-tattooed) checkout girl. Without a word, she handed me a tissue, and I thanked her.

"Shopping can be *really* emotional," she said as she handed me the bag with the dress safely tucked inside.

I wiped my eyes and thanked her again, not at all sure if she was being sarcastic or sincere. But then again, I didn't care.

Because Thomas is actually going through with his talk at the museum gala, Louise Tollingham insisted that he bring his entire family along—not realizing, I'm sure, just how many kids he has. Thomas and I have to be there an hour before the six-thirty start, so Blake, who somehow talked his way out of being a volunteer, has been given an impossible task: He is in charge of getting Nate and Jack bathed, dressed in something other than shorts and T-shirts, and delivered to the museum on time, in like-new condition, and with smiles on their faces.

The fact that I'm wearing a dress and the likelihood that we'll be there until well after dark makes bikes a less-than-perfect option, so Les Findlay gives us a ride in his golf cart, which is painted in Vietnam-era camouflage. On the dash-board are a row of switches and big red buttons, all of which Les warns us not to touch. He explains, in the vaguest possible way, that they all have something to do with a complex heating system for the winter, but I've seen enough James Bond mov-ies to know what's *really* going on. Rocket launchers, machine guns, lasers—for all I know this golf cart can transform itself into a submarine. Or a fighter jet. Or both.

On the museum's front lawn, an enormous tent covers twenty round tables with crisp white tablecloths, an even two hundred white folding chairs, a stage, a dance floor, and a pair of well-stocked bars. Musicians and bartenders are busy setting up, but they all turn and smile as Les drops us off in front of the museum.

"Thank you for the ride. Nadine's on her way to the house now," Thomas tells Les. "You can pick her and the boys up at six thirty. And Pip. Don't forget Pip."

"Yes, sir," Les says. "I'll get them here safe and sound." He pushes one of the red buttons as he steps on the accelerator, and the air is suddenly filled with the sound of a helicopter taking off.

I take a step back and duck involuntarily, fully expecting the secret retractable rotor to appear overhead. "You're sure you trust him with your kids," I say to Thomas.

He forces a smile. "They'll be fine."

"Mm-hmm."

Thomas doesn't make it ten feet inside the door before Louise Tollingham grabs him by the arm and leads him away to meet a VIP, leaving me standing there by myself. Across the room, I spot a group of volunteers—a few my age that I recognize from soccer camp, but mostly high school kids I don't know. A girl with fashionable glasses, a streak of blue in her hair, and a clipboard (always a sign of someone in charge) waves me over.

"Are you a volunteer?" she asks. "Hi, I'm Allison, the volunteer coordinator."

As I introduce myself, Owen Cheever's head spins away from the conversation he's been having with a soccer friend and toward me. He does an actual double take when he sees me, and then stares until he catches himself and turns away. And that's when I see it: He's wearing a bow tie that is not only *exactly* the same shade of green as my dress, it looks like the same fabric.

Allison leads all of the volunteers out onto the patio, where she goes through the various jobs expected of us: acting as greeters and impromptu tour guides, picking up empty glasses and plates, helping to pass hors d'oeuvres—basically everything except serving drinks, which we're not allowed to do. Each of us is assigned a partner for the evening, and naturally, the second that Allison realizes that Owen and I are wearing color-coordinated outfits, she makes us a team. When she calls out our names, Owen's friend smiles and nudges him with an elbow. Owen shushes him with an elbow of his own, then steals a glance at me.

"Just remember," Allison says, "smile, and try to be helpful. Don't bother people, but don't be afraid to ask if they need anything. If somebody has a question that you don't know the answer to, find me or Ms. Tollingham. Oh, and there's brochures about the museum and becoming a member in the lobby. Right now, you should get together with your partner and make sure you both know where everything is—the kitchen, the bathrooms, whatever. Get something to eat and drink now, because you shouldn't be eating in front of the guests."

The rest of the volunteers pair up and wander off in all directions, leaving Owen and me standing awkwardly in the center of the patio.

"So," we say simultaneously after a long silence.

"Go ahead," he says.

"I was just gonna say, have you done this before? 'Cause I

really don't know what I'm doing."

"I did it last year," he says. "It's no big deal. Mostly you just stand around."

"I'm still not sure why they even asked me," I say. "I don't even live here."

"That's easy. I mean, why they asked you. There's just not that many pret—er, nice-looking girls here," he says, his cheeks reddening.

I feel myself blushing in response, much to my chagrin. How dare he almost compliment me. We're saved momentarily by Allison, who stops by to check up on us.

"I *love* your dress," she says. "Lucky you, Owen. Your partner's the prettiest girl here. Everyone's asking me who she is. Did you guys know each other before tonight?"

"Y-Yeah," Owen mumbles. "Sort of. We're both in summer soccer."

"Oh, cool," Allison says as she starts to move on to the next group. "Well, I just wanted to say how great you two look together. Like something out of a catalog."

We stand there for a few seconds, avoiding eye contact, before Owen speaks up: "She's right, you know . . . about the dress. It's . . . you have, you know, green eyes . . . and the color is . . . you look really nice."

"Thanks," I say quietly. The GHT is that he looks pretty good, too, not that I would admit that to him in a million years. I have trained myself to observe my fellow humans in a purely objective way, and empirically speaking, as we scientists like to say, he is an attractive boy. Maybe he is dressed a little too preppy for me (that green bow tie!) and the boy-bun *definitely* has to go, but he's still better-looking than any of the boys at my school. I pinch myself on the underside of my arm to bring me back to reality. It is, after all, Owen Cheever I'm talking about.

The museum gala is a snapshot of the people of Swallowtail Island—at least the summer population. According to Les Findlay, most of the locals, himself included, "wouldn't go to something like the gala on a dare." A few minutes after seven, the patio starts to fill up with "summer people" as Owen calls them, and Allison steers a young couple our way. With a glance at our name tags, she smiles and introduces us. "Owen and Lark, these are the Porterfields. This is their first summer on the island. Could you give them a quick tour? Maybe show them Captain Cheever's study and Ada's room for now?"

"Sure," says Owen. "Just follow me."

The Porterfields fall in behind him, silent, and in Mr. Porterfield's case, glum. He looks as if he would rather be anywhere else in the world, but his wife, genuinely interested in the museum and in Captain Cheever's story, pretends not to notice his sulking and pulls him along by the sleeve of his seersucker blazer. After leading them through the two rooms with his well-practiced patter, Owen stops at the top of the stairs.

"And we're back almost where we started," he says. "I hope you enjoy the party."

"Thank you so much, Owen. And Lark," Mrs. Porterfield says. "That was lovely."

"Where's the bar?" Mr. Porterfield demands as he yanks her down the stairs. "I need a drink."

"*Charming*," I say when they're gone.

"Seriously," says Owen. "What a loser."

I start down the stairs, but stop and turn around when Owen says, "Wait a second. I . . . want to . . . say something. Can you . . ." His eyes go from me to his shoes, back to me, and finally to a spot on the wall next to me.

"What?"

"Look, I know you must think I'm like the biggest . . . jerk ever . . ."

My right eyebrow rises involuntarily. "Yeaaahhh?"

"I just wanted to say, you know, about that day at the beach . . . with your brother and all that . . . I don't know what happened . . . I kind of freaked out, I guess." He rubs his face with his hands and shakes his head. "It's just that . . . I've always been the best at . . . lots of things, but especially soccer, and then you come along, and you're a . . ."

"A *girl*?"

"Yeah, that. And you're new, and . . . anyway, I don't expect you to forgive me or whatever, but I still want to say . . . I'm *really* sorry."

"It's okay . . . for me, anyway. I know all about losing it out there. Last year, I . . . well, let's just say there's a reason I'm stuck with this old phone. But the person you need to apologize to is Blake. Because . . . I mean, you called him—"

"Is he . . . here?" Owen asks.

"Not yet, but he's coming. They're *all* coming. The whole fam damily."

"Okay. You're right. I'll find him."

"Maybe I should talk to him first," I say as I start down the stairs. "So he doesn't think you're gonna, you know, *hit* him or something."

Back out on the patio, the party is in full swing; the band is playing really old songs, like from the '70s and '80s. Meanwhile, an army of servers in white shirts and black vests circulate with trays of champagne flutes and hors d'oeuvres. It doesn't take me long to spot Jack and Nate in their navy blazers, chugging bottles of lime-green soda—sorry, *pop*—and attacking a chip-and-dip platter. Nadine is at a table on the back edge of the tent, talking to Simon Stanford (dapper as usual), and someone whose face is blocked by a freakishly tall man in a seersucker suit and a straw hat. Luckily, someone calls to him and when he teeters off in pursuit, I see the third person: It's Dinah, and a small crowd is starting to gather around her.

"Hey, I have to go say hi to someone," I tell Owen. "Back in a minute."

When I get to the table, Simon stands to greet me. "Lark. You're a *vision*. Absolutely *stunning* dress, my dear."

GHT: Simon is such a gentleman that I would curtsy if I knew how. "Thanks—Nadine helped me pick it out. Dinah! I didn't know you were coming." I hug her, and add, "I saw you every day this week. You didn't say anything, even when I told you about my dress."

"I still have a few surprises left in me," she says with a wink.

"Do they have you working hard?" Nadine asks.

"Not really," I say. "You won't *believe* who my partner is. Owen Cheever."

Nadine puts a hand on my shoulder. "How's that working out?"

"It's . . . different. Not what I expected, I can say that."

"That doesn't sound so bad," says Nadine.

"We'll see. It's still early. He *apologized*. It was weird."

"It's a start. It's possible he's not like his father. Or any of his ancestors," she says with a nod toward Simon. "Maybe he takes after the captain, another branch of his family tree. We can hope."

Simon starts to say something, but his soft voice is drowned out by a drumroll and someone testing a microphone on the stage where the band is set up. It's Louise Tollingham, attempting to get the attention of the crowd.

"I'll see you guys later," I say, and slip through the crowd to rejoin Owen at the back edge of the patio.

Louise gives a long introduction of Reginald Cheever, the board president, who steps up to the microphone to a smattering of polite applause.

"Oh, boy. Here we go," Owen says with an eye roll. "We shoulda sat down. My dad and a microphone. *Not* a good combination."

"Welcome to the twenty-fourth annual summer gala," Cheever begins. When he finally finishes thanking all the people who helped make the event such a success blah blah blah, he pauses, removing the microphone from its stand so he can walk around with it.

"Here comes the sales pitch," Owen says, nudging me as if we're best buds. When I turn to look at the spot where his shoulder touched me, he looks embarrassed and puts a few more inches between us. "Oh. Sorry. I was just . . . I'm sorry. That was . . ."

I shake my head, laughing. "You're such an easy target, now that you're trying to be nice to me and all. What, did you think I was going to punch you again?"

"I-I don't, I didn't . . . are you always so . . . hard to figure out?"

I shrug. "Pretty much."

His father continues with his speech: "My friends, and fellow supporters of this fine institution, change is coming to Swallowtail Island. Progress. My great-uncle, Captain Edward Cheever, who died seventy-five years ago this summer, and whose home has become a symbol of the island, would be very pleased with the plans we have for the future."

I search the crowd until I find Nadine, who gives me a knowing nod when we make eye contact.

"In a few weeks, we will be breaking ground on the first phase of a project that will bring the island up to par with places like Nantucket and the Hamptons. I'm talking about more than a hundred new homes, a championship golf course, a world-class clubhouse—and that's just phase one!" Cheever pauses, clearly expecting more applause than actually comes.

"Don't count your chickens," I say under my breath.

"What—what do you mean?" Owen asks.

I shake my head. "Nothing. It's still Dinah Purdy's land."

The look on his face tells me that he has no idea what I'm talking about. Which, when I think about it, is not that surprising. I mean, just because he's a Cheever doesn't mean he knows everything, or even *anything*, about his family's business. After all, he is only twelve years old. If I hadn't gotten personally involved with Dinah and the whole situation, the fate of some land on Swallowtail Island wouldn't have mattered even a little bit to me.

Cheever clears his throat and goes on: "Some—maybe

even some who are here tonight—might have you believe that development is bad for Swallowtail, but I'm asking you to trust me. It's progress, and that is *good* for the island and the people who live and work here. So, in the spirit of putting our money where our mouth is, I'm happy to announce that the Cheever Construction Company is donating the sum of one hundred *thousand* dollars to the museum, to be used for a new addition to be named in honor of one of Swallowtail's most esteemed citizens: Miss Diana Purdy!" Louise Tollingham whispers something in his ear, and he quickly corrects himself. "Miss *Dinah* Purdy."

*Well* played, Reggie. I didn't see *that* coming. And judging by her reaction, neither did Nadine. Or, for that matter, Dinah. You'd think that if someone was going to name a building after you, they'd let you know. Especially if they're basically stealing your land to build it on, right?

Meanwhile, the crowd cheers loudly and the applause goes on for a long time. Cheever wraps up his speech with an appeal to everyone to make donations on behalf of the new Dinah Purdy Wing of the museum.

He hands the microphone over to Louise Tollingham, who calls on all volunteers to join her on the stage to receive packets to hand out to every guest.

"I guess that's us," Owen says. He leads the way, and I make eye contact with Nadine again. She turns her hands palms up, shrugs, and shakes her head.

Owen and I pick up our envelopes and work our way through the crowd as we pass them out while Louise introduces Thomas, standing stiffly at her side and looking a bit pale. During her introduction, two volunteers set up an easel holding *Deux Belles Jeunes Filles* to Thomas's left. He adjusts the height of the microphone, clears his throat, and starts to talk about his background and career highlights, earning a few thoughtful nods and "ahs" when he name-drops Winslow Homer and Norman Rockwell as two artists whose paintings he has restored. GHT? He's actually not bad. Much better than I expected, anyway, and people seem genuinely interested in what he has to say. Even Owen, who has ended up with some friends on the edge of the patio, is paying attention.

"The painting here on the easel was done by James Liggett-Smith, who studied at the atelier of John Singer Sargent, in my opinion the greatest artist America has ever produced," continues Thomas. "This is the aptly titled *Deux Belles Jeunes Filles*, which translates, of course, to *Two Beautiful Young Girls*."

When he points out some of the (until recently) hidden details of the painting of Dinah and Ada, the crowd pushes forward for a closer look. "We'll leave it out so everyone can have a closer look," he says. "The girl on the left is Ada Cheever, daughter of Captain Edward Cheever. Sadly, Ada died shortly after this portrait was painted, the same year as her mother, Julia Cheever, who is the subject of another fine painting currently undergoing restoration. On the right is a fellow guest tonight—the

198

aforementioned Dinah Purdy, who was a close childhood friend of Ada's. If you have a chance to come up for a closer inspection, take a look at Ada's right hand. This area was completely obscured by dirt and varnish over the years, but there's no question about it now, though: She's holding a key, a very symbolic object. When we look closer, we can see that the round glass door that covers the clock face is slightly ajar, suggesting that she is about to use the key to wind the clock. Symbolically, this is fascinating, and typical of Liggett-Smith. It's as if he's saying to us, 'Time is running out!'"

Many in the audience nod solemnly; they are eating out of Thomas's hand. I make eye contact with him and *roll* mine, which makes him smile. It's not that I don't believe that artists use symbolism, but sometimes I think Thomas's interpretations are a bit over the top. The more I think about his words, though, the more they ring true: When it comes to solving this mystery and saving Swallowtail Island from the Cheevers, time really *is* running out. Dinah's rights to her own land end in three days.

Thomas drives me crazy, quoting those Greeks and Romans all the time, but with the clock ticking, it's like Cicero himself is whispering in my ear: *While there's life, there's hope.* And the last time I checked, I was still breathing.

With the speeches finally over, the two bars are suddenly packed with thirsty guests. Owen and I return to tour-guide duty, taking couple after couple upstairs to the study where we make sure to point out the table that is featured in the painting of Ada and Dinah.

"And that's the clock from the painting, too," Owen says. "It's over a hundred years old. Someone has wound it once a week ever since the captain died. When I was a really little kid, my dad used to try to scare me. He said that if I was in this room when the clock stopped, I would be haunted by the captain's ghost. I'd have to listen to him moaning and shaking chains and all that ghost stuff every night for the rest of my life." Owen laughs at the memory and then holds up a hand to quiet everyone down. "Hang on, it's gonna chime in a few seconds."

As the minute hand reaches the twelve, everyone stops talking and the clock's bell rings out. Instead of eight single rings, though, there are four pairs, like this: *ding-ding! ding-ding! ding-ding! ding-ding!*

"Ah, eight bells," says a man in a hideous plaid sports coat. "End of the watch. Takes me back to my navy days."

"Looks like it's a few minutes behind," says another visitor, making a point of showing off his enormous gold watch. "I have eight-oh-five."

"When you're a hundred years old, you'll be lucky to be only five minutes behind," says the man's wife.

"Did your dad really tell you that story about the clock?" I whisper to Owen as we lead a couple down the stairs.

"That's my dad," he says with a sly smile.

Several tours later, Allison, still gripping her clipboard, brings Nadine and Thomas to the top of the stairs and delivers a welcome piece of information: This is the final tour of the night.

"Thank goodness," I say. "'Cause I can't fake one more smile."

"Thomas Emmery," Thomas says, holding a hand out to Owen. "And this is, well, you probably already know her. Nadine Pritchard."

"Hi. I'm Owen. Or, thanks to *her*, my new name is Under. Under A. Cheever."

It's Thomas's turn to roll his eyes at me. "Laaark."

"It's okay," Owen says. "My dad says it fits."

"Somehow I doubt that," Thomas says. "You ready to head out, Lark? Dinah's already gone—she said to be sure to tell you good night and that she'll see you Monday."

"Oh! You're . . . going?" Owen asks. "It's just . . . after the party, all the volunteers . . . hang out for a while. Kind of a tradition. It's fun. The caterers give us all the leftover food."

I'm about to say thanks, but no thanks when Thomas speaks up. "Sounds like fun, Lark. What do you think?"

"I . . . dunno . . . I'm . . ." I'm plumb out of excuses is what I am. I really don't want to stay, but for the life of me can't come up with a reason *not* to.

"You have your phone, right? Just text me when you're ready and I'll come get you," Thomas says. "I think I can get Les to loan me his cart. It's like high school all over again—borrowing Dad's car. Except Dad's car wasn't done up in camo and heavily armed."

"Y-You don't have to," Owen says. "I can give her a ride. I have my own cart."

I grit my teeth and glare at Thomas, wordlessly but oh-so-clearly telling him in my best Obi-Wan Kenobi way: *That is NOT fine with you. It is NOT okay for Owen to give Lark a ride home.*

"Perfect," Thomas says, and part of my brain explodes. So much for the Force.

Behind us Captain Cheever's clock starts to chime as the hands strike nine o'clock: *ding-ding!*

I wait for the other seven bells, but nothing happens. "I don't get it. It only rang twice. Why did it stop? It can't be broken—it was working at eight o'clock."

"I dunno," Owen says, shrugging.

Thomas claps his hands together. "So, we're all set. Owen will give you a ride home. How about by . . . ten thirty?"

"Yes, sir," Owen says.

While Thomas and Owen chat away like long-lost friends, Nadine gets my attention and mouths the words *Call me tomorrow.*

I give her a thumbs-up and immediately feel self-conscious;

the GHT is that I have been known to mock people for that very gesture. What is *wrong* with me?

I lead the way down the stairs and back out on the patio. Nate and Jack run toward us but slam on the brakes when they see Owen. Nate gives me a "how could you" look and kicks at the bluestone.

It's pointless to try to explain, so I say, "I'll see you guys in the morning. Where's Pip?"

She appears as if on cue, her mouth falling wide open at the sight of Owen.

"Oh, for crying out loud," I say.

"What. Is. Going. On?" Pip asks.

"We're leaving as soon as we find—ah, there he is," Thomas says, spotting Blake and waving him over.

Like the others, Blake is confused and/or alarmed by Owen's presence. "Oh. Heyyy. Are we going or what? Where's Les?" He takes a step back, putting more distance between himself and Owen.

"On his way. Lark's staying for a while," Thomas announces. "There's a little get-together for all the volunteers."

"It's not *just* for volunteers," Owen says, and I'm pretty sure he's lying. "Why don't you stick around, too?" He addresses this last question to Blake, who doesn't respond; it's as if Owen had spoken the words in Elvish.

"Blake?" Thomas says. "What do you think? You want to stay, and ride back with Lark?"

Blake catches my eye and I nod vigorously, hoping that the Force will have more impact on a younger, weaker mind: *Yes. You do want to stay.*

"Uhhh . . . okay, I guess," Blake says.

Yes! Thank you, Obi-Wan.

A few seconds later, Thomas climbs into the front seat of Les's cart with Jack on his lap. Pip and Nate ride in the back, giving me the stink-eye as they disappear down the road.

Owen looks at me, then at Blake, and then back at me. "Can you, uh, give us a minute?" he says. Suddenly, his bow tie looks really tight around his neck and his face reddens noticeably.

"What? Oh. Yeah. Sure."

It's Blake's turn to do the Jedi mind thing. *You cannot leave me alone with this maniac.* He doesn't blink for a long, long time.

"It's cool," I say as I start back towards the patio. "Owen has something he wants to say."

From my seat on the stone wall, I can see Blake's face and hear most of what Owen says, and it is, seriously, the most awkward thing I've ever witnessed.

"Look," Owen starts. "I know you must think I'm a complete . . . I'm an idiot. I'm just a spoiled crybaby who was mad because he didn't get what he wanted. I just want to say that I'm really, really sorry about . . . what I said. And the way I acted. And I swear, I'm not just saying it. I am. I . . . I hate myself for what I said. I just hope that you can . . ."

Blake fidgets, not sure what to do with his hands. He pushes his hair back from his eyes. He rubs his cheeks, and then the back of his neck. His face, like Owen's, is bright red.

"It's okay," Blake says quietly. "Thanks. I mean, I am pretty bad at soccer."

"You're not that bad," Owen lies. He lowers his voice, but I still hear the next part: "Don't tell her, but your sister decking me like that was probably the best thing that ever happened to me."

"Okay, okay," I say, getting to my feet and waving my arms around like a referee ending a boxing match. "Enough. I can't take any more. Geez. I'm embarrassed for you. *Pathetic*. Now, is everybody good? Good. Let's go before you decide you need to hug or something to add to the humiliation."

# CHAPTER
# 11

OKAY. I'M JUST GOING TO come right out and say it: It's entirely possible that I've been wrong about Owen A. Cheever.

I know, I know. Nothing he does is ever going to make me forget how he has acted in the past, but the fact is—and this is *really* hard to admit—that I am actually, gulp, *glad* that I stuck around for the after-party. It is pretty much the way Owen described it: a bunch of kids hanging out around the fire pit on the museum patio, talking and eating and listening to music. It's the first time I've been to a party with high school kids, and it is nothing like the ones I've seen on TV or in the movies. First of all, nobody is dancing, which I have always assumed was part of every teen get-together. Second, nobody is making out. Yeah, there are some couples sitting close together, but there's nothing awkward going on.

Blake and I end up on the "young" side of the party with Owen and seven or eight other local kids. Because we're from exotic Connecticut, everyone has lots of questions for us. Even Owen has a hard time believing that I'm only twelve, and going into eighth grade, as is Blake, who is almost two years older.

"No way," Owen says. "You're, like, six feet tall."

"I skipped a grade," I say.

"Her mom was really tall, too," says Blake.

"Wait. *Her* mom? I thought you guys were . . ." says Owen. "I mean, the way you . . ."

I shake my head. "His mom died, then his dad married my mom. After my dad died. And then my mom died."

"Oh. Wow," Owen says. "That—"

"Explains a lot?" I say, smiling. "About all my 'issues'?"

Flustered, Owen blurts out, "No, no, that's not what I mean. That's . . . that must have been hard."

"*Is*," I say quietly.

"Right." He's quiet for a moment, then changes the subject to a safer topic. "So, do you live anywhere near Houghton?"

"Um, yeah. I mean, it's like an hour away. There's a school there, Carton Academy."

"Lark might go there," Blake says.

"*Maybe*," I say. "There's, like, a *chance*."

"They've been recruiting her," says Blake. "For soccer. But not just soccer. She's smart, too. I mean, obviously. They offered her this big scholarship." He almost sounds proud of me.

"That is so . . . weird," says Owen. "My parents want me to go to boarding school out east, and so far, Carton is my favorite. I was just there a few weeks ago."

"Wouldn't it be crazy if you guys were there on the same day?" Blake wonders.

"So, are you serious . . . about boarding school?" I ask.

Owen nods enthusiastically. "Yeah, anything to get away from my dad. And he thinks it would be good for me. What about you? Do you want to?"

"I haven't decided. I'm not even sure they still want me after . . ."

"The *Incident*?" says Owen.

"Wait. What? How do you . . ." My head spins to look Blake in the eyes. "Did you . . ."

"He didn't say anything, I swear," Owen says. "After that first day at soccer, I was curious. You wore a shirt with your school's name on it, so I did a little research. My cousin goes to school in Middletown. You're actually kind of famous. I'm still not clear on all the details, but after that day on the beach, I have a pretty good idea of what went down." He grins and rubs his nose for effect.

"Don't believe everything you hear," I say. "People exaggerate. It wasn't that bad. Shut *up*, Blake." Poor Blake hasn't said a word, but suddenly the Force is strong in him, and what he's thinking is coming through loud and clear.

"Don't worry—I'm not going to say anything," Owen says.

"Seems like everybody already knows," I say with a shrug.

Fortunately, someone arrives with trays of sliders and California rolls, so the conversation about the ISF is over, at least for the moment. By the time the food and drinks are all gone, the musicians have packed up and gone and the fire is nearly out.

"I guess it's time to go," I say as the crowd around the dying fire dwindles.

"My phone's dead," Owen says.

"Mine's in my bag, inside," I say.

One of the musicians, wearing a Merchant Marine Academy sweatshirt, is passing by on his way into the museum. Owen asks him the time.

The musician stops and checks his watch. "Going on five bells."

"What?" Owen and I say together.

"Oh, sorry," he says, grinning broadly. "Forgot where I am. Ten twenty-five."

"We need to get going," Owen says. "You're supposed to be home in five minutes."

"I wouldn't worry too much about it," I say. "That's just Thomas being . . . *fatherly* or something. Especially since Blake's with me."

Owen is not convinced. "Yeah, well, I still think we should . . . come on." He hurries off to his golf cart, bright red with the Cheever Construction logo on the hood. I ride on the seat next to him while Blake sits on the backward-facing rear seat.

It's only a few minutes to the Roost, and no one speaks until Owen pulls to a stop a few feet from the kitchen steps. Thomas is inside, putting away dishes.

"Thanks for the ride," Blake says, hopping off the back.

"Sure," says Owen.

"See you Monday," I say.

"Hey, uh, wait a second. I'm having a beach party at my house next Friday. . . . Why don't you . . . you, too, Blake . . . why don't you come? There's gonna be a *huge* bonfire and, you know, the usual stuff. Hot dogs, s'mores . . ."

"I-I don't know," I say. "I don't really know anybody —"

"There'll be lots of kids from soccer. And from tonight. C'mon. It'll be fun."

Blake looks at me and shrugs. "Um . . . I guess it's up to Lark."

"We have to ask Thomas, anyway," I say.

"Okay, okay," Owen says. "No pressure. I mean, if you don't want to have any fun . . ." He drives off with a wave.

"Why is it up to me?" I ask Blake when Owen makes the turn out of the driveway.

"He doesn't want me to come. Or, if he does, it's only to make sure that *you'll* come."

"What are you talking about?"

"Holy crap, Lark—are you blind or what? The way he looks at you. He *likes* you."

"You're crazy. He's just being nice. He's trying to make up for . . . well, for a *lot* of things."

"Uh-huh. Right."

While I'm getting dressed in the morning, I hear voices outside. When I realize that it's Les Findlay, I hurry down to the kitchen. Thomas has invited him in for coffee, and they're sitting at the table, along with Pip and Nate, when I come in.

"Hey, can I ask you a question?" I say to Les, outfitted in head-to-toe khaki.

"How about we start with 'Good morning, Mr. Findlay,'" Thomas says.

*Oh. Right. Manners, Lark.* "Good morning, Mr. Findlay."

"Mornin' Lark," he says. "Have a good time last night?"

Thomas refills Les's coffee cup and pours me a glass of orange juice. "Good question. How was it—the after-party? Blake's still in bed."

"He's *always* in bed," Nate says. "I like getting up early." He grins at me, letting me know that he's forgiven me for talking to Owen Cheever.

"It was fine, I guess," I say.

"That's it? *Fine?*" Pip says. "Your first high school party and all you can say is, it was *fine*. How was . . . O-wennn?" She makes a face when she says his name.

"He was fine."

"Well, thanks for that *comprehensive* description of things," says Thomas. "I don't know about the rest of you, but I have a *wonderfully* clear picture of what it was like."

"Are you done? Can I ask my question *now*?"

"Go right ahead, tiger," Les says, leaning back in his chair, his intense blue eyes fixed on me.

"You were in the navy, right? Do you know anything about the clocks?"

He continues staring at me as if he hasn't quite heard the question. Finally, he says, "The *clocks*. What do you . . . I don't think I understand the question."

"You know. The ones with bells. Navy clocks. Like at the museum."

"Ohhh, right, right. Got you. Ships' clocks. What do you want to know?"

"So, last night I was in the captain's study at eight o'clock, and the bell rang eight times."

"So far so good," Les says, smiling because he knows where this is going.

"Then, I'm back in the same room an hour later, nine o'clock, and it starts to do its thing. But then . . . I think something's wrong with it, because it only rings twice, like, ding-ding. And then later, we asked this guy for the time and at first he says it's almost five bells. Then he says it's ten thirty. We're, like, *what*?"

Les lets out a single, booming *Ha!* then says, "Sorry—the look on your face takes me back to my first time aboard a navy ship, on my way to Vietnam. The first few days, I never knew *what* the heck time it was. Six bells? Two bells? Didn't mean a darned thing to me, but all the old-timers seemed to know."

"Did you figure it out?" I ask.

"Oh, sure. It's really simple once someone explains it to you. On ships, not everybody is on duty all the time. The day is divided into shifts that are four hours long. But you don't dare call them shifts in the navy. They're *watches*. The watches start at twelve, four, and eight. So, let's say you go on watch at midnight. Every half hour equals one bell. So, at twelve thirty, one bell rings. At one o'clock, you get ding-ding—two bells. One thirty is three bells, two o'clock is four bells—you're halfway through the watch. And so on."

I let that sink in for a few seconds. "Wait. One o'clock is two bells, and two o'clock is four bells. So . . . three o'clock is six bells?"

"Yes, ma'am. Ding-ding, ding-ding, ding-ding."

"And four o'clock is eight bells."

"Now comes the tricky part," Les says. "What about four thirty?"

"N-Nine bells?"

"Guess again. Your watch ended at four, and another one *started*. So, it's—"

"One bell?"

"Exactly! This time around, five is two bells, six is four bells, and so on, till eight o'clock, which is eight bells."

"Ohhh. That's what . . . the clock in the museum last night. And nine o'clock *was* two bells. So there's nothing wrong with the clock."

"And ten thirty?" Les asks.

"Five bells! Just like that guy said. Huh."

"There you go. That's all there is to it. Just remember twelve, four, and eight are all eight bells."

"Cool. Thanks."

"Afraid it's not much use unless you're in the navy," Les admits.

"You never know," I say.

For the last hour of soccer camp on Monday, Owen and I are on the same side as we're practicing corner kicks. When it's my turn to do the actual kicking, I blast the ball right into the crowd in front of the goal, where Owen leaps up and heads it past the goalkeeper and into the net. Since we scored, we get to go again, so I tee up the ball and send it flying. This time, it hits Owen in the chest and bounces to the ground in front of him, where he dribbles once, fakes, and then chips it into the far corner of the goal. On my third attempt, I send a short, snappy pass to my nearest teammate, who taps it back to me. I hold the ball for a second, drawing the defense toward me, and then lob it over their heads to the waiting Owen, who bashes it into the goal. Three corners, three goals.

Owen runs toward me, and for a moment I'm terrified that he's going to hug me, but—thank *goodness*—he stops short and high-fives me instead.

"That was *insane*!" he screams.

I'm much more blasé: "Yeah. Pretty cool."

His face falls at first, as if he's embarrassed by his enthusiasm, but he recovers quickly. "Pretty cool? I don't care what you say. That was *awesome*."

On the way back to the sidelines for the final meeting of the day, he asks if I've thought about the beach party Friday.

"Oh. No. I forgot. I need to ask Thomas."

"But you're going to, right?"

"Uh, yeah. I guess. I mean, sure."

"*Man*. What does it take you get you, like, *excited* about something?"

Luckily, the coaches are waiting at the sideline to congratulate us for the corner kick drill and I don't have to answer him. The truth is, there are plenty of things that get me excited, and winning at soccer is only one. But at the moment, my brain is preoccupied with finding Edward Cheever's missing will, which is *not* something I want to share with the person who stands to benefit the most if I *fail*.

When soccer camp breaks up for the day, I ask Pip, Nate,

and Jack how their day was. Nate regales us with a much-embellished story, which has Pip and Jack interrupting every few seconds to challenge him on some detail or another.

"That's not the way it happened, Nate," Pip says. "You're such a liar."

Nate ignores her, continuing with his tall tale, which ends, naturally, with him scoring the game-winning goal and then being carried off the field by his teammates.

Pip throws up her hands in disbelief. "I was *on* your team, Nate! Nobody carried you anywhere."

I lean toward Nate and offer a high five. "Don't mind the haters, dude."

"Aaarrrgg," says Pip, climbing aboard her bike and pedaling away. "I give up."

"Better go get her, guys," I say. "Maybe you can tell the story again later. I'm sure your dad will love it."

As they take off after Pip, I pick up my own bike.

"You're not going home with them?" Owen asks from the seat of his golf cart, parked a short distance away.

"Oh. Didn't see you. No, I have a job. Afternoons."

"Really? Where do you work?"

"Remember the woman with Thomas on Saturday? Nadine? She was a friend of my mom's. I'm sort of her assistant."

"Wow. A job," he says, as if the concept is completely foreign to him. "Nadine *Pritchard*, right? My dad and her, they don't really . . ."

"Yeah. I know. Well, I gotta get going. See ya."

Nadine is on her phone, pacing around the yard when I get there. She waves me into the house where I help myself to iced tea and a couple of gingersnaps on my way to the war room. My current assignment is to go through a dozen boxes of miscellaneous papers from Albert Pritchard's old office building—things that someone (probably Gilbert Cheever) had boxed up and shoved into a dark corner of the attic. The building had remained in the Cheevers' hands until a few weeks ago, when they sold it to a local realtor who will have her office on the ground floor and live in the apartment above. In the process of cleaning out the attic, she found the wooden boxes buried under decades of dust, cobwebs, and mouse poop. Lucky for us, she's a friend of Nadine's and when she saw the Pritchard name on a document she pulled out, she called Nadine immediately.

It's *extremely* unlikely that there's a copy of the will lurking in them. That would have been Gilbert's first task after ensuring that Albert was dead: Find his brother's new will and destroy it. Instead, I'm looking for any correspondence between Albert Pritchard and Captain Edward Cheever that refers to a new will, something that Gilbert may have overlooked. After going through two boxes, I had a single sheet of paper with the captain's name on it—a letter he had written to Pritchard from aboard a freighter and postmarked in Buffalo a few months before he died. It's not enough to take to a judge, but it certainly makes it clear that Edward didn't trust Gilbert.

He was concerned—*very* concerned—about Gilbert working in Pritchard's office where he might have access to Edward's files. He then says that he wants to meet with Pritchard to draft a new will when he returns to Swallowtail. Unfortunately, he doesn't mention any details.

"Sorry about that," Nadine says as she sweeps into the room. "I've been talking to my lawyer about getting an injunction against the Cheevers."

"What's that?"

"It's an order from a judge saying they have to stop whatever they are doing. Thanks to you, we know they're moving construction equipment onto land that doesn't belong to them. Unfortunately, even if we get it, it's only temporary. The judge might . . . *might* give us the injunction if we can show evidence of another will, or that fraud was committed during the probate process. We don't have to be able to prove it, just show that it's likely that we *will* be able to prove it. Or something like that. My lawyer says that she can argue that it's in the public's best interest to delay things until we know for sure. Kind of a crapshoot, but we're running out of options."

"And time," I say.

"Right. You have to hand it to Reggie Cheever. Making a big donation and naming a new wing of the museum for Dinah. *Brilliant.* He looks like Mother Teresa. And when we try to stop them, we're going to look like—"

"Jerks."

"I was going to say something a lot worse, but yeah, jerks for sure." She rubs her forehead as she takes in the pile of papers in front of me. "All right. Focus, Nadine. How is all this going? Anything more?"

"Not yet, but I still have a lot of boxes to go through," I say. "There was one, so there could be more, right?"

"Fingers crossed," Nadine says. "Tell you what. I need to call my lawyer back in a few minutes, but then I'll sit down and help. What time is it?"

I check my watch and do the calculation. "Um . . . almost three bells."

Nadine's head tilts steeply to starboard. "It can't be three o'clock. Can it?"

"One twenty-five. Remember the clock in the study at the museum, how I thought something was wrong with it because it only rang twice at nine o'clock? I asked Les Findlay—he was in the navy, so I figured he'd know—and he taught me about how a ship's clock works. In navy time, one thirty is three bells."

"Learn something new every day," Nadine says. "And from Les Findlay, no less. He must like you. He's not known for being especially . . . friendly, let's say. Scares most people half to death. Okay, let me get this call over with."

Nadine goes back outside for better cell-phone reception and I dig my hand into the center of the pile on the table before me, closing my eyes and mentally crossing my own fingers. "This one!" I say as I tug a trifolded sheet free from the pile. I unfold it and quickly toss it aside when I realize it's yet another bill from the boatyard that did the work on Albert's boat.

A few minutes later, though, I pull out a surveyor's plan, folded into a small, thick packet. I unfold it to its full size, about two by three feet, and printed across the bottom is "Proposed Subdivision of Lands of Edward A. Cheever, Gladdon & Sons, Surveyors."

The plan shows only the west end of Swallowtail Island, starting at the little harbor and going north to Rabbit Ear

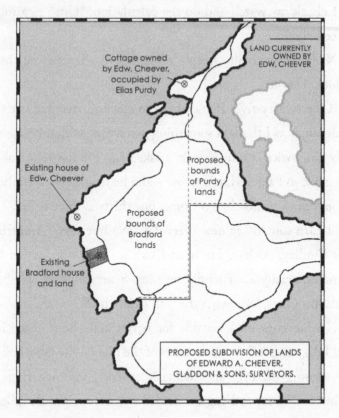

Point. I trace my finger along the line that marks the western shore until I arrive at an X, which is labeled "Existing house of Edw. Cheever." Following the same line north and east toward Rabbit Ear Point, I come to another X with a note that reads "Cottage owned by Edw. Cheever, occupied by Elias Purdy."

There's another house marked on the plan, but this time the X is within the borders of a two-acre lot right next to the captain's land and is labeled as the "Existing Bradford house and land." It's a few seconds before these two facts sink in: The house is the Roost and the Bradfords are my great-grandparents.

A solid line shaped like a backward Z is drawn across the island, starting at a point at the top of the little harbor and ending on the shore a half mile north of Nadine's farm. According to the key at the top of the plan, that solid line represents "Land currently owned by Edw. Cheever." But it's the *dotted* line that makes my heart beat faster: It divides Edward Cheever's land into *two* parts. The eastern half includes Dinah's house and this, in small print: "Proposed bounds of Purdy lands."

And then it gets weird. The note about the western half, which includes the captain's house, reads "Proposed bounds of Bradford lands."

"Wait. What is this?" I say.

Nadine is still on the phone when I find her, so I go back to digging through the pile, hoping to find something that will help to explain the plan.

Ten minutes later, I'm down to the last paper in the stack

and almost pass it by without a look when lightning strikes again. This time I know exactly what I'm looking at. It's an invoice for legal work from Albert Pritchard's office with PAID stamped across the top in red letters. It is addressed to Edward Cheever and is a description of the services provided.

> Consultation and drafting of Last Will and Testament of Capt. E. Cheever.
>
> Original and one fully executed copy enclosed. Additional copy to remain in safe at offices of A. Pritchard, Esq.
>
> . . . . . . . . . . . . . Amount Due: $17.50

I'm already on my feet and on my way out of the war room when I spot a handwritten note in the margin at the bottom of the page: "Dear Albert, I greatly appreciate your timely attention to this matter. Yours, Edward Cheever. Cheque enclosed."

"Nadine!" Once again, I almost run her over in the hallway. I wave the paper at her. "Look!"

"Is that —" Her eyes are as big as dinner plates.

"Almost." I hand her the invoice. "It's not the will, but it's *proof* that there was another will."

"Ohhh, this is gooood. And look at the date! Two months before he died. You're right. It's the next best thing to having the actual will. Yes! There they are. The magic words: 'Original and one fully executed copy enclosed.' The captain got two copies! I need to send a picture of this to my lawyer. Our chances for an injunction just improved by a bunch. Well done, you!" She hugs me and pumps her fists.

"There's one more thing," I say, spreading out the surveyor's plan in front of her. "I found this, but I don't know . . ."

Nadine studies it, her fingers tracing the lines as mine had. "*Proposed* subdivision . . . around the same time he wrote the new will. What was he . . . this is *truly* bizarre. What is *in* that will? And these people—was he planning to sell all this land to them? She taps her index finger on the X marking the Bradford house. "Wait. That's—"

"My house," I say.

"Omigosh, you're *right*! How did I miss that? The Bradfords. Of course. Your . . ."

"Great-grandparents."

"It looks like they were going to buy almost half of the captain's land. But he must have died before the sale went through. That's why this plan was never filed with the town. I doubt anyone knew about this. What's wrong? You have a funny look on your face."

"Something about it doesn't make sense. My great-grandfather died in World War II, before this thing was made. So why would . . . "

"His widow buy a big chunk of land on Swallowtail Island? I see what you mean," says Nadine. "You'd think she'd be *selling*, if anything. We need to follow up with this. This surveying company is long gone, I'm afraid, but maybe there's somebody around who remembers something. It's worth a shot."

Nadine's phone rings and her smile disappears when she sees who is calling. "It's the fire department . . . let me . . . Hello? Yes, this is Nadine Pritchard. What's . . . oh, no. When? Where is she? Is she okay?" Nadine drops into a chair, listening and alternately nodding and shaking her head. "Oh, thank you . . . yes, yes. And you'll wait for me? Good. Thank you for calling. Tell her I'm on my way. I'll be there in ten minutes, tops."

She presses the button to end the call, and I wait, holding my breath, afraid to speak.

"It's Dinah," she says. "She fell and broke her arm . . . apparently she was out in her yard . . . luckily she flagged down the mail carrier and he called nine-one-one. . . . They took her to the clinic in town, but they're insisting on taking her by water ambulance to the hospital in Port Clinton."

"Is she . . . okay?" I ask.

"Sounds like it. She may have broken some ribs, too. I'm sure they're just being supercautious because of her age. Okay, I need to run. I'm going to ride over with her." Nadine is darting around the room, picking up keys and searching frantically for her handbag. "Can you lock up here for me? And check the barn. Make sure the horses have water and hay. Argghhh! Where *is* my bag?"

"Here!" I say, spying it under the table and handing it to her.

"Go! Don't worry, I'll take care of everything here. Call me when you know . . . anything."

"Thank you, thank you." She's out the door and halfway to the barn when she turns around to shout, "Can you go out to Dinah's, too? Make sure the house is—I'm going to leave my golf cart down by the ferry dock—use it. Keys will be under the seat!"

# CHAPTER
# 12

THE WINDOWS AT DINAH'S HOUSE are wide open, and a building northeast wind has the curtains fluttering nervously. The sky had been an uninterrupted expanse of vivid blue when I waved goodbye to Nadine, but an hour later, an army of gray clouds marches steadily toward me, churning up the lake in the process. I hadn't noticed it as I approached the house, but now, looking out the windows, I see that the trees around the house are once again filled with birds, but this time is different: they're silent, and strangely still.

On the table sits a plate of cookies, the glass Dinah always sets out for me, and a worn, leather-bound hardcover with a pair of bookmarks sticking out—no doubt marking Dinah's "quotes of the day" that we were meant to discuss. Curiosity gets the better of me and I open it to the first marked page. In faint pencil are brackets around these words: *"Never,"* said my aunt, *"be mean in anything; never be false; never be cruel. Avoid those three vices, Trot, and I can always be hopeful of you."* The second passage, appearing much later in the book, appears to be the words of the narrator: *My meaning simply is, that whatever I have tried to do in life, I have tried with all my heart to do well; that whatever I have devoted myself to, I have devoted myself to completely; that in great aims and in small, I have always been thoroughly in earnest.* Dinah has double-underlined the phrase "in great aims and in small" and written "words to live by!" in the margin.

I close the book, looking for the title, but the lettering on the spine is worn and no longer legible, so I open to the title page. It is *David Copperfield* by Charles Dickens. Weird, right? It's like the cosmos, or perhaps the ghost of Mr. Dickens, is trying to tell me something. I drop into a chair to read both passages again, and to imagine what Dinah would have said about each. I'm about to set it back on the table when I peek at the inside front cover, and, despite the late afternoon heat, a chill runs up my spine when I see this now-familiar stamp, in the same green ink:

CRACKENTHORP BOOKS
59 DOVER STREET
MAYFAIR, LONDON

But the *déjà vu* moment doesn't end there. In the center of the cover is the same inscription, written in the same hand and in the same color ink as the one in Mom's copy of *The Pickwick Papers*:

*ex libris*
*T. P. & P. C.*

"What is going *on*?" I say aloud, weighing the odds against my mom and Dinah both owning books by Charles Dickens, originally from the same bookstore in London—and later from the library of whatever T. P. & P. C. is. I suppose it's possible that both books were in that box at the junk shop, and Mom gave one to Dinah. But that explanation fails when I read the inscription written on the first page, opposite the cover:

*To Dinah, with all my love!*
*I found this copy in a bookshop in London!*
*I hope you love David as much as I do.*
*Thank you for turning out to be the hero of my life!*
*Merry Christmas!*
*Ada*

Reading Ada's words and knowing that she died so young makes me incredibly sad, and I find myself gripping the book tightly to my chest and wishing Dinah was sitting across the table from me, telling me stories about her childhood. Her cottage seems very empty as I open *David Copperfield* to Chapter 1, which is titled (strangely, I think) "I Am Born." I guess Mr. Dickens is serious about starting at the beginning. I make it through exactly one line—*Whether I shall turn out to be the hero of my own life, or whether that station will be held by anybody else, these pages must show*—before I stop and flip back to Ada's inscription to Dinah.

"Ahhh," I say, wondering what it means that at twelve years old, Ada had already decided that she wasn't the hero of her own life. I'm not surprised. I've only known Dinah for a few weeks, but I can see the impact she's had on my life. It's hard to imagine how many others she's touched in her ninety-three years. Hundreds. *Thousands.* As much as I admire her, though, I can't help thinking that if anyone's going to be the hero of my life, it's going to be me.

Before I get to the second sentence, my phone rings. (At this rate, I will finish *David Copperfield* sometime in 2072.) It's Nadine, calling from the hospital in Port Clinton. "She's going to be fine. The poor thing—she fell face-first onto some rocks, so her face looks like somebody beat her up. Two broken ribs. And, of course, a broken wrist, probably when she tried to break the fall. But she's in good spirits. She's most upset that she's going to have to spend the night here and miss your session."

"Tell her we can have a makeup session next week."

"I will. Look, I hate to ask, but can you check on the horses in the morning? I'm going to spend the night here. Tomorrow . . .

we'll see how things are. I'd ask the Wimd—, er, my parents, but I can't count on them to remember. Is that okay?"

"Yeah, absolutely," I say. "Don't worry. I'll bring Pip with me. She'll know what to do."

"Oh, that's perfect. Thank you. You're a lifesaver. And if there's anyone you can think of to talk to, you know, about that plan you found . . . or the invoice, or *anything* . . . I don't care about the Cheevers or lawyers or injunctions anymore. I just want to be able to tell Dinah that her house is really *hers*. Think what that would mean to her."

"Maybe she'll put in that swimming pool that she talks about. I'll go to the museum right now, before Thomas leaves. There has to be *something* I can do. Call me later, okay? And tell Dinah that I miss her and that we still have a *lot* of reading to do. I just started *David Copperfield* and it's, like, eight hundred pages."

"I'll tell her," Nadine says. "David is my favorite of all the orphans. You're going to love him. Now, go. And be careful, okay?"

"I promise."

Thanks to Nadine's golf cart, I'm at the Cheever Museum five minutes later. I'm hoping to sneak past the front desk where Louise Tollingham is sitting behind a desk, intent on her computer screen, but the door squeaks as it closes and she spins around in her chair and recognizes me.

"Oh. Hello, Robin."

"Lark."

"Right. Of course. I knew it was a bird. What can I do for you?" She stands, eyeing me suspiciously, like I'm going to run off with the silverware.

"I'm here to see Thomas."

"Thomas Emmery?"

Sheesh. How many Thomases are working there? "Uh-huh."

"Right. Of course." She glances at her watch. "He's *working*. Are you sure you want to interrupt him?"

"I'm sure." I feel my hands clenching and unclenching involuntarily, and I take a deep breath. "It's *very* important."

There's a long silence while she stares at me before finally giving in with a sigh. "Follow me," she says, holding open the door to the hallway that leads to Thomas's workshop. When we arrive at his door, she announces, "You have a visitor."

"Mmm?" He continues dabbing at the *Deux Belles* painting with a cotton swab, his nose mere inches from the surface.

"It's me," I say, causing him to look up.

"Lark! Hi. Is everything okay?"

I look at Louise, hoping that she'll get the hint and leave us.

"Right," she says. "Well, I'll leave you two." She leaves, but she's not happy about it.

"What is her *problem*?" I say when she's gone. "Do I really look like I'm going to rob this place?"

"It's not you," Thomas says. "She has a problem with kids in general. Which is pretty strange when you think about it.

Dealing with school kids has to be part of the job. Anyway, sorry—what's going on?"

"It's Dinah—she's in the hospital."

"Oh, no! What happened?"

I tell him everything I know, adding, "I mean, I know it's not like when Mom . . . but, well, you know.

"Aww, Lark, I'm so sorry. I know how much she means to you . . . all the time you've spent with her the past few weeks. I'm sure she's going to be fine. Is there anything I can do? Do you want me to go with you over to the hospital in Port Clinton? Blake can man the fort for a few hours."

"No, no . . . at least, not yet. I have stuff to do here. This is gonna sound weird, but you know how we talked about that missing will, the one that the captain's brother stole?"

Thomas nods in spite of his obvious confusion about where this conversation is going.

"The thing is . . . The thing is, don't ask me *how* I know it, but there's another copy of that will somewhere in the museum. I know it's here, but I don't know exactly where to look. If I could just sit at the captain's desk to, you know, put myself in his place for a while . . . "

"Unfortunately, you can't, not today," Thomas says. "There's some kind of private event going on in the upstairs rooms, supposed to last until eight or nine tonight. Something to do with the new development out on—"

"On *Dinah's* land," I say.

"Yes, I suppose so. Apparently, it's people who have been invited to get first shot at the best lots, I guess."

"This is *so* unfair. I know, I know. Life is unfair. But this really sucks."

"You can try tomorrow," Thomas says, trying to be helpful.

"Tomorrow's the deadline," I say, my eyes straying to the face of the young Dinah in the painting.

"Look, it's . . . what time is it?" Thomas asks.

I'm examining the clock in the painting when I answer, "Five o'clock."

Thomas says something in response, but his words don't register. It's as if the words "five o'clock" are echoing around the room. *Five o'clock.* I check my watch, and, oddly enough, it *is* five o'clock—on the dot.

"That's it," I say. "That's it! It's five o'clock!" There is, I swear, a light bulb blazing an inch above my head like I'm a cartoon character.

"What's so important about five o'clock? Are you supposed to be someplace? Lark?"

I go to the painting, pick up a magnifying glass from the table, and aim it at Ada's hand. "The other night you talked about the key in Ada's hand, the one for winding the clock." I can barely contain my excitement. "Where is it? Do you know where that key is? Is it here? In the museum?"

"I-I suppose so. I've never seen it, but it must be here. Somebody still winds the clock. What's going on?"

I step back from the painting and set the magnifying glass on the table. "I know where the will is."

"You do? Where?"

I shake my head. "I'll explain later. I only have one day to prove I'm right. I need a plan. Not just *a* plan. The perfect plan."

"To do . . . what?"

"It's better if you don't know," I say, and run out the door.

After dinner, I coax the three boys into joining Pip and me in our room.

"I need your help," I say. "On a secret mission."

"Cool," says Nate. I knew that he would be easy to convince, but I need all three boys and Pip.

"You don't even know what it is," Blake says, his arms crossed. "You have to think before you say yes to everything, Nate."

Nate shrugs. "No, I don't."

"Guys, just listen for a minute, then you can decide." I outline the plan for them and give them a moment to consider it.

"And *why* are we doing this?" Blake asks. "I don't get it."

"Because," I say, waiting a beat before continuing, "this is literally the only chance to stop a . . . an *injustice* of . . . *epic* proportions from happening. To somebody who is pretty freaking *amazing*. But it's not just this bad thing that you'll be helping to stop. You're going to be part of something really *good*. Look, this one time, can you just trust me that it's super-important? And you can't say anything about it. To anyone."

Pip and the boys all look at each other, and one by one they all nod.

"What about Dad?" Jack asks.

"No!" I say. "You can't tell him. Promise me, Jack."

He squirms a little, but with everyone staring at him he agrees to the rules. "Okay. I promise."

"I still don't understand what *you're* going to be doing while we're doing all that other stuff," Blake says. "But fine."

"I promise I'll tell you all about it later," I say. "I don't want to jinx it by talking about it first. It's possible—*possible*—that I could be wrong, but I really don't think so."

The boys file out of the room, leaving Pip and me on my bed, below the bird mobile's slowing spinning menagerie. Between us, Pogo dreams of chasing rabbits, her legs and nose twitching like crazy. My own brain skitters from topic to topic: What if I'm wrong about the will? What if someone spoils my big plan—someone like Louise Tollingham? How is Dinah doing? And what if I find the will? What then? What am I supposed to do with it? Oh, no! Nadine's horses! I almost forgot that I have to check on them first thing in the morning.

"I'm excited about tomorrow," Pip says. "It's like a family project."

"Mmm. Yeah, sort of."

"I think your plan is going to work perfectly," Pip says,

brimming with confidence that I wish was contagious.

"I hope you're right, for about a million reasons," I say. "Remember, when Mom was sick, she used to say that the gods owed her one really good day? Well, they still owe *us* one. Tomorrow would be a good time for them to come through."

My phone vibrates on the table next to the bed. "Hi, Nadine!"

"Oh, good, you're still awake. I was afraid you'd already gone to bed. Just wanted to update you on Dinah, and see how your day went. Dinah's doing great, but they're definitely going to keep her here for another day or two. The broken ribs make them nervous, I think."

"Well, tell her I'll see her tomorrow."

"Oh, you're coming over? That's great. She'll be so excited. Sounds like the weather's going to be wild, though. You might have a rough ride over on the ferry."

"That's okay. I'll survive."

"Listen, Lark . . . I hope you're okay about . . . *not* finding the will. We did the best we could. And thanks to you, we know a lot more than we did. You have a lot to be proud of. The important thing is that Dinah's okay, and you're okay, and . . ."

"Um, yeah. About all that. I have *big* news."

"Oh? What's up?"

"I know where it is."

"Where what is?"

"The will."

"What! Are you sure?"

"Pretty sure. Ninety-nine point nine percent." I tell her the story about how I figured it out, and then share the basic details of The Plan.

"Wow," she says when I finish. "I am . . . flabbergasted. You're amazing, and you've put a lot of thought into this. Now, this plan of yours, the museum and the clock and all that—you're sure? And all your siblings? Because it's a little . . . I mean, just be careful, okay? I take it you haven't told Thomas *everything*."

"Ha! No, we can't. He would totally lock me in my room if he knew. I'll tell him later, after it's all over."

"As long as you promise me that you won't do anything crazy. Or ask any of your siblings to."

"Promise."

"All right, then. I guess I'll see you at the courthouse tomorrow afternoon. Good luck."

"Thanks. I'm gonna need it."

When I set my phone down, a brilliant flash of lightning illuminates the sky, followed a few seconds later by a long, low rumble of thunder. Pogo lifts her head momentarily, weighing her dislike of thunder against her degree of comfort at that moment. Comfort wins out, and her head drops back onto the bed with a thud. Pip snuggles up next to me and I wrap a protective arm around her. For a long while we lie there together, wordlessly staring out the French doors as the fast-moving storm grows closer and closer.

At three in the morning, I'm awakened by the sound of the French doors slamming shut as the wind, now howling from the northeast, lashes the rain against the windows and siding. Sandwiched between Pip and Pogo, both of whom could sleep through a thermonuclear attack, I sit up in bed and listen to the storm for a while. When I realize that I'm not sleepy, I flip on my light and pick up *David Copperfield*.

This is intended merely as a statement of fact, and in no way as criticism, but midway through Chapter 3 ("I Have a Change"), I fall back asleep with the book on my chest. When the alarm sounds at six thirty, the sun has theoretically risen, but looking out across the lake, I see no evidence of it. A bank of clouds, dark and dense as cast iron, hangs low in the sky, and the lake is an angry greenish-gray, punctuated by gashes of white, windblown spray.

"Time to get up, Pip," I say, nudging her. She curls into a tight ball when she hears the rain assaulting the house. "C'mon, we have to check on Nadine's horses before soccer. And then— it's going to be a crazy day."

Actually, "crazy" doesn't *begin* to describe it.

I stack our bikes on the back of Nadine's golf cart and head off across the meadow to the path that leads to her farm. At times, the wind is so strong in our faces that the cart slows to a crawl, and I wonder if we're going to make it before the batteries die completely.

When Nadine's house comes into view, Pip points at a spot in the sky beyond low-lying Cattail Island, tucked in just off the northeast shoreline of Swallowtail like a barge anchored in a cove. An armada of battleship-gray clouds bears down on us, dumping rain by the bucketful, but in the midst of all that darkness is a pinprick of rose-colored light—as if someone has poked a hole in the sky. Involuntarily, my foot comes off the accelerator and the cart stops. Pip hops off and runs toward the shore, where she stands for a long time, leaning into the wind and ignoring the rain. A lone swallow circles above her, and for a second, maybe two, Pip's face reflects the pink light.

And then it is gone, the hole in the clouds plastered over by unseen hands, the swallow carried off by the wind. Pip, though, is so perfect, so perfectly *sweet*, that I feel a sudden urge to hug her, to hold her forever. The thought of her growing up, of becoming a surly teen, someone like . . . well, like *me*, makes my chest ache.

"It's so beautiful," she says. "It's a sign. Just think—we're probably the only people in the whole wide *world* who saw that speck of light. It was meant for us." She notices my expression. "What's wrong? Why are you looking at me like that?"

"Nothing's wrong, I promise. You just . . . look, do me a favor and don't grow up, okay?"

"Are you *crying*?"

"No-oo," I lie. "In case you haven't noticed, it's *raining*. Anyway, have you seen enough? If we don't get moving, we're both going to catch pneumonia."

Pip's mouth opens into a perfect O, but no sound escapes—or maybe it does but is lost in the roar of the wind.

"What is it? What's wrong?"

"When you said that . . . about catching pneumonia? You sounded *exactly* like Mom. For a second I thought . . . I got goose bumps—look." She pushes up the sleeve of her raincoat. "See?"

I take her hand in mine and lead her to the horse barn. She

stops before we go inside and glances back at the sky where the rosy spot had appeared, and then up into my eyes. "No matter what else happens," she says, "*we're* going to be okay."

I'm soaked through and shivering from the storm, but Pip's all-too-familiar words jolt me like I've stuck a finger into an electrical outlet.

# CHAPTER

# 13

BECAUSE THE WEATHER IS SO bad, we spend the first part of the day at soccer camp watching videos of pros teaching a variety of skills, and then move into the high school gym to practice them in small groups. With everything going on in my mind, I have a hard time focusing on the ball, something that Owen notices, and, being Owen, feels the need to point out.

"What's *wrong* with you today?" he says after I miss-hit yet another easy ball in the last drill of the day.

"Nothing," I snap. "Believe it or not, I'm not perfect."

Owen holds up his hands. "Whoa. Sorry. *Kidding.*"

"Yeah, well . . . never mind." I kick the ball to him, this time right on target.

"So, have you thought about Friday?" he asks.

"Friday?"

"Beach party? My house? Remember?"

"Oh. Right. That. Yeah."

Owen's face breaks out in a huge smile. "Really? You're coming?"

"What? No." Owen's smile disappears as quickly as it had appeared. "I mean, I don't know. I forgot . . . there's a lot going on right now. It kinda depends on, I still need to talk to Thomas. Maybe."

"I'm sure he'll let you come, especially if your brother comes."

"Okay, okay. I'll talk to him, all right?"

Neither of us says anything for the rest of the drill, which is fine by me. Owen pouts a little, but keeps his mouth shut, even when I drill a ball into his . . . well, let's say it hits him below the waist. I do my best to hide my smile.

The session finally ends, and I immediately dig my phone from the pocket in my backpack to check for messages from Nadine. She had left a voice mail only a few minutes earlier: "Hi, Lark. The good news is that Dinah's fine. She's in a little pain, but they've got it under control. The bad news is that they want to keep her another day, maybe two, because of the broken ribs. They want to make sure she can get around on her own. So, I'm going to stay here. Don't worry about going to the farm this afternoon. A woman who boards a couple of horses with me will check on the barn—I already talked to her. And if there's any change, I'll let you know. Oh, and Lark? Good luck tomorrow. Fingers crossed that the plan works out. Call me when you're on your way on the ferry. I'll meet you at the courthouse. Okay? Give me a call if you need anything. Bye for now."

"Pip!" I call out, seeing her chatting with a group of girls. "Where are the boys? It's time to go. We have work to do."

From my tone, she knows I mean it, and in under a minute, the four of us are on our bikes, riding directly into a gale, the rain coming down so hard it stings my face.

"Lark!" calls out a voice from behind me.

I turn to see Owen running toward us, squinting at the rain and wind. "Keep going!" I shout at Pip, Nate, and Jack. "I'll catch up." I squeeze the brakes, and Owen stops next to me, water pouring off his face.

"Leave your bikes here," he says. "I'll give you a ride on my cart."

"No thanks. We're already wet. Look, we—I'm in a hurry."

"I heard about that old lady," he says. "Mrs. Purdy. I'm sorry. I know you . . . I . . . look, I just want to help you, okay? If there's anything I can . . . "

I try to read his face, not an easy task with the rain pelting us both.

"Thanks . . . really. But there's nothing you can do. She's gonna be okay. I'll see you tomorrow, okay?" As I hurry to catch up to the others, I sneak a peek back at Owen, who's still standing on the path watching me.

As planned, Blake is waiting for us at the turnoff to the

house, but he does not look happy about it. "This is insane," he says. "It's a freakin' monsoon."

"It's not that bad," says Nate, turning his palms skyward. "It's hardly raining anymore." The words are barely out of his mouth when an especially violent gust of wind knocks him sideways off his bike and onto the grass. He comes up smiling. "That was *so* cool!"

"You're an idiot," says Blake.

"C'mon," I say, standing on my pedals and accelerating away from them. "We're almost there. And Nate? You're not exactly filling me with confidence."

He waves me off. "No problem. I'm ready. I promise."

"Okay, this is it. It's all or nothing. Stick to the plan," I say as we drop our bikes outside the entrance to the Cheever Museum and run inside, shaking the rain from us like a pack of sheepdogs. As I had feared, Louise Tollingham is working the front desk, and she stands, horrified, when she sees the puddle forming on the polished hardwood floor.

"Oh my goodness," she says, forcing a smile. "We certainly are . . . wet. Let's try to stay on the mats, shall we? At least until you . . . what can I do for you today? Are you here to see your father?"

"These guys haven't seen the whole museum yet," I say, pointing at the boys and Pip, "and today seems like a perfect day for it. Not much else to do."

Louise closes her eyes for a moment, gathering her strength.

"I see. Yes, I suppose you're right. Shall I let your father know you're here?"

"No!" I say, a little too quickly. "I'm sure he's busy. Don't bother him. We see him all the time," I add with a fake smile.

"I wanna see the captain's room!" says Jack, darting around the room and touching everything he can reach. "Was he a *real* sea captain? Did he hafta fight pirates? Did he make them walk the plank? Can we see his sword?"

"Easy, Jack," says Blake. I smile to myself because Jack is following his script perfectly.

Louise tries to hide her pained expression with a smile of her own, but she's not fooling me: she is hating every second of this. She can't really deny us a museum tour, though, so she leads us up the stairs and into the study.

"Here we—" she starts, turning just in time to see the five of us scatter in five different directions. "No! Come down from there! Don't touch those!"

Too late. Jack is already on the top step of the ladder and ringing the two ship's bells with everything he has. Before she can get to him, he's gone, disappearing under the captain's desk.

"Sorry," I say to Louise. "He can be a handful. He *usually* doesn't break anything, though."

Meanwhile, Pip is pulling Captain Cheever's logbooks down from the shelves and leafing through them. "Where are the pictures?" she asks.

"Pictures of what?" Blake asks, looking over her shoulder.

"Trees, of course. They're *log*books, get it?" She falls to the floor and rolls around, laughing hysterically.

"Children. Please. Stop." Louise's eyes are wild with a combination of fear and fury. "Those. Books. Are. Irreplaceable. Put them back this instant! No! Don't touch them. Let me do it."

"Geez. Make up your mind, lady," Blake says.

She doesn't get a chance, because Nate has unlatched the French doors, which bowl him over as the gale winds swing them nearly off their hinges and into the room.

"Whoa!" he says, running out onto the balcony and immediately climbing onto the railing. I'll say this for Nate: The kid has the balance of an Olympic gymnast. Incredibly, he's walking across the top of the railing like it's a balance beam, ignoring the wind, the rain, and the screams of Louise Tollingham.

"Stop that!" she cries as the rest of us clamber out onto the balcony after him. "Get him!"

"Careful!" I shout. "Don't knock him off. Nate?"

"What?"

"Do you think you should come down?"

He shrugs. "D'you think I could do a cartwheel on here?"

"No!" Louise screams. "Do. Not. Do. A. Cartwheel. Please come down. I'll let you pick something from the gift shop, anything you want."

"*Anything?*" he says. He's swaying to and fro with each blast of wind, and Blake reaches up to steady him.

Louise hesitates, thinking, I'm sure, of the reproduction of

Captain Cheever's brass telescope that sells for three hundred and fifty dollars and wondering why Blake doesn't simply grab Nate and pull him down. "Yes. Anything."

"Deal!" says Nate, smiling broadly at Louise and taking two steps toward her. "No, wait. I just *hafta* do a cartwheel." He's getting himself into position, mapping out his steps and peering down at the ground beneath him.

"Nate," I say. "It's time."

"Here I go!" He flexes his muscles, takes a half step back, two stutter steps forward and then, with help from a swirling, whirling gust of wind, leaps into the air and right over the railing, his cry of *yeeeeaaaaaaa!* trailing him all the way down.

"Nooo!" Louise screams.

I'm the first one to the railing. Although the balcony is a good ten feet off the ground, there is a large, well-trimmed shrub directly below it—and Nate has landed dead center on the top of it, exactly as planned. He looks up at me with a goofy grin and then rolls off the shrub onto the lawn, where he lies, sprawled out with arms and legs going in all directions.

Louise eventually manages to get past the rest of us to look over the edge. "Oh, no. No, no, no. Is he . . . Someone call nine-one-one!"

"I'm doing it," I say. "You'd better get down there! But don't move him! Go! Go!"

Louise, Blake, Jack, and Pip run inside and down the stairs while I slip my phone back in my pocket and get to work.

Before I go on, though, I think it's important to set the record straight: That leap from the balcony was *entirely* Nate's idea. All I did was ask for a diversion that would give me a few minutes alone in the study with the ship's clock. Maybe it wasn't the *safest* plan ever conceived, but you know what? It worked.

Okay. On to the clock.

First, I need to find the key used to wind it—the one in Ada's hand in the painting (*"Ada holds the key"*). A quick search of the area tells me it's not in plain view, but I'm confident that it's not far. After all, according to Owen, in the seventy-five years since Edward Cheever's death, the clock has never stopped. Kneeling on the carpet in front of the table where it sits, I examine the wood closely and immediately spot two vertical gaps in the carvings: a drawer! I slide it out and sure enough, a shiny, T-shaped key is there waiting for me. It looks to me to be a one-of-a-kind creation. The bottom of the T is hexagonal, a tiny socket wrench made to fit into two holes in the face; one to wind the clock spring and the other to wind the mechanism that rings the bells every half hour. The top of the T, the handle, is four inches of heavy steel, tapering almost to a point at each end. In my hand, it feels like a weapon.

"Okay, good," I say aloud. "Keep moving, Lark." I lift my head to listen for signs of anyone coming back upstairs to the study, but all is quiet.

The actual clock is circular, about eight inches in diameter and four inches thick, and made of polished brass. It was made to last, no doubt about that—and it has. On a ship, it would have been attached to a wall with bolts, but for display on a table, it rests in a wooden, custom-made clock stand. The top part of the stand is concave so the round clock sits securely in place. Below that is a simple but elegant carved base, which in turn rests on four brass "feet" with thick felt pads. Taking a deep breath, I lift the clock out of the stand—it's even heavier than it looks—and set it on the carpet beside me.

My eyes dart back and forth from clock base to key, over and over. I lift the base and turn it over and around in my hands, looking for the secret that I *know* is there.

And how do I know this?

All right. A brief time-out to fill you in. Remember when I was with Thomas in the studio? He asked me the time and I said, "Five o'clock" because I happened to be looking at the painting of Ada and Dinah—specifically, at the *clock* in the painting—at that exact moment. And that's when it hit me: In ship's time, five o'clock is *two bells*. Two bells. Everyone assumed that Edward Cheever's final words had something to do with the two brass ship's bells on the mantel, but it was another two belles, Dinah and Ada, all along. Maybe

Edward hoped that the housekeeper would share those words with Dinah's father, Elias Purdy, and that he would know which "bells" Edward was referring to, *and* know where to look.

Since he never had that chance, it's now up to me.

I press on every surface, waiting for a tiny door to pop open, but the stand remains stubbornly solid. I shake. I twist. I tap. Nothing.

"Come on. *Think*," I say, clasping the key in my hand and rubbing its polished surface between my fingers like a lucky charm. I close my eyes for a second, and when I reopen them, the answer is staring me in the face: the feet! Turning the clock stand upside down, I unscrew one of the brass feet. When it is off, I do the same to the other three, and then examine the holes in the wood panel. I hold it up to the light for a better look, but still can't see anything.

"I need something to stick in . . ." The key! Suddenly its strange design makes perfect sense. It wasn't made only to wind the clock. It has another purpose! When I slide one of the tapered ends of the handle into the hole, I hear it make contact with metal. Then I give it a little push, and something inside gives way, followed by a distinct . . . *click*! I forget to breathe as I repeat the action in the other three holes, and each time, I am rewarded with that same satisfying sound.

My heart feels like it's in my throat when the entire bottom panel of the clock stand falls free onto the carpet, exposing a secret compartment that is only an inch or so deep. And folded so that it fits perfectly in that space is an envelope. With trembling fingers, I pry it loose, unfold it, and turn it to read the printing in the upper left-hand corner: *A. Pritchard, Esq.* If I had any doubts about what I held in my hand, *Will* is written across the front of the envelope in cursive that I recognize as the captain's.

Of course I can't resist peeking inside the envelope in order to confirm that it really is Edward Cheever's Last Will and Testament, and that it's the one we've been looking for. There's no time to read the whole thing right now—it's several pages long, and I need to get it to Nadine, so she can file it at the courthouse. As long as it's filed while Dinah is alive, the terms of the will have to be followed. It may take some time (and lots of lawyers, Nadine said), but if the will says what we *think* it says, every bit of land that the Cheevers hope to turn into condos and golf courses belongs to Dinah. And that is going to *kill* them.

The envelope is still in my hand when Louise Tollingham's voice rings out from the doorway behind me.

"Have you called—" she starts, looking panicked about Nate. Then she spots the clock and dismantled pieces of its stand scattered on the floor around me. "What are you *doing*? Your brother is down there—" She stops, her face contorting as she begins to grasp the reality of the situation. "Why, you little . . . you planned that whole thing so you could . . . what is *that*?" She's pointing at the envelope.

"N-Nothing," I say. And yes, I totally get how dumb that sounds.

"Give it to me. This instant." She moves toward me and I shove it deep into the front pocket of my shorts, scanning the room for an escape route.

"Sorry. I can't do that."

"Whatever it is, it belongs to the museum, or to the Cheevers. Don't make things worse for yourself. There's only one way out of this room, and you're not getting past me. I will tackle you if I have to."

I edge around the table where the clock sat for all those years, keeping its secret safe.

"You can't stop me," I say. "*This* changes everything. It's Edward Cheever's will—the *real* one, not the one that was used to cheat Elias Purdy. And by the way, there's one more thing you're wrong about."

"Oh? And what is that?" she asks.

I breathe in deeply and steel myself for what's coming. "There's more than one way out of here."

I make a break for the balcony, barrel-rolling over the captain's desk and knocking over a candlestick and an inkstand in the process. When I reach the balcony, I shout, "Look out!" to my coconspirators on the ground below and, in one quick motion, I'm standing atop the railing, which seems considerably higher than it had a few minutes earlier. Unfortunately, there's no time to reconsider; from where I stand, there really is only one way down.

Louise reaches the French doors in time to see yet another of Thomas Emmery's kids pretend to be a bird and soar off the balcony.

Pip screams my name as I make the leap. Unfortunately, my adrenaline level is sky-high, and I overshoot that oh-so-important shrub, the one with the imprint of Nate's body across its top, by a good five feet. Instead of soft branches, I slam into the wet, hard ground, hearing a strange popping sound from my right arm the split second before my head hits the grass with a thud.

# CHAPTER
# 14

I BLACK OUT LONG ENOUGH to have all three boys and Pip hovering over me and looking very relieved when I open my eyes.

"She's okay," Nate says. "Did you get it?"

My brain feels like it missed a part of a movie and now I need to rewind it and watch it again. I stare up at them all for a few seconds, and then leap to my feet. I pat my pocket and almost faint from the pain in my arm. "Yeah. I got it."

"What's wrong with your arm?" Pip asks. "It's all funny . . . Oh. Oh. Oh." She looks like she's going to pass out, or puke, or both—and I may join her.

"It's fine," I lie. "I have to get out of here before they . . . my bike. Where's my bike?"

"Right here," Blake says. He's unable to take his eyes off my arm. "But you can't —"

"I *have* to! What time is it? Exactly!" My arm is throbbing, and I shiver with pain.

"Ten minutes, no, nine minutes to three," Nate says.

"I've called the police!" Louise calls out from the balcony. She's wagging her finger as her hair flies crazily in the wind. "Don't you children move!"

With my good arm, I turn the bike toward the driveway and throw a leg over the bar. "You guys . . . get out of here. If the police . . . remember what we talked about. Tell Thomas I'll explain later. I'll call from . . . I have to hurry. Ferry leaves in . . ."

The wind is mostly at my back, but the drenching rain continues as I race toward town and the ferry dock on my bike. Take my word for it: a probably broken arm, a bumpy road, and a heart close to bursting from pedaling as hard as I can is *not* a good combination.

The ferry, still loading and tied to the dock, is in sight and I am hurtling down the last stretch of pavement when a woman battling the wind for control of a *ginormous* umbrella steps off the curb, right into my path. If I had two good arms gripping the handlebars, I might be able to swerve to miss her, *and* stay in control.

However, I don't, I don't, and I don't.

I jerk the handlebars to the left and jam on the brakes

with everything I have. It's the front brake, and on a dry day, I would have been airborne for the second time in the span of ten minutes, somersaulting over the handlebars. Lucky for me, though, the brakes don't grip on the wet rims, and rather than an acrobatic finale, I run straight into a concrete planter. The crash sends me skidding across the pavement, leaving me with a decent-sized cut on my chin, skinned knees, and a front wheel that is bent beyond repair. But like a zombie that just won't stay down, I scramble to my feet and shake myself off. The good news? It could have been *so* much worse. On top of that, pretty much every part of my body hurts, so I hardly notice the throbbing in my arm.

I leave the bike where it is and run the rest of the way. When I rush through the door at the ferry terminal to buy a ticket, a flock of tourists gets one look at my bloody face and immediately splits in two, both halves gasping in perfect harmony.

"I need . . . a ticket," I say, struggling to catch my breath.

"Round trip?" the agent asks without looking up from her screen.

"Uh, yeah. How much is that?"

"Twelve fifty," the agent says, her eyes bugging when she finally looks up and sees my bruised and bloodied face.

Using my one good arm and hand, I reach deep into my pocket, pull out a twenty, and slide it across the counter to her.

She stares at it, reluctant to make a move to take it. "Is there somebody with you? An adult? They definitely won't let you board alone with, uh, if you're bleeding."

Out on the dock, the *Niagara*'s horn sounds. A few seconds later a dockhand sticks his head in the door of the terminal and shouts, "Five minutes! Ferry leaves in five minutes! Due to the conditions out on the lake, the Coast Guard says this will be the last boat of the day. Last boat to Port Clinton!"

I plead with the ticket agent, who pushes my money away. "C'mon. Please. I'm *fine*. It's one little cut. You don't understand. I *have* to get on that boat. It's life or death."

"You're not getting on any boat today, sweetheart."

It's a man's voice, and I turn to find my old nemesis, Officer Pawlowski, standing barely six inches away and towering over me. When I ran into him on the way back from Dinah's house that night, I didn't realize how tall he is, easily six foot four. The water dripping off his plastic poncho is forming a massive puddle around his enormous shoes.

"My stepdad is gonna be here any second," I lie. "We're

going to Port Clinton. To the hospital. I think I broke my arm." I hold it out for him to see, and his face goes white.

"Geez, kid. That is . . . how did you—"

Before he can finish, Reggie Cheever bursts through the door, shouting and pointing at me. "That's her. Good work. Have you arrested her?"

"No, sir. Not yet. She's, um, injured. Looks like a broken arm. Says her stepfather is on his way to take her to the hospital in Port Clinton," Pawlowski reports.

"I don't care if her arm falls off," Reggie sneers. "She's not going anywhere until I get my property back. Search her. This *instant*. If you don't, I will." He takes a threatening step toward me.

I back myself against the counter. "You touch me, I'll scream." To Officer Pawlowski, I add, "I don't know what he's talking about."

Pawlowski steps between Reggie and me. "Let's just everybody calm down. I'm not sure I'm even allowed to search her. She's a minor and . . . I mean, I didn't actually witness anything, so right now, anyway, it's just your word . . . did you actually *see* her steal something?"

Reggie's face turns as red as Owen's does when he's angry. "Are you *kidding* me? You believe *her*? This common . . . criminal, instead of me? I'd be very careful if I were you, officer. Maybe you're forgetting exactly who signs your checks. If I say she stole something, she stole something."

"But you didn't see it?"

"What difference does that make!" Reggie shrieks. "Louise Tollingham saw it and she told me. Then I told you. It's very simple. Even *you* should be able to follow that. Arrest her. Search her!"

"Tell you what," Pawlowski says, glancing at me. "We're gonna wait and see if anybody shows up. The boat leaves in a couple minutes. I don't want her dad showing up and thinking she got on the boat without him. In the meantime, have a seat while I get you an ice pack for that arm."

Reggie stammers and grumbles something about respect and having Pawlowski's badge, but he's cut off by the ferry horn.

"Last call for the ferry!" cries the same dockhand as before. "This will be the last boat of the day."

Directly behind Officer Pawlowski is a window, and through it I see a bird swirling high above the dock. I move to the window for a closer look; from the shape of its wings, I recognize it as a swallow, struggling to fly directly into the wind.

"He's probably trying to get to Cattail Island," I say.

"Uh, yeah," Pawlowski says. "If you say so." The look on his face tells me that he thinks I'm crazy. Or delirious from pain. Or both.

The woman behind the counter has found an ice pack and hands it to Pawlowski, who shakes it up and gives it to me. "Hold that on your arm. It'll help with the swelling. And maybe the pain."

I thank him and press it against the spot that hurts the most, sucking in my breath when it makes contact. "Oww-oww-oww."

Pawlowski cringes as if he's the one in mortal agony. "Oh, man. I'll bet that hurts."

"You think?" I say as I consider making a run for the ferry, but quickly realize that it would be a wasted effort, and would probably make things worse. Pawlowski would simply drag me off the boat and to the police station. No, I need another plan, and I need it soon.

While Reggie is preoccupied with his phone, I motion to Officer Pawlowski to come closer. He bends down and I whisper to him, "I need to use the bathroom."

He squints at me in an attempt to see if I'm lying. "Is it . . . can you wait till we—"

I shake my head vigorously. "No, it's an . . . *emergency*." I'll let him interpret that any way he wants.

"Okay," he says. "Quick, while Mr. Cheever's on the phone. Just don't try anything. I'll be watching the door."

Pointing at my arm and the ice pack, I say, "Where am I gonna go?" and dart for the ladies' restroom.

I've only been in the restroom at the terminal once before, on the day we arrived on Swallowtail, but I clearly remember a row of narrow windows above the sinks. I toss the ice pack out the window first, and then climb up onto a sink, praying that it will support me. With the window open all the way, there is just enough room for me to squeeze through. The only problem is that my only option is to crawl through headfirst, so I drop to the ground and roll like a cat burglar, stifling a scream when my broken arm briefly hits the ground.

It won't be long, I know, before Officer Pawlowski panics and barges into the restroom looking for me, so I grab the ice pack and run as fast as I can away from the ferry dock and toward the crowded-together houses in the downtown area. I can temporarily disappear in the fenced-in gardens and back-yards where I need to come up with a plan to get the will to the courthouse in Port Clinton. By now, they're searching every nook and cranny of the ferry, so it's not an option, but I am not about to give up. I have to find another way off the island. If anything, that creep Reggie Cheever has made me even more determined to succeed. I scramble over a picket fence surrounding a bright yellow house and duck inside the open door of a toolshed in the backyard. While I catch my breath, I fumble in my pocket for my phone, which immediately warns me that it is less than 20 percent charged.

"You have *got* to be kidding," I say as I pull up Nadine's number.

She picks up after the first ring. "Lark? Where are you?"

"Hello? Nadine!"

"Hello? Lark? Can you hear me?"

"Yes, yes. Can you hear . . ." And then . . . nothing. The call drops and my phone warns me that I'm now at 10 percent.

"How is that *possible*?" I scream as I hit REDIAL.

"Hello?" This time, Nadine sounds like she's at the end of a long tunnel.

There's no time to explain everything, so I shout, "Courthouse! Meet me at the courthouse!"

"Did . . . say . . . house? Lark? Lark?" She's gone again, but at least there's a chance that she heard the word "courthouse" and would wait for me. Now all I have to do is get myself and the will there, too.

I stare at my phone, considering my options and talking out loud: "This is the problem with living on a stupid island. You need your own boat. Or airplane. Or at least, someone who isn't afraid of a little storm. Someone who has seen worse. Much worse. Someone like . . . Les Findlay! Yes! He's just crazy enough to do it." I scroll down through my contacts until I find him, and then hit CALL. I'm not the least bit religious, but I say a little prayer that he answers—and he does.

"Les Findlay," he announces in his no-nonsense voice.

I take a deep breath and launch into my speech: "Mr. Findlay, this is Lark Heron-Finch, you know, from the Roost? This is gonna sound crazy 'cause I know there's, like, a hurricane out there, but . . . could you take me to Port Clinton on your boat, like right now? It's an *emergency*. I *have* to get there, and the ferry's not running, and I can't think of anything else . . ."

Two seconds of silence, maybe three, then, "Sure." He sounds no more concerned than if I'd asked him to change the station on the TV.

"Omigosh! Thank you! Where is it, your boat?"

"I'm in the cut between Swallowtail and Cattail, up by the old breakwater—you know where that is? Directly across from Miss Purdy's place. Where are you? You want me to pick you up?"

"No! I'm in town. Don't come here, they're looking for . . . Don't move. I'll meet you there. It'll be faster. And safer. I'll be there in ten minutes. Thank you!"

I'm about to hang up and figure out exactly *how* I'm going to get there in anything close to ten minutes when Les says, "Does your, uh, does Thomas know about this?"

It's my turn for three seconds of silence while I consider the best answer. I close my eyes and go with the truth. "N-No. But if he knew what I know, he would want me to go. And so would you. Really."

This time Les matches my three seconds and raises me one—long enough for me to convince myself that I've blown it by sticking with the truth. Finally, he says, "Good enough for me," and I can breathe again.

As I end the call, my phone is at 7 percent. I curse all those long silences—they cost me a percent at least. If only there was a way to connect the stupid thing to my heart, which feels as if it's going to break right through my chest, it would be at 100 percent in about ten seconds.

"One more call. Please, please, have your phone, Pip."

She answers before the first ring finishes. "Lark! Where

are you? Are you on the ferry?" she says, the words running together like machine-gun fire.

"No, I'm in town, in a shed. Listen—"

"Why did—"

"Wait! No questions! Please. Just listen. I don't have much time. Are you home?"

"Yes, but—"

"You need to get here as fast as you can and give me a ride out by Dinah's. Not on your bike. On Tinker. Okay?"

"But you hate—"

"Pip! I can't explain. Just hurry. I'm at the yellow house on Ash Street. And be careful, it's crazy out here. Promise?"

"I promise."

The phone battery is at 6 percent. Me? I'm 100 percent charged. Maybe more.

I park my broken-down body on a bench inside the shed, happy to be out of the weather for a few minutes to concentrate on holding the ice on my arm. The wind is so fierce that the rain is horizontal, though, and I'm still getting soaked. Not that it matters. I can't get any wetter than I already am, and besides, in a few minutes, I'm going to be out on a small boat in conditions so extreme that the Coast Guard won't allow the ferry to run. That is, *if* my sister is able to get me there on her *horse*.

Good plan, Lark. *Brilliant.* Maybe if I close my eyes for a few seconds, my situation won't seem so hopeless.

The rumbling of thunder to the north jolts me back to life. Except it's not thunder—it's the clatter of hooves on pavement, and it's getting louder by the second. When it finally comes into view, I pinch my leg to convince myself that I'm not hallucinating, because coming straight at me at a full gallop is a piebald pony, and on its back, a girl in a hot pink raincoat and matching sou'wester hat, shouting my name. Paul Revere has nothing on my little sister.

Pip brings Tinker to a halt inches from my dazed and broken body, patting her on her neck. "Good girl." When she spots the gashes on my face, still bleeding, she opens her mouth to speak.

*"Don't,"* I say. "I know. I look terrible. And believe me, I feel like—I feel terrible. But we need to get to Dinah's, up by that old breakwater. Les Findlay's gonna meet me there." As I'm standing on a tree stump, ready to climb aboard, I ask the question that I should have asked earlier: "Can she carry us both?"

Pip nods and points at my arm. "Yeah, but can you hold on with only one arm?"

A golf cart whizzes through the intersection at the end of the block, completely ignoring the stop sign. Officer Pawlowski is driving and Reggie Cheever is in the passenger seat. They don't see me, but there's no doubt that they're going to keep looking. "Shoot. We need to go. Now. Scooch up, there's no room for my butt."

"I'm scooched as much as I can," Pip says.

"Okay. Here goes." Holding on to Pip with my good arm, I swing one leg over the saddle and push off with the other. Somehow it works, and the two of us are squished into a saddle meant for one, small, person. I wrap my arm around her waist. "I'm in. Go, go, go!"

As Tinker surges forward, I peek over Pip's shoulder and spot Pawlowski and Cheever, headed straight for us in that souped-up cop cart. They are so focused on finding me, and so certain that I'm on foot that they really aren't even looking at Tinker and Pip. As we pass by in opposite directions, though, Cheever does a double take when he realizes there's another passenger, and that passenger is me.

"Hey!" he shouts. "Stop!"

"Go, go, go!" I say.

Cheever screams at Pawlowski to turn the cart around and then resumes yelling at me.

"Isn't that the cop that —" Pip says.

"Yes. Just go. Faster."

"Are you sure?"

"Yes! Go!" Behind me, Pawlowski hits the brakes so hard that Cheever is launched from his seat and ends up face-planted on the hood as the cart skids to a stop. He recovers quickly, though, pummeling the poor cop with his fists and screaming like a maniac until Pawlowski resumes the chase. "They turned around! You have to outrun them."

"What if they start shooting?"

"They're *not* going to start shooting," I say, and for the most part, I believe it.

"Hold on!" Pip cries as she urges Tinker into a canter and we start to pull away from the golf cart. "I know a shortcut."

"Are you sure?"

"Pretty sure."

"Pretty sure?" Even though I'm practically screaming in her ear, I don't think Pip hears me. Her face is split by a huge smile and it hits me that she has waited all her life for this moment: Pip and her pony, saving the day.

The roads are deserted because everyone with any sense at all is indoors, so Pip keeps Tinker in the middle where there's less water and debris brought down by the wind. Above us, the trees sway so wildly that I can't believe they're still standing. When we take the left turn onto Alder Street, Tinker breaks into a full gallop and I squeeze even harder.

"I can't breathe!" Pip says.

"Sorry."

"That's better. Where are they? Can you still see them?"

I turn my head enough to peek behind us. The cart is nowhere in sight. "I can't see them, but don't slow down."

We pass a sign that reads No Exit. "Piiiip! Where are you going?"

"Trust me," she says as Tinker heads for the woods at the end of the road.

The pavement ends at a yellow-and-white-striped gate, which we could easily have gone around. But this is Pip's fantasy, so we go *over* it with her screaming, "Wheeeee!"

"Is there a trail?" I ask when my heart finally leaves my throat and returns to my chest. "I don't see——"

"Not really. I told you, it's a shortcut. Just hang on. There's lots of trees down we'll have to go . . . over! Good job, Tink!"

She's not kidding about the trees; we spend more time in the air than on the ground. But she's also right about it being a shortcut. There's a small clearing just ahead, with the main road just past it and in the distance, waves crash over the breakwater, sending spray flying high into the air.

"Pip, you're my hero! That *was* an amazing shortcut!" I say, kissing her on the cheek. "Thank you. And thank *you*, Tinker. Oh! There's Les!"

His boat is anchored only a few feet off the beach and he lifts his head from a place deep in the bilge when he hears us approaching. He is battle ready in a full suit of army-green foul-weather gear. His head, however, is bare; apparently, his lawn mower-cut hair repels water.

I let go of Pip for a second to wave with my one good arm,

and at the same moment, Tinker veers sharply left, almost sending me flying yet again. I manage to hold on, awkwardly pulling myself together before swinging my leg over and dismounting. I give Tinker a pat on her rump. "Good girl."

"Not the most graceful entrance I've seen," says Les, who looks me up and down, shaking his head. "You look like something the cat dragged in."

"Thanks. I feel worse than I look, believe me." I wade out to the boat and climb in.

"Oh, well, that's a relief," he says with a wink at Pip. He points out at the lake beyond the breakwater. "You're sure about this? It's blowin' the dogs off the chain out there."

"I'm sure. Although I-I thought your boat would be bigger." *And newer*, I think but don't say. It looks like it's been through a war—maybe two.

"Don't let her looks fool you. She's built like a brick outhouse. Find yourself a life jacket. They're under the seat. There's some rough-water gear in the starboard locker. You can't go out there dressed like that."

I peel the bottom of my ripped and grass-stained polo shirt away from my stomach and wring it out, but the rain is coming down so hard that it's soaked through again in seconds.

"Holy—what'd you do to *that*?" Les says, pointing at my arm.

"What?" Digging through the locker, I find a slicker that had once been yellow. It smells like gasoline and is many sizes too big, but it feels good to pull it on—until I have to get my right arm into its sleeve. I turn my back to Les so I can wince without him seeing it.

"Your *arm*, smarty-pants."

"Nothing." I lower myself onto a bench seat from an old school bus and strap on an orange life vest. "C'mon. Let's go. We have to hurry. Time's running out."

"Nothing, my eye. I seen broken arms before. You need a doctor."

"Fine. Take me to a doctor—in Port Clinton."

"All right, all right. S'pose it's just as fast to take you there as back to town. And there's an actual hospital."

At that moment, the police golf cart appears over Les's shoulder. "We have to go. Now!" I shout.

Les turns and spots the cart, blinking his eyes a few times to get a clear look. Reggie Cheever is waving his arms and shouting, but the sound of his voice is lost in the midst of the wind and wave noise. "What on earth are *those* two morons up to?"

"I'll tell you later," I plead, tugging on his arm and looking him square in the eyes. "Please. Just get us out of here. As fast as you can."

Les holds my gaze for a couple of seconds, nods, and then turns the ignition key. Two enormous outboard motors rumble to life.

MICHAEL D. BEIL

"Hold on tight!" Pip says, watching waves crash over the wall. Her eyes are wide, frightened. "Even tighter than you held me."

"I will. Pip—thank you. You and Tinker really are my heroes. I promise to explain it all later. You'll understand then. Now, get out of here! Go home and don't answer the door if anyone comes looking for me."

Les casts off the lines. "Where to, lady?" he says, gunning the engines and throwing me against the seat back.

# CHAPTER
# 15

INSTEAD OF HEADING NORTH TOWARD the breakwater, though, Les turns south.

I pound on his back with my good hand and scream over the wind, "What are you doing? Where are you going?"

"No choice," he says. "Have to go around Cattail. Too rough to go through the opening in the breakwater. Don't worry. I'll get you there."

"Isn't that a lot farther?"

"About four miles. We'll have flat water for the first couple miles, while we're between the islands. After that, it's gonna get rough."

He's not kidding. As we approach the opening at the east end of Cattail Island, the waves get bigger and bigger, tossing Les's boat around like a child's bathtub toy.

"Wrap your good arm around that armrest!" he shouts as we make the turn north, heading straight into the wind and waves. "It's going to be a wild ride. Haven't seen it like this since seventy-eight."

"What happened in seventy-eight?" I ask, immediately regretting the decision.

"Storm hit during the regatta in August. Six boats sank. Including the race committee boat—a sistership of this old girl."

"Great," I say, too quietly for him to hear.

"Don't worry," he says. "It was being run by an inbred moron. Cousin of the Cheevers. I'll get you there in one piece." He glances down at my right arm, hanging limp on my lap, and smiles. "Well, in the same number of pieces you boarded. Hold on, big wave!"

We both duck as a wall of green water washes over the bow, threatening to swamp us. Behind me, the engines whine as the propellers momentarily lose their grip on the lake. Les turns the wheel sharply, the stern drops, and we lunge forward.

"Like a roller-coaster ride. Hope you have a strong stomach."

I really wish he hadn't said that, because a moving vehicle is my kryptonite. You name it, I've puked in it. Cars. (There's no calling shotgun at our house, because everyone knows what's going to happen if I ride in the back. They all just step aside and let me have the front seat.) Buses. Roller coasters. Trains. Planes. And yes, boats. *Lots* of boats. The fact is, with all the other issues I have at the moment, I haven't even thought about the possibility of motion sickness.

Until now. Within thirty seconds of Les opening his big mouth, I'm retching over the side of the boat with him holding on to the hood of my borrowed coat, my face inches from the passing waves.

"At least you know enough not to puke into the wind," he says, grinning, when I lean back into the boat.

"I have a lot of experience," I say, wiping my chin with the greasy sleeve of my borrowed jacket.

Les throws his head back with an explosive laugh. He's actually *enjoying* being out here. "C'mon back up here. Hold on to the wheel with me, and focus on the horizon. Having something to do is the best cure. There's two stages to seasickness, you know. In the first, you're so sick you're afraid you're going to die. In the second, you're so sick that you're afraid you *won't*."

Luckily, I tend to recover quickly and this time is no exception; even three miles of stomach-churning ups and downs from the east end of Cattail to the northernmost tip of Rabbit Ear Point doesn't get me to stage two.

When we make the turn at the top of the island, everything changes. Now we're going with the wind and waves, but it is far from a comfortable ride. The boat rocks from side to side, feeling like it's about to capsize, and then pitches wildly when the bow sticks into the back of a wave, or slides sideways down a wave after the stern is lifted high in the air. If anything, it's even *harder* to hold on, because it's so unpredictable.

For the first part of the trip, ours is the only boat on the water, which is not surprising, considering the conditions. But as we pass Dinah's house, another boat roars out of the cove behind little Egbert Island. Les and I spot it at the same moment. It's long and sleek and bright yellow, and headed right for us. A huge wave sends its bow high in the air and then drops it just as suddenly with an enormous splash. I immediately recognize the two men standing at the steering wheel: Officer Pawlowski and Reggie Cheever.

"No. Way. Where did they come from?"

"That's Cheever's boat. Keeps it in Egbert Cove. That's where the new yacht club is going to be. Or so they say." Les looks right at me. "I don't know what you did to him, and to be honest, I don't really care, but boy, he is *mad*. If he's willing to come out in these conditions, in *that* boat, you have seriously gotten under his skin. Just tell me one thing: Does this have anything to do with Dinah Purdy and her land?"

"*Everything* to do with it. If I can get to the courthouse in Port Clinton, I can prove that the land really does belong to Dinah."

"Good enough for me."

"Can you outrun him?" I ask.

Les laughs. "No, not even close. But I didn't survive three tours in Vietnam for nothin'. Still got a few tricks up my sleeve. Do you trust me?"

"I don't really have a choice," I say.

"I suppose that's true," says Les, smiling. He pulls the throttle handle back all the way and the boat surges forward in the waves. Meanwhile, the yellow boat is a couple of hundred yards behind us and closing fast.

"They're getting closer," I say.

"Good," says Les. "I want them close. Just not too close."

"You have a plan?"

"I do. Right now, I want to stay directly in front of them. Let me know if they turn at all."

"Okay. They're still catching up, but not as fast."

"Good. Lucky for us, they can't really open it up in these waves. Boat like that just isn't made for it. Just need to hold him off for a little while."

"Then what happens?"

"Karma, I think they call it." He sees the puzzled look on my face and winks at me. "Stand right here, next to me, and hold on tight."

Dead ahead of us, peeking out from the rain and the mist and the spray, and bobbing up and down in the waves is the buoy at Ada's Reef. It's not dark enough to see the flashing light, but every few seconds I catch a brief glimpse of red paint against the gray water.

"That's Ada's Reef, right?" I say.

Les nods. "It is." He checks the speed and then his watch. "Three minutes away, I'd say. Plus or minus a few seconds."

Behind us, Cheever's boat is getting closer, its bow riding high in the air.

"You see that?" Les says. "The way he has to keep the bow up like that? The boat's new to him. Never had it out in anything close to this. He's afraid he'll swamp if he lets it down too far."

"How can he even see where he's going?" I ask.

Les grins. "Good question."

Ada's Reef grows closer and closer, and still, Les is aimed right at the buoy. The rain is coming down so hard that I lose sight of it for a while, but when we are the length of a soccer pitch away, it shows itself through the haze. The yellow boat is close enough behind us that I can hear Cheever shouting at us, but I won't give him the satisfaction of even *thinking* that I'm concerned about him.

"Whatever you do," Les says as the buoy grows close enough for me to read the number painted on its side, "don't make any sudden movements, and don't point at the buoy. Okay? And hold on with all you got . . . just in case."

In case *what?*

I get an answer to that question in a hurry.

Les heads straight for the buoy until we are only a few boat lengths away, and then starts a gradual turn. But he doesn't turn out into the lake, away from the rocks, which I can now see, thanks to the breaking waves. He turns left, *toward* the rocks.

"Leeessss! What are you doing?" My left hand is holding on so tightly that it's completely white.

"Trust me," he says as we slip past the buoy. "They still behind us?"

I sneak a peek over my shoulder. "Uh-huh." Just ahead of us, the water looks to be boiling as waves break over the rocks.

As a huge whitecap lifts our stern, Les opens up the throttle and spins the wheel hard to the left. We miss the rocks by inches, and he makes a hard right turn, and then a left as he avoids more obstacles.

Les looks over his shoulder at the yellow boat and laughs. "He was so busy watching me and trying not to swamp, he never even saw the buoy. Followed me blindly. It's like a mine-field, but I have two advantages: a more maneuverable boat, and I know where the mines are." With that, he turns the wheel hard again to the left, aiming his bow at the center of Reggie Cheever's boat.

Officer Pawlowski frantically scans the lake for rocks, while Reggie roars obscenities at Les and me. In the end, though, instinct wins out, and he guns his engines and turns to avoid a collision.

He has, as they say, chosen poorly.

A second later, the yellow boat lurches to a stop as a wave lifts, and then drops the heavy fiberglass hull squarely onto a jagged boulder with a loud crunch. The next wave nearly rolls them over before it washes them off that rock and onto others, but the damage is done. They are sinking.

Officer Pawlowski grabs a bucket and starts bailing, while Reggie Cheever points his finger at Les, threatening to kill him and then sue him.

"If you're smart, you'll sue me first!" says Les, spinning his boat around while keeping it clear of the other boat and the rocks, which are still a threat to us. Slowly, he navigates his way back through the rocks to the safe side of the buoy where he uses his portable radio to call the Coast Guard. "Boat on the rocks at Ada's Reef. Going to need an inflatable to make the rescue. No immediate danger. Captain and crew are safe. I'll wait outside the light till you arrive. Over."

"Are they . . . really safe?" I ask. Reggie Cheever isn't exactly my favorite person, but I don't want the guy to drown.

"They're fine," says Les. "Worst case, the boat swamps completely. They could practically walk to shore from there."

"It's kind of crazy, isn't it? Him crashing on *these* rocks. Like, ironic."

"What goes around, comes around," says Les. "Sometimes it takes longer than others."

"Seventy-five years seems like a long time to wait," I say.

With the Ada's Reef buoy dancing wildly on the waves between us, Reggie Cheever, knee-deep in water aboard his battered and sinking boat, shakes his fist at me.

The Coast Guard arrives minutes later. Cheever and Pawlowski climb into the small inflatable rescue boat while the wreck of the yellow hull bounces up and down on the rocks. Reggie continues to rant and rave in our direction, but thankfully the wind and waves completely drown out his voice. It looks like he's trying to get his rescuers to take him to us, but they keep pushing him down into his seat.

"Looks like they have this under control," says Les. "Let's get you to Port Clinton, what do you say?"

"I say yes."

After the craziness of the first part of the trip, the second half is a piece of cake. Still, I breathe a sigh of relief when the breakwater at the mouth of the Portage River comes into focus through the haze. Les pushes the throttle forward, slowing us as we approach the markers at its end, but the wind and waves continue to push us along until we reach the trees that mark the natural shoreline. Once we cross that threshold, the water is smooth and I release my death grip on the armrest. We made it.

"D'you know where you're going?" Les asks. "I'll dock right behind that green boat—he's a friend of mine. You're going to cut through that parking lot, then cross over the street. You're looking for Madison. It's just a couple of blocks thataway. Courthouse'll be on your left. Look for the big radio antenna. Good luck with . . . whatever you're doing."

"Yeah, thanks . . . really. I can't believe you did this for me."

He shrugs. "Girl says it's important, I believe her. Just do me a favor, okay? Let me take you to the hospital when you're done. At least then I'll be able to look Thomas in the eye. I'll wait for you at the courthouse entrance. Promise?"

I nod, and when the boat bumps against the dock, I actually clamber over the rail and onto the dock without falling into the river. Now all I have to do is make it to the courthouse without getting run over, washed away in a flood, carried off by a tornado, or crushed by a satellite falling to Earth. *Two blocks*, Les said. I'm reasonably confident that I can do that.

My phone buzzes in my pocket; the screen shows that it's Nadine but goes black before I can answer.

"I'm almost there!" I shout at the dead phone and then bolt into the street without looking—directly into the path of a hulking SUV.

The driver lays on the horn and hits the brakes, skidding

on the slick pavement. Instinctively, I cower and throw up my good arm in front of my face, sending my phone skittering across the pavement and down a storm drain while I wait for a collision that never comes. When I lower my arm, the SUV's grille is inches away, and I find myself looking directly into the eyes of its passengers. In one of the weird coincidences of all time, it is the family that Nadine and I *almost* had lunch with that day at Em's Docksider. Mikey, the poor kid that they teased so badly, leans over the front seat and stares at me with wide eyes. The father, behind the wheel, shakes his head and then swings his door open.

"Are you okay?" he asks. "Hey, I *know* you. From the restaurant."

I am either unable, or have no idea *how* to respond, so I stand silently in the middle of the road, paralyzed.

"Hop in. We'll take you where you need to go," he says.

I shake my head slowly and take a step back. "It's okay. I'm not going far."

"Come on. It's the least we can do. I almost ran you over."

Maybe I'm just tired and not a hundred percent sure my poor body can take much more, but when Mikey opens the back door of the SUV, I climb inside where it is warm and dry.

"Thank you," I say as Mikey slides over to make room for me. "Do you know where the courthouse is? On Madison?"

"Between Third and Fourth," says the father, stepping on the gas. "I'm on it."

Less than thirty seconds later, we skid to a stop.

"Are we there already?" Mikey asks. He sounds disappointed.

"That's it," his father says, pointing across a wide lawn to a stone building. "You're sure you're okay? You don't look so great. Is somebody meeting you here?"

"I'm good," I say, fumbling with the door handle until Mikey finally reaches over me and opens it. "Thank you guys *so* much." I give Mikey a friendly pat on the shoulder as I step back out into the rain and wind and, for some reason, before closing the door, I add: "I'll see you around," even though that seems *really* unlikely.

As I jog across the long sidewalk toward the courthouse, I turn and wave once more at the father, who has rolled down his window to watch me, and almost run straight into a woman in a raincoat and matching hat pulled down almost over her eyes.

"Lark?" It's Nadine, with an utterly bewildered expression on her face. "What are you doing here?" Mikey's family waves to her from the SUV, adding to her confusion. "Is . . . Is that the family from Em's? And, omigosh, what *happened* to you?"

"It's a really long story. Yeah, that's them. They gave me a ride from the dock. Are we too late?"

"Too late? For wha—wait! You *found* it? Come on. Let's get out of the rain."

The moment we're through the courthouse door, I reach deep into my pocket and pull out a damp packet of papers.

Carefully unfolding it, I show Nadine the cover page: "The Last Will and Testament of Edward Cheever."

Her hand flies to her mouth and her knees buckle as she drops to a bench placed against the wall in the hallway. She flips through the pages quickly, mouth open in disbelief at what she's reading, and then stands up suddenly. "We have to hurry. Probate closes at four thirty. We have . . . omigosh, four minutes! Come on! You're a genius," she adds, tugging me down the hall.

"Dinah. Is she . . . Is she okay?" *Please, please, please be okay, Dinah.*

"She's fine. At the moment, she looks better than you, I think. How did you *get* here, anyway? The ferry stopped running. When you weren't on the last one, I tried calling. I thought it was over. I thought the Cheevers had won again. I gave up, at least on the idea of finding the will. I'll never stop fighting them."

"There's no way I was giving up," I say. "Even when I was under arrest—"

"What!" Nadine exclaims, leading the way through the door to the probate division.

"I'll explain later. Anyway, the cops have me, and the ferry stops running, and then, I don't know. It sounds crazy, but I'm looking out the window and I see this swallow trying to get home to Cattail Island—or at least that's what I imagined she was doing—and suddenly I realized that getting the will here was bigger than me getting in a little trouble, or being in a little pain from a broken arm—"

"A broken arm! Lark! You promised . . . "

"—it was like the universe was screaming at me to finish the job, so I had to, you know, improvise."

"May I help you?" the woman behind the counter asks. Behind her, the clock reads 4:29.

"Yes, please," Nadine says. "You may, indeed."

Suddenly everything is a bit blurry and my head feels as if it's been pumped full of helium. "I think I need to sit down for a minute," I say, dropping into a folding chair as Nadine slides Edward Cheever's will across the counter.

Ten minutes later, Nadine, beaming, turns to me and holds up a photocopy of the will and the forms she has filed.

"It's done," she says as I climb to my feet. "The wheels of justice, as they say, are in motion. And I am taking you to the hospital this instant. And then I'll call Thomas and let him know that you're—Lark!"

# CHAPTER
# 16

WHEN I OPEN MY EYES, the first face I see is Thomas's.

"Well, look who decided to join the party," he says.

"About time," says Nate.

I sit up in an unfamiliar bed, and crowded around me, in addition to Thomas and Nate, I see Pip, Blake, Jack, Nadine, and, waving from his spot in the corner, Les Findlay.

"Welcome back," Nadine says. "You were out for a long time."

"W-Where am I?"

"The hospital in Port Clinton," Thomas says.

Something about my right arm feels different, heavy, and I realize that it's in a cast from my wrist to just below my shoulder.

Pip comes to my side and puts her hand on the cool plaster. "It's broken."

"In two places," adds Nate. "I saw the X-rays. It's awesome."

Thomas wags an index finger at me. "It took me a while, because nobody wanted to tell me the truth, but with Les's help, I finally pieced together everything you went through to get here. You are *certifiable*. But I am . . . we are *all* really proud of you, Lark. And for the record, Aristotle is right again. 'There is no great genius without some touch of madness.' Nadine has been filling me in on what it all means. In addition to being insane, you're a hero."

"What about that lady at the museum?" Blake says. "She wants to have her arrested. And Owen's dad. He wants to have her *killed*, I think. She sank his boat."

"She didn't sink anybody's boat," says Thomas. "At least, I don't *think* she did."

"The issue with the museum is under control," Nadine says. "I've already talked with the police and the county prosecutor. Nothing was damaged. And besides, the museum doesn't belong to the Cheevers. The family gave it to the town back in the eighties. Of course, the new will proves that it wasn't theirs to give away in the first place. But that's the least of their problems."

"The will," I say. Slowly, piece by piece, the craziness of my day is coming back to me. "Dinah! How is Dinah?" I raise my head too quickly and immediately feel dizzy, so I drop it back onto the pillow.

"Easy, there," Thomas says.

"I'm just fine, young lady," Dinah says, squeezing between

Thomas and Nadine and reaching out to touch my face. Her left arm is in a cast and her right cheek is badly bruised, but her eyes are as bright as ever and she's smiling broadly. "A little banged up, but not as bad as you. You look *terrible*."

"Thanks," I say.

"I don't know about you all," Nadine says, "but I think it's time Lark heard the rest of the story. And when she's feeling a little better, she has to tell us her version of what went on out there on the lake."

"Just an ordinary day on Swallowtail Island," says Les.

"What's going on?" I ask. "How long have I been asleep?"

"Going on twenty-four hours," Nadine says. "Do you remember collapsing in probate?"

"N-Nooo. I remember telling you about the swallow . . . and then . . ."

"You should be the one to tell her," Thomas says to Nadine.

"Tell me what!"

Nadine sits on the edge of the bed and unfolds the photocopy of the will. "Well. It's probably a good thing you're sitting. Well, maybe not sitting. Lying down."

"Nadine!" I say.

"Okay, okay," she says. "But I have to warn you first: Everything I'm going to say is what is *supposed* to happen. There's still a lot that can go differently, once a judge and lawyers get involved. You understand that?"

I nod. "Got it. Just tell me!"

"In some ways, Captain Edward Cheever's will is what we expected. He makes it absolutely clear that Gilbert is to get nothing—no land, no money, no anything. And there's no mention of a life estate for Elias and Dinah Purdy—the land he leaves them is *theirs*, no strings attached. So far, so good, right? Well, hold on to the bed, because it gets better. But rather than read from the will, I'm going to summarize, if that's all right.

"Not long after Edward's wife and daughter died, a young couple bought the house down the road from him. They were from New York, and only spent a couple of months a year on the island, but Edward became very fond of them. When the war broke out in nineteen forty-one, the husband enlisted and was sent to Europe, leaving behind his wife and a young daughter who reminded Edward of Ada. Unfortunately, the husband died in Europe, leaving his family in difficult circumstances. So, Edward became a benefactor to the woman and her daughter, paying her school tuition, maintaining the house on the island, sending her gifts, and so on. Shortly before he died, Captain Cheever decided to change his will completely, dividing all of his land on Swallowtail into two parts, exactly like it's shown on that old surveyor's plan you found. Elias Purdy would get one half, and the rest would go to the young widow and her daughter. He wanted them to live in his old house. In addition to the land, he left them a third of his money. Elias got another third, and the last third went to the Mariner's Church in Detroit."

"That widow and her daughter were your grandmother and your great-grandmother. Lillian and Abigail Bradford," adds Thomas.

"Wait, wait, wait," I say, my head swimming. "I don't get it—what does . . ."

"It means we're *rich!*" says Pip. "And so is Dinah!"

"*Easy*, Pip," Thomas says. "You're not rich yet. *Maybe* someday. Or maybe not. The Cheevers are not likely to give up without a fight."

"*That* you can count on," Nadine says. "It could go on for years."

"I can't think of anything I'd rather do than battle the Cheevers in court," Dinah says. "I'm officially coming out of retirement. They won't know what hit them."

Thomas tries to run his fingers through his tangled mop of hair. "Lawyers. Just what I need."

Suddenly everyone is talking at once, and my hospital room sounds like a school cafeteria. As for me, my brain is so fuzzy that I'm having trouble understanding how all the pieces of Nadine's story add up to Pip and me being rich. Finally, I hold up a hand to make them all stop.

"I-I don't get it," I say. "How could Mom leave us something she didn't even know she had?

"It doesn't matter that she didn't know," Nadine says. "Only that she left you and Pip *her property on Swallowtail Island*, just like *her* mom did for her. Not that we need another reason to be grateful to have Dinah in our lives, but without her holding on to that little cottage out on the point for all these years, the Cheevers would have divided up all of your land and sold it to a hundred different people. Even if the will had turned up later, it would have been too late. The new owners would have built houses and there's not a judge in the world who would try to undo a mess like that. Thanks to Dinah's good genes and her love of birds, you and Pip own more than three *hundred* acres of prime land. It's worth a fortune. Dinah's share is smaller, *only* about two hundred acres, but it might be worth even more because so much of it is waterfront."

Pip sits on the edge of the bed and puts a hand on my cast. "I guess the gods heard you."

"What do you mean?" Thomas asks.

"The other night, Lark said that the gods owed us one good day, because they never got around to giving Mom the one they owed *her*."

"I could have done without *this*," I say, holding up my cast. "But overall . . . I'll take it."

Because of the bump on my head, the doctors make me spend another night in the hospital. Thomas sends the boys and Pip home, but he stays, sleeping in one chair with his feet up on another. When I protest, insisting that I'm fine and that he doesn't need to stay, he puts an index finger to his lips.

"Don't argue with me. I made a promise to your mom to take care of you the best I can," he says. "I am not leaving you alone in a hospital room in Port Clinton, Ohio. Besides, I've had a lot of practice at this. One night? Piece of cake."

"I'm really sorry, Thomas," I say, losing the battle to hold back tears. "I messed everything up for you. I'm sorry I'm so difficult. Your life would be so much easier without me. Now you're gonna get fired—"

He comes to the side of the bed and kneels, taking my hand. "Lark, don't. The fact is, you and Pip . . . I couldn't have made it through the past few months without you. Losing your mom was one of the hardest things I've . . . but I am *so* thankful that I have the two of you in my life. You've made my life—you've made *all* our lives better."

With one arm in a cast and the rest of my body battered and bruised, it's not the easiest thing in the world to do, but this is one of those moments in life when, let's face it, only a hug will do.

# Epilogue

TWO WEEKS LATER, ON THE tail end of a mid-August heat wave, my legs are tucked beneath me in a wing chair at Dinah's cottage, *David Copperfield* on my lap. Dinah sits across from me, listening intently as I begin Chapter 22: "Some Old Scenes, and Some New People." Nadine is out on the porch, on the phone with her publisher, discussing details of the launch of Dinah's biography.

In Chapter 22, David comes across Steerforth, his popular but troubled friend from school, in a dejected mood: *"David, I wish to God I had had a judicious father these last twenty years!"* When David asks him what the matter is, Steerforth responds, *"I wish with all my soul I had been better guided! I wish with all my soul I could guide myself better!"*

I stop reading and look up from the page as Nadine joins us inside the cottage.

"Do you want to stop for the day?" Dinah asks. "Are you tired?"

"No, no. I'm fine. I . . . it's . . . Steerforth reminds me of Owen Cheever."

"*Really?*" Nadine asks. "How?"

"I guess I think he's not *entirely* bad," I say with a shrug. "Owen, I mean. I know he's rich and all, but I kind of feel sorry for him. I don't think he likes his father very much. *He's* the real bad guy, not Owen."

"You won't get an argument from me there," Nadine says. "Reggie Cheever is a first-class twit. You may be right about his son. Even if the fruit doesn't *fall* far from the tree, sometimes it rolls down a hill away from it."

"Maybe he should be your next project," Dinah says, looking straight at me. "He's not beyond redemption. You could show him the way."

"*Me?* No. Way. If he wants to turn himself into a decent human being, that's up to him. I just said he reminded me of Steerforth, not that I want to help him. I'm *done* with the Cheevers. Besides, I'm going back to Connecticut in a couple weeks, and he's probably off to boarding school someplace. Nate says Owen missed some days at soccer and the story was that he was visiting schools. I'll probably never see him again."

"Oh, I wouldn't count on *that*," Nadine says. "It's a small island, and you're coming back next summer, aren't you? The heck with Owen—*I* need you."

Outside the cottage, bike tires crunch on the gravel drive, joined by the *clip-clop clip-clop* of Tinker's hooves and the nonstop chattering of Pip and Jack.

"*Those* are the true sounds of summer," Dinah says. "Bicycles, horses, and children laughing. Some things don't change, even after nearly a hundred years."

"It's the whole fam damily," I say, looking out the window. "Even Thomas and Pogo. Only one missing is Bedlam."

Dinah stands and straightens her dress. "Oh, dear. And I look a proper mess. Well, invite them in."

"I don't think they're expecting a fashion show," says Nadine, pulling me toward the door and whispering in my ear, "I hope I'm that vain when *I'm* ninety-three."

"I heard that!" Dinah says, checking her face in a mirror. "I'm not vain. Well, no more than anyone else expecting a gentleman caller."

I stick my head back in the door to tell Dinah, "I don't think anyone has called Thomas *that* before."

Pip climbs down from Tinker and runs to hug Nadine. "Isn't Tink beautiful?" she says.

"She looks well cared for," Nadine agrees. "She's never had so much attention. I don't know what she'll do when you're gone."

Pip's head swivels to look at Thomas, and then I realize that all three boys have turned in his direction, too.

"All right. What's going on?" I ask.

"Nothing," Pip says.

I shake my head. "You're *such* a liar. But Jack will tell me, won't you?" I push him gently against a tree.

Jack's eyes search for someone to help him. "I don't know anything!"

"Fine. So, if there's nothing going on, why did you all ride out here?" I ask.

Thomas holds up a square envelope. "This came for you this morning. Thought you might want to read it."

"It's not my birthday," I say, eyeing it suspiciously.

"It's not going to bite you," Thomas says. "Why don't I take it inside so you can read it, and I can say hello to Dinah."

"She's very excited to see you," Nadine says. "She's fixing her hair. 'A gentleman caller,' she said."

Thomas strikes a modeling pose with a *Zoolander* face. "I've still got it."

"You are *so* weird," I say. "Can I at least *see* the envelope?"

"It's from England," Pip whispers.

"England? I don't know anybody—ohhh, wait."

Inside, Dinah bustles about the kitchen, setting out "the good stuff"—a small round of cheese with fancy crackers—along with a bottle of wine for the adults and sweet iced tea for the kids. Thomas opens the wine, and after a toast, Dinah leads the way out to the front porch.

"I think it's the nicest day of the summer," she says. "Look at that *sky*! Have you ever seen anything so blue? Now, what brings you all out here today?"

"A special delivery for Lark," Thomas says. "And I wanted to see for myself how you're doing."

"Oh, pish. I'm good as new," Dinah says. "Tell me more about this special delivery."

Thomas (finally) hands me the letter and I turn it over to read the return address, embossed deep into the flap of the envelope. "Crackenthorp Books. I can't believe they wrote back."

"Why does that name sound familiar?" Dinah asks.

I point out the stamp inside her copy of *David Copperfield*. "Mom's copy of *The Pickwick Papers* has the same stamp *and* it also has this same writing, 'from the library of T. P. & P. C.' And, you know, that silver swallow that I told you about. So I wrote to them to see if they knew anything about it."

"Open it!" demands Blake, about to explode. "You're driving me crazy."

"Okay, okay," I say, slipping a finger under the flap and lifting.

"And read it out loud," says Pip.

"Oh, yes," agrees Dinah.

The letter is the first one I've ever received that has been typed on an actual typewriter:

Ms. Lark Heron-Finch
The Roost,
Swallowtail Island, OH 43456

Dear Miss Heron-Finch,

Your letter came as quite a surprise to me, and brought back many fond memories. It has been many years since I last thought of Swallowtail Island. My father, Samuel Crackenthorp, who took over this shop from his father in 1930, met Edward Cheever and the two maintained a written correspondence for many years.

In 1941, when the Blitz was on and invasion by Germany seemed imminent, my father sent many of his most valuable books to friends in America and Canada for safekeeping. According to his records, two books were sent to Mr. Cheever that year: The Pickwick Papers and Little Dorrit. However, based on the publisher's information in his notes, both books were modern editions and not valuable themselves. As for the unusual secret that you describe within the pages of Pickwick, there is not a word, and my father died during the war, so the records and the correspondence ended there. In light of all this, if I were to venture a guess, it appears that the two books were simply a gift to

Cheever, and that the changes to the book occurred after its arrival in America. This is merely speculation, and if you learn otherwise, please let me know; my curiosity has definitely been piqued.

The inscription, "ex libris T.P. & P.C." refers to a long defunct women's group, The Procne & Philomela Club, whose headquarters were near here, on Dover Street in Mayfair. A number of books from their library landed here and were sold secondhand. Other than that its members were women and that it appears to have disappeared around 1920, I can tell you nothing else about the club. Perhaps a group of suffragettes?

I'm sorry not to have been more of a help to you, but will contact you should I learn anything more.

Yours sincerely,
    Archibald Crackenthorp

I can't hide my disappointment. "Well, *that* was a letdown. So, basically, he doesn't know anything."

"Not true," says Nadine. "Maybe he doesn't know about the swallow, but he gave you some good information. It's up to you to push the stone along the path. Don't forget: A few weeks ago, everybody thought that Albert Pritchard's death was an accident."

I read the letter again, nodding. "You're right. The first thing is to look for this other book: *Little Dorrit.*"

"That's Charles Dickens, too," says Thomas.

"It came here in nineteen forty-one. What are the odds that it's still here?" I ask.

"Fifty-fifty," Nadine says.

Dinah reaches over and touches my hand. "I came long before that and I'm still here."

"I still have a couple weeks before we go back to Connecticut," I say. "I guess I can look for a book with one arm."

"About that," Thomas says, and once again, the boys and Pip turn uncharacteristically quiet.

"What? What is going on?" I'm on my feet, indignant, because it's clear that I'm the only one present who *doesn't* know.

Thomas motions for me to sit back down. "I haven't been keeping anything from you. I didn't even know myself until a few hours ago. How would you feel about staying on Swallowtail, going to school here? Don't say anything yet. We could try it for a year, and next August, if we hate it, we can go back to Connecticut. And in a year, you may be heading off to boarding school anyway. With all that's going on with the will and lawyers and motions and injunctions and things I don't understand very well, it seems like the right thing to do. But we're a family. It has to be unanimous. Everyone else has voted. Now it's your turn."

Eight pairs of unblinking eyes (yes, even Pogo has joined in) are on me as I let the idea of living on Swallowtail sink in for a full ten seconds. I shake my head slowly. "Let's not," I say, watching seven faces fall in unison before adding, "go back."

It takes a moment for what I've said to sink in. Thomas is the first to get it, putting his hand to his heart. "Whew. For a second there, you scared me."

The porch shakes from the eruption of cheering and high-fiving as the others catch on.

"I have to tell Tinker!" Pip cries, throwing her arms around me. "Thank you thank you thank you!"

"You know what would make this moment *perfect*?" Thomas says.

"Champagne?" Nadine guesses.

"No, but that's not a bad idea," he says. "The eight of us— no, *ten* of us, can't forget Pogo and Tinker—we're a family now. And that means we need—"

"Don't say it, Thomas!" I say. "No!"

Thomas grins and places his hands on my shoulders, spinning me so that I'm facing the door. "C'mon, everyone outside.

It's time for a family picture. With the *whole* family."

"Oh, no," I say, taking my place in the back row. "What have I *done*?"

Standing there with my good arm around Dinah's shoulders while Thomas sets the timer on his camera, my thoughts turn to, of all people, Aristotle. I looked up that line about the swallow that Thomas quoted the day we arrived on the island, and it turns out there's more to it than "one swallow does not make a summer, neither does one fine day." Aristotle also insists that one good day, or a brief time of happiness does not make a person completely happy. But you want to know the GHT? *Today*, here on Swallowtail Island, posing for a picture with my crazy, mixed-up, complicated, maddening, and beautiful family, I *am* happy.

# Acknowledgments

Lark's story has had a more tortured path to publication than my previous middle grade novels. I was ready to try something completely different, so I began an experiment: a darkish YA novel with a supernatural element, set on an island.

Well, so much for that. The island stayed where it is, but along the way, almost everything else about the book changed—for the better, I hope.

I would like to take this opportunity to thank everyone who helped me bring Lark's tale to life:

First, I've been fortunate to have three very special early readers, each of whom read multiple drafts and provided valuable feedback:

Gretchen Mills: I hope I can return the favor one day when you write your first novel. And yes, I mean *when*.

Erin Flaherty: Thank you for the "local knowledge" about life on Put-in-Bay you passed along, courtesy of all those summers on the island. Long live The Frosty Bar!

Teresa Ramoni: You have the eyes of a copyeditor, but it's your ear for dialogue that saved me from myself on multiple occasions.

As a relative newcomer to the world of soccer (COYS!), I'm grateful to these soccer-specific readers for their help with those scenes: Claudia Langsam, Olivia Alexander, Liam Stapleton, and Ozzie Bennett.

A resounding thank you to Bethany Buck and everyone at Pixel+Ink for inviting me to be a part of your grand new venture. Your enthusiasm for the book convinced me that I had found a new publishing home. Here's to many more adventures on Swallowtail Island!

Extra-special thanks, with a cherry on top, to my agent, Rosemary Stimola, for her patience, persistence, and perspicacity. Without you and all the wonderful folks at Stimola Literary Studio, this book would be nothing more than a few megabytes of data taking up space in a Google Docs file.

And finally, what more can I say about my wife, Laura Grimmer? It's your love and brilliance and support and sense of humor and perhaps most of all (as Thomas refers to it), your baloney detector that make all things possible. As I said at our rehearsal dinner in 1993, I can't wait to see what comes next. As long as you're there, I know it will be amazing.

# About the Author

In a time not long after the fifth extinction event, Edgar Award–nominated author MICHAEL D. BEIL came of age on the shores of Pymatuning Lake, where the ducks walk on the fish. (Look it up. Seriously.) For reasons that can't be disclosed until September 28, 2041, he now lives somewhere in Portugal with his wife and their two white cats, Bruno and Maisie. He still gets carsick if he has to ride in the back seat for long and feels a little guilty that he doesn't keep a journal.

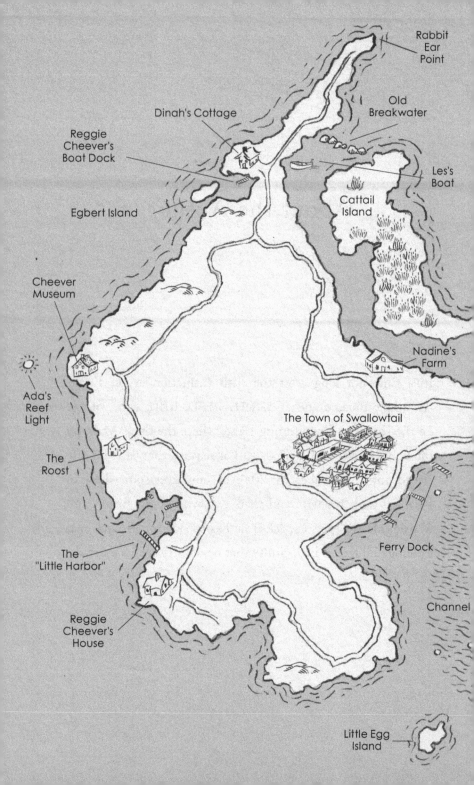

# SWALLOWTAIL ISLAND

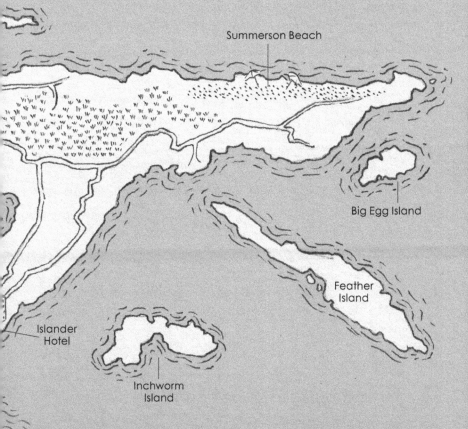

Summerson Beach

Big Egg Island

Feather Island

Islander Hotel

Inchworm Island

SWALLOWTAIL ISLAND